THE HUNTED

ALSO BY WAYNE BARCOMB

Undercurrent

Blood Tide

All Are Naked

WAYNE BARCOMB

THE HUNTED

MINOTAUR BOOKS ❧ NEW YORK

This is a work of fiction. All of the characters, organizations, and events portrayed in this novel are either products of the author's imagination or are used fictitiously.

A Thomas Dunne Book for Minotaur Books.
An imprint of St. Martin's Publishing Group.

THE HUNTED. Copyright © 2009 by Wayne Barcomb. All rights reserved. Printed in the United States of America. For information, address St. Martin's Press, 175 Fifth Avenue, New York, N.Y. 10010.

www.thomasdunnebooks.com
www.minotaurbooks.com

ISBN-13: 978-0-312-37075-6
ISBN-10: 0-312-37075-X

First Edition: April 2009

10   9   8   7   6   5   4   3   2   1

To my wife, Susan, who lets me cash in on her many years
of editorial publishing experience—a great lady and a superb editor

ACKNOWLEDGMENTS

So many people have helped in so many ways in the research and writing of *The Hunted*, it's hard to know where to start. But a few come immediately to mind.

First and foremost is my agent, Mel Parker, who goes far beyond the norm with his professionalism and thoroughness in everything he touches. Mel is a jewel and a delight to work with.

Martin Levin, former president of the Times Mirror and former chairman of the Association of American Publishers, for his encouragement and for recommending Mel Parker.

My editor, Marcia Markland, and associate editor, Diana Szu, at St. Martin's for their help and guidance throughout.

And my thanks to the many law enforcement people who helped me understand how cops operate so effectively: Detective Lieutenant T. J. Moroney of the NYPD's Midtown North Precinct showed me around New York's 12th precinct from which my fictional cops operate, helping me to create realistic visual images. Lieutenant Moroney also read the manuscript and provided insightful, helpful observations.

Detective Sergeant Chris I'Orio of the Sarasota Florida Sherrif's Department for always having been there when I had a procedural question, no matter how big or small.

Edgar Award winners Stuart Kaminsky and John Lutz, who read the manuscript and offered critical advice.

And finally, a man who has become my good friend, former FBI agent Charles Walsh, who perhaps more than anyone taught me the things a mystery writer needs to know. The week I spent with Charlie at the FBI Academy in Quantico, Virginia, attending his lectures on CSI (crime scene investigations) and interviewing some of the serial-killer specialists, has been one of the highlights of my writing career.

THE
HUNTED

SHE NEVER TRULY hated her father until that night. It began as the others had. The voices awakened her around midnight. She buried her face under the pillow but the voices found her.

"You stupid cow. You're so dumb, you still don't know how to do it right, do ya? Do you?"

A loud slap. "Paul, please."

The light from the kitchen intruded into her room, highlighting her small three-drawer dresser covered with Snow White and Cinderella stickers. She wished her bedroom had a door. She would close it to shut out the sounds. The screams were the worst.

"Paul, please," her father's voice mocked her mother's plea. "I'm sick of your whining. Shut up!" More scuffling, another slap. "No? OK, I got a better idea."

The little girl raised her head from under the pillow, sat up and looked out the open window, and wished she could climb out and go far away. Her eyes closed and she was walking with her mother in the warm night. A shiny car stopped, and a tall, handsome man with a kind voice asked her if she and her mother would like to go away with him. He said her mother was the most beautiful woman he had ever seen.

He stepped out, took her and her mother's hands, and helped them into the car, and they drove away with the handsome man. She did not know where they were going, but it would be far away and they would be forever happy.

"Oh, Paul, it hurts so much, please. Please. Oh! God! God, help me. I can't stand it."

The child slipped out of bed, tiptoed to the doorway, and peered into the kitchen. She saw her mother lying on her back on the linoleum floor she had waxed earlier that day, the room still smelling of the wax. Her father sat on top of her, his hand up her skirt. She knew where her father's hand was.

She stood staring at her mother and father. Her mother lay between the radiator and the refrigerator, one shoe on, one lying under the small kitchen table. Her blouse was torn, and she could see one of her mother's nipples. Her left eye was swollen, and the rest of her face was red and wet from tears. Her father's hand was over her mother's mouth.

She smelled her father's sweat and whiskey. He was probably already drunk when he got home. When he was like that she wished he would go away and never come back. But he was her father and she was ashamed of those thoughts.

"You bit me. You bitch!" her father screamed. He pulled his hand away from her mother's mouth, and blood trickled from the side of his index finger.

She stood in the doorway, watching, as her father pulled his other hand from her mother's skirt and slapped her hard. A wine bottle rolled out from under her, and her mother's legs sent it clattering across the floor. It came to rest at her feet, and she stared down at it.

Her mother suddenly came to life, arched her back, and rolled her father off. Her knee shot into his groin, and she started to get up. Bellowing with pain and rage, her father grabbed an ankle.

She watched her father drag her mother until he could get his hands on her throat. He began choking her and banging her head against the floor. She tried to slide away and got as far as the radiator. Again he grabbed her and pounded her head against the edge of the radiator. Blood gushed and formed a small pool on the floor.

She rushed to her mother, who lay still, the color draining slowly from her face.

A blow sent her sprawling. When she focused her eyes, her father stood over her. "You get in your bed now, Tookie! You hear me? Now! You say one thing—one thing and you'll get the same thing your mother just got. Now get in there!"

Never taking her eyes off her father, she slid across the kitchen floor to her bedroom. When she reached her room, she grabbed two of her dolls and dropped on the bed, sobbing.

Through the doorway she could see her father leaning and swaying over her mother's body. She watched him feel her wrist with his fingers. He stood over her mother, weaving, sucking on the knuckle of his finger. His eyes seemed to be everywhere, and then she saw him look toward her room. She was afraid and closed her eyes and made believe she was asleep.

"Tookie, wake up, sweetheart. Daddy wants to talk to you."

She moaned and stirred.

"Wake up, Tookie. Talk to Daddy."

She opened her eyes and looked straight into her father's bloodshot eyes. They always bulged, and they scared her. She squirmed and tried to turn away from him but he held her fast. The hard bristle of his unshaven face scratched her cheek. The mole behind his ear brushed against her neck. The mole was big and hairy, and she hated it. She wanted to be free, to go to her mother. But he held her face next to his.

"Tookie?"

She hated that stupid name he called her. Her mother called her Lucky. Her lucky charm. She liked that.

"I want you to listen to me, sweetheart. Daddy's gonna call the police and tell them about Mommy. They'll come over here in a little while and talk with me, and they'll talk with you, too. Now here's what happened, and here's what we're gonna tell the police. Mommy and Daddy were sitting at the table in the kitchen. We had a little argument, and Mommy got mad and hit Daddy in the face. Then Daddy hit Mommy back, first in the face and then here." He touched her breast.

"Then Daddy hit Mommy once in the eye. You were standing in your doorway and you saw it. Mommy saw you and jumped up to go to you to put you to bed. She slipped on the magazine on the floor and fell. When she fell, she hit her head on the radiator, and it got cut open. That's what happened, sweetheart, and that's what we're goin' to tell the men when they come over to talk with us."

She wanted to get away from him, wanted to be out the window with her mother and the handsome man. But he held her arms hard, smiling and nodding. Her arms hurt and she hated looking at his ugly gold tooth.

"But, Daddy, that's not true."

Even before he hit her, she knew it was coming. She closed her eyes and felt the pain as his open hand smacked across her face. Tears filled her eyes, but she was afraid to open them.

"Now you listen to me and you listen good. You're gonna tell me exactly what I just told you, or you'll get a lot worse than you just got. You hear me?"

She opened her eyes. He was still holding her by the arms, his eyes bigger than she had ever seen them. Traces of spit trickled down the sides of his mouth. She stared and nodded her head slowly.

"That's better. Now you tell me what happened."

She slowly, haltingly repeated the story.

His face softened, and the grip on her arms relaxed. "That's a good girl, sweetheart. Now let's do it a couple more times just to be sure." Three more times he had her run through the story. Each time she told it more convincingly.

"Oh, that's my girl, sweetheart. Daddy's gonna take good care of you."

She closed her eyes again, but the smells of her father were making her sick. She struggled to hold back the vomit in her throat as his hands touched her where they always did.

"Now, Tookie, I'm going to call the police and tell them about the accident, and they'll be comin' over soon. You stay in bed. They will probably want to talk with you after they talk to me. You be sure and tell them just what you and me went over together, right?"

She nodded. Her father went back to the kitchen and she lay in bed, hugging her dolls, trying not to cry.

She listened to his movements and sounds and crept out of bed and peeked into the kitchen, watching him. He picked up the wine bottle, washed it off, and smashed it in the trash can. Then he pressed a magazine hard against her mother's bare foot and placed the magazine near the radiator. He picked up her mother's shoe from the far side of the room, put it under one of the kitchen chairs, removed the other shoe and set it next to the one under the chair. With a damp paper towel, he washed off traces of blood between her legs and inner thighs. He tore her stained panties into shreds and flushed them along with the paper towel down the toilet.

Her father stood hunched in the middle of the kitchen. He poured some more whiskey, drank it, picked up the phone, and called the police.

Tookie heard him tell the policeman there'd been an accident. She wiped her nose and eyes with the sleeve of her nightie and watched her father as he hung up and sat at the kitchen table. She wanted to go to her mother again, but she was afraid.

She went back to bed and was almost asleep when the doorbell rang. Her clock said ten minutes after one.

"Mr. Gale? I'm Detective David McNally, and this is Officer Gamache."

"Yeah. Come in. Come in." Gale fumbled in his shirt pocket for a cigarette and clumsily worked the pack out.

Tookie could see the two policemen standing in the middle of the kitchen looking at her mother's body sprawled across the floor. The man in the jacket knelt and felt her wrist, at the same time looking at her puffed eye. "I'm afraid she is dead, sir." He rose and faced her father.

When she heard the man say her mother was dead, she buried her head under the pillow. She didn't want to see or hear any more.

Gale flicked the sweat from his forehead, never taking his eyes off McNally. He'd dealt with cops before, and he knew he would have to be on his guard. McNally appeared to be in his late thirties, good-looking, even seemed kind of gentlemanly. Not like other cops he had known. Nice leather jacket, white turtleneck. But cops could fool you. The guy's handsome face showed an intelligence that unsettled him.

"Can I use your phone, sir?"

Gale nodded.

"Hello. McNally here. The lady's dead. Get the medical examiner over here and the state police and the photographer." He hung up and looked over at the body again. "Mr. Gale, could we go sit down in the other room? I'd appreciate it if you could tell us what happened. I'm sorry. I know this is difficult for you."

"Sure, sure. That's OK. I understand. I . . . I . . ." Gale sobbed and swallowed hard, closing his eyes.

McNally and Gamache glanced at each other and back to Gale. "Thank you, sir," McNally said.

McNally nodded to Gamache, and Gale led them into the small living room off the kitchen, sparsely furnished with a floral-print couch and a worn armchair facing a TV set. He snapped on the overhead light. Still holding his crumpled pack of cigarettes, he pulled one out and held the pack out to the two cops. "Cigarette?"

They declined.

McNally made Gale uneasy, but there was something about Gamache that he just didn't like. He looked like all cops: cocky, big-shot attitude. Blue uniform stretched across his fat belly, gun and nightstick hanging off him.

"Mr. Gale, can you tell me what happened here tonight?" McNally asked, a gentle friendliness in his voice.

Gale was careful. He knew cops too well. They were just like those pricks in the Merchant Marine. You get in a little trouble and they suck you in by making you think they care about you, being nice to you. Then just when you start to trust them, they grab you by the balls.

He had told the investigating officer in the Merchants why he had beaten the woman in Madrid. He trusted him and thought he would understand. Before he knew it, they had kicked him out, telling him he was lucky he wasn't going to jail. Now he had to deal with these two fucks.

"I came home from work about midnight, Officer. I worked late, and then I stopped for a few beers. My wife likes to wait up for me if I'm late. She was sittin' at the kitchen table, sleepin'. When I come in she woke up in a bad mood. She was pissed at me for comin' home so late without callin', you know?" He nodded at the officers but got no response.

"Anyway, I tried to ignore her. I poured myself a little nightcap and suggested we go to bed. But she kept at me, gettin' herself all worked up. So, we had some words, and she throws a magazine at me. Then, all of a sudden, she sucker punches me in the face. I'm caught by surprise, and I hit her back, first in the chest and then the face. I mean, hey, she really belted me.

"Then I look up and I see my little girl standin' in the doorway. Sarah, my wife, saw her too and jumped up from the table to put her back to bed. She slipped on the magazine on the floor and fell backwards and hit her head on the radiator. That was it. It all happened so fast. Her head hit that radiator and she started bleeding like a pig." He ground the cigarette out and looked back at the officers.

Both men stared at Gale. He squirmed, crossed and uncrossed his legs. *For Christ sake, say something, you assholes.*

Finally McNally spoke. "Mr. Gale, how long had your daughter been standing in the doorway?"

"Quite a while, I guess. I noticed her right after I hit her mother the second time. She sort of whimpered, and when my wife saw her, she jumped up to go to her, to put her back to bed. That's when she slipped on the magazine."

McNally glanced at Gamache. "What happened then?" asked McNally.

"Well, I run over to her, and so did my daughter. Sarah was moaning and bleeding from her head where she hit the radiator. I could tell from the gash in her head and from the blood that she was hurt bad. A few seconds after I got to her, she stopped moaning and passed out."

"Passed out?"

"Yeah. Her eyes kinda rolled back and her head slipped to the side, and she was gone."

"What do you mean, gone?"

"I mean she was dead."

"Didn't you think she was maybe just knocked out or something?"

"No, I seen dead people before, when I was in the Merchant Marine. I knew she was dead."

"What did your daughter do?"

"She ran to her mother. When she saw the blood she started screaming."

"And then?"

"Well, I didn't know what to deal with first. My wife is layin' dead on the floor, and my kid's hysterical. I picked my daughter up and carried her into bed, calmed her down, and told her I'd take care of Mommy. Then I went back to Sarah and felt her pulse. I couldn't feel none, and that's when I called you."

McNally nodded. His eyes never left Gale.

Gale wanted a drink.

"Mr. Gale, can we go back into the kitchen?"

Gale was tired. He wanted Sarah out of here. He wanted the cops out. He wanted to go to bed. "Sure."

The investigative unit arrived and went to work. The photographers began taking pictures while the medical examiner worked with the body, and a technician videotaped the death scene. A paramedic sat at the kitchen table filling out forms.

Gamache sat next to the paramedic. McNally and Paul Gale stood in the middle of the room. Gale watched the crowd of people taking over his kitchen like they owned it and wanted them the fuck out of his house. He started to say something but McNally interrupted him. "Mr. Gale, can you describe for me just how your wife stepped on the magazine and how she fell? Could you show me how it happened? Walk me through it?"

"Look, Officer, what do you want from me? I mean, my wife is layin' dead in front of me. It's one-thirty in the morning. My eight-year-old daughter's in there, maybe asleep, maybe not. I got seven strangers in my kitchen, and I'm dead tired. I been through a lot tonight. I just don't want to talk no more." His voice broke, and he closed his eyes.

McNally covered his face with his hands and rubbed his eyes.

"Uh, Dave."

When McNally looked up, Gamache was standing by the little girl's bedroom. She stood in the doorway, her eyes red, tears trickling down her cheeks.

McNally looked at Gale. "Your call, Mr. Gale. Do we talk to her now?"

Gale looked at his daughter. Their eyes locked. He nodded his head slowly, and she nodded back.

McNally looked from Gale to the little girl.

Her eyes remained transfixed on her father.

"Sweetheart, Mr. McNally would like to talk with you for a minute. Can you come out and sit down?"

Tookie stared at her father. She knew what she had to say, and she knew she could do it. She walked into the kitchen and looked around for the first time.

She saw her mother lying on the floor. The policeman standing by her bedroom smiled at her. She could see the window in her bedroom, and she wished she could float through it again. Suddenly the handsome man was in her house, standing in the kitchen, smiling at her. She looked back at him, and she knew that everything was going to be all right.

He smiled again, and he spoke. "Honey, can you tell us what happened here tonight? Can you?" The handsome man's voice was soft like her mother's.

The little girl stared straight ahead. "My father did it. My father killed my mommy."

2

THE YOUNG WOMAN lay in bed. She was tired but unable to sleep. She opened her eyes and was still for a moment, staring into space. But there was no space, only the bedroom walls.

Her headache arrived as expected. She squirmed in bed, flailing her legs until the bedcovers lay on the floor. Her temples throbbed, and she squeezed them until her fingers ached.

The sun streaming through the window raised her spirits, and she willed the bad thoughts away. But they would come back.

Ten-thirty A.M. She couldn't remember when she'd slept so late. She sat up and stretched. Her bedroom glowed in the bright sunlight of a beautiful Saturday.

She eased herself off the bed, padded into the bathroom, and took a Percocet. The hot shower warmed her body and calmed her. She closed her eyes and turned her face upward into the cleansing waters, waiting as she did every morning for the water to wash away the foulness. Her headache gradually receded, taking with it some of the hostility.

But the ugliness never really left. No matter how hard she tried, how busy she kept herself, how many years had passed, the memories were always there. Waiting.

She dressed slowly, donning a Saturday outfit of form-fitting jeans, a wide belt with oversize buckle, lightweight black turtleneck, and her New Balance sneakers. Thinking of ways to spend the day, she remembered the Monet exhibit at the Metropolitan. She would take a long walk in the sunshine and spend a few hours with her favorite artist.

Taking a long walk on a perfect mid-October day was just what the doctor ordered. She smiled at the metaphor as she zigzagged her way through the crowded streets, walking briskly with long, graceful strides past the shoppers and the street vendors hawking their knockoff Kate Spade and Coach handbags.

When she reached Forty-second Street and Sixth Avenue she stopped in front of the public library, where she decided to treat herself to a little side trip. Bryant Park, the back porch of the library, as some referred to it, was one of her favorite places, a French classical–style urban oasis. She loved the little park, one of the most sensual, graceful open spaces in New York.

She strolled along the football field–size lawn, enjoying the colorful fall flowers. Autumn in the Bryant, her refuge of peace and calm. Relaxing in the garden, nibbling on her bagel and sipping her Starbucks coffee, she felt the rest of her earlier hostility gradually fade away.

She finished her coffee and bagel sitting at one of the small tables facing the imposing figure of the park's namesake, William Cullen Bryant. His bronze statue, sitting atop a marble pedestal in an archway flanked by two Doric columns, lent an air of dignity to the park.

After sharing several minutes with the poet in the warm sunshine, she resumed her stroll, reveling in the forty-block walk, absorbing the sights and sounds of the city—the sidewalk merchants displaying their purses and scarves, the smell of pretzels and hot chestnuts under the yellow and blue Sabrett's umbrellas, distant sirens, and the constant horns of New York drivers.

She reached the museum and stood in front for a moment. No matter how many times she visited, it was always a thrill gazing up at the enormous ornate columns bracketing the graceful arched entrance. People sat around the outdoor benches and steps enjoying the atmosphere and the warm sunshine. A thirty-foot-long banner announced the Monet exhibit.

She took the stairs two at a time.

Inside the museum, its quiet peacefulness and the beauty of Monet worked the magic she had hoped for. The paintings took her breath away. All the Monets she had studied and loved in college were there. The series of haystacks, Rouen Cathedral in morning sunlight, and the Cathedral in full sunlight. The pure color harmonies of his water lilies, the naturalism of his Gare Saint-Lazare, and the dreamlike colors of "Impression: Sunrise."

"That's the painting generally regarded as the one that gave Impressionism its name," she heard a man's voice just behind her. She turned, not sure if he was talking to her. A sandy-haired man of about thirty, wearing rimless eyeglasses, stood directly behind her, looking over her shoulder.

"A hostile art critic wrote a negative article about an exhibit that included this painting by Monet. He said they were all just a series of impressions: 'slap happy daubers,' he called them. He coined the term Impressionism from the title of Monet's 'Impression: Sunrise.' " He said all of this quietly, matter-of-factly, and stood smiling, awaiting her response.

"You're quite an authority," she said.

"No, not really. It's just one of those isolated facts you sometimes remember from a college course. I love Monet, though, do you?"

"Yes, I do." She looked at him curiously. He was a few inches shorter than she, slender, almost frail-looking. *Boyish* came to mind. "Well, I just got here," she said, moving away from him toward the haystack series. "I've got a lot more to see. Thanks for the lecture."

"I guess it wasn't much of a lecture, but it was nice talking with you. Enjoy the exhibit." He turned and headed in the other direction.

She watched him, hands in pockets, bounce off on his toes.

She was absorbed by the paintings and followed the taped Monet lecture on her rented earphones. Three hours of concentrated art history left her tired and hot and longing for the beautiful day outside. She yawned and half promised herself to come back tomorrow.

"How'd you like it?" a familiar voice asked from behind her.

She turned. Her quirky friend from the exhibit skipped down the stairs two at a time. "I liked it," she said, and continued walking.

He caught up to her, smiling broadly, his sandy brown hair sticking up in back. His hands were stuck deep into the pockets of his chinos, and he rocked back and forth as he spoke. "I went over to the Egyptian exhibit, then came back here for some more Monet and was just finishing up when I saw you. Three hours in here on a day like today is enough for me. But I'm really glad I finally got to see Monet and I love the Egyptian exhibit. I'm going to come back and spend some more time when the weather isn't so beautiful." He nodded toward the front door. "Are you leaving now, too?"

For a moment, she was tempted to say she wasn't. He had already committed himself to saying he was leaving. It was a perfect chance to get rid of him. "Yes, I am," she heard herself say.

"Good, I'll walk out with you, if that's OK," he said.

She shrugged and headed for the door.

"Uh, my name is Jack Beatty," he said, holding out his hand.

She shook it. "Hi."

They reached the front door, and Jack tried to maneuver himself into position to open it for her. She beat him to it, opened it herself,

and was out into the now fading late-afternoon sunlight. She dug her
sunglasses out of her purse without breaking stride. "Well, I'm heading down this way," she said, starting toward Fifth Avenue.

"I'm going that way, too. Do you mind if I walk with you?"

She looked at him. He was still smiling, but he looked uncertain,
vulnerable. "Sure, why not," she said.

He scurried along to keep up with her long strides. "Uh, could we
slow down a little? I'm not much of a jogger." He stuck his tongue out
in mock panting.

"Sorry, I always walk fast." She slowed down.

"Oh, that's much better, thanks. I think I might make it now. By
the way, what's your name?"

She hesitated. "My friends call me Lucky." The name tumbled
out. It was so weird.

"Lucky? What a great name. Well, it sure is nice meeting you and
having a chance to chat with you," he said, his head bobbing awkwardly.

The blocks ticked away as they made their way downtown in that
twilight area between fading daylight and soon-to-be darkness. The
streets bustled with late shoppers and people hurrying to wherever
they were going.

Jack was a talker. He was one of those people who were funny
without trying to be. *Comical* was the word her aunt liked to use. The
herky-jerky movements, his hands thrust deep into his pockets, and
his wide-eyed enthusiasm amused her.

He still had difficulty keeping up with her long strides, causing
him to run a little, getting slightly ahead of her, and then jogging
backward to make eye contact.

Along the way he had laid out his life's history. "I'm from Iowa. Got
my BA in art history from the University of Iowa. Been in New York
for just a year. After graduation, I stayed in Iowa City and worked as a
designer at the University Press. Boy, was that a bore. I really think I've

got some talent. New York is where the real opportunities are for
people like me."

His head bobbed and nodded again, and she had to suppress a
chuckle at how intense and serious he was.

"You ever been to Iowa, Lucky?"

"No, I haven't. Someday maybe."

Jack laughed. "Iowa's not a place anyone goes to on purpose, like
Hawaii or California. Iowa is a place where you live or visit because you
have to, like business or something. Uh, you like living in New York?"

She walked with her head high, body erect. Jack kept turning,
leaning toward her, looking up at her face to get her attention.

"It's OK," she replied without looking at him.

"Don't mind me. I'm just inquisitive about people. Probably too
nosy. Sorry."

She glanced over at him. He had dropped his head sheepishly. He
was cute, in a dumb, boring kind of way. No sex appeal. But harmless. That was it. That's why she let him walk with her. He was cute
and harmless. Kind of just right for the mood she was in today. It was
OK to let herself be distracted by him for a while. When he became
too tiresome, she would get rid of him.

"I love New York," he said, starting up again. "I feel like I'm in
heaven. I'm starting to do pretty well now, too." His head went up
and down again in that way she was beginning to find both appealing
and annoying.

"That's good."

"I'm a freelance designer. I do mostly interior and cover designs
for magazines."

They had walked about twenty blocks when Jack said, "Hey, you
know walking with you is stimulating in more ways than one. I've
really worked up an appetite. It's five-thirty. Uh, you think you might
like to get a bite to eat?"

She was about to say no until she turned to look at him again. He had this uncertain grin on his face, his eyes arched hopefully. He sure was different. She was beginning to get kind of a kick out of him. She was hungry and the idea of heading back home to fix herself something had no appeal. "Sure, why not?" she said and smiled.

"Oh!" He sounded surprised.

He took her to a nondescript Italian restaurant in the sixties between Sixth and Seventh avenues. The place was a cliché that seemed to fit him. Each table was covered with a red-checked cloth and an empty Chianti bottle holding a drip candle. A small, flat dish held salt and pepper shakers, grated Parmesan cheese, and a cruet of olive oil.

"I found this little spot one Saturday afternoon after the movies. They start serving at five. Pretty unusual for New York, and the food's not bad."

She was tired and hungry, and the pasta tasted good. Jack had a couple of martinis before dinner, which made him even more talkative. He ordered a glass of wine with dinner, and halfway through the meal he ordered another.

"Who's your favorite author, Lucky?" he asked.

She noticed his face was flushed and he was talking louder. "I like a lot of authors."

"But who's your favorite? Everybody's got a favorite."

"John McPhee."

"You gotta be kidding. I don't believe it. He's one of my all-time favorites," he proclaimed loudly.

She gave him a quizzical "oh, come on now" look.

"No, it's true," he protested.

She put her finger to her lips. "Jack, keep your voice down."

"Oh, sorry, Lucky. I've got a little medical condition, I'm not really supposed to drink much . . . and I don't, let me hasten to add. Guess I'm overdoing it a little, I'm enjoying you so much."

"It's been fun, Jack, but I do have to go in a few minutes."

His eyes fell. "Oh, damn. Well, anyway, I still can't get over our taste in authors. I've got every book McPhee ever wrote. *A Sense of Where You Are*, *The Headmaster*, *The Pine Barrens*, *Coming into the Country* . . ."

"You have *Coming into the Country?*"

" 'Course, why?"

"Nothing."

"Well, how come you asked about it?"

"It's just that I've been looking for that book and haven't been able to find it. Probably out of print."

"Well, look no further. You can borrow mine."

"Thanks, but I'm sure I can get it at the library."

"Listen. Tomorrow's going to be a lousy day. Supposed to rain all day. Perfect day to read. I only live a block and a half from here on Eighth Avenue. Five minutes. Walk over with me and I'll get you the book." He was bobbing and nodding again.

God, he read my mind, she thought. Relax and do nothing but read all day. Nothing good at home and it was true that she'd been dying to get her hands on *Coming into the Country*.

"Come on, Lucky. Give me five more minutes with you. I'll get you the book and put you in a cab home."

Actually, it was no big deal, and it was an interesting coincidence. It would be worth an extra five minutes. "OK," she said. "Let's go."

His building was a dilapidated old brownstone like thousands of others in the city. "Are you up for a little climb? I'm on the fourth floor."

She hesitated. He'd been slurring his words on the walk over and he no longer struck her as cute. She was about to ask him to run up and bring down the book when it started to sprinkle.

"Come on, Lucky. We're going to get wet."

She shrugged and scurried in with him out of the rain. Jack led the way up the dimly lit stairs. The rickety railing swayed when she grabbed it.

The building was quiet except for the scuffing of Jack's shoes on the bare stairs and his puffing and mumbling just above her. By the time they reached his door she wished she hadn't come. She stood watching him fumble through the pockets of first his coat, then his pants, looking for the key.

"Aha! Success."

The front door opened directly into a small living room, dominated by a large sofa and bookcases running the length of the far wall. She was impressed with his collection of art books.

"Here, why don't you sit for a minute, and I'll go hunt for the book." He disappeared down a small corridor that probably led to his bedroom.

Instead of sitting she wandered over to the bookcase. There were several by McPhee but no *Coming into the Country*. She wondered why he wouldn't keep them all together. Maybe he'd been reading it. She discovered two others she hadn't read and pulled them out and sat on the sofa.

Jack returned carrying a bottle of wine and two glasses. "I can't put my hands right on that damn book, but I know it's around here somewhere. Let's take a break in the action, though, and have some wine. Then I'll find it for you." He sat next to her, his shoulder and knees brushing hers.

She moved away. "Jack, I came up here to get the book you offered, not to watch you drink. Forget the book. You're drunk. I'm going home." She started to get up.

Jack put his hand on her shoulder. "I'm sorry. Please don't go. I'll get the book for you now." As he stood, he leaned over her, putting his arms on the back of the couch, one arm on either side of her head. "But first, I just want to do something I've wanted to do ever since I first saw you. I want to kiss you, Lucky."

She started to get up again, but he moved his arms closer, each arm holding her head firmly against the couch. He leaned closer, his face now inches from hers.

"Goddamn you!" she yelled.

She tried to slide her head out and under his arms but he held her firmly. Then he straddled her. Before she could move again his lips were caressing her face. His breath stank of alcohol, and she could smell the musky odor of his perspiration. She managed to move her head away. His big eyes moved in on her face. One hand slid down between her legs.

"No, no!" she screamed, and rolled him off her. In the same motion, her hand found the wine bottle. She hit him with it. He rolled onto the floor and she brought the bottle down again.

The bones in his nose crumbled and blood poured out and into his mouth. He lay on the floor, his eyes rolling crazily. She grabbed his head and smashed it on the hardwood floor, now slimy with his blood and pieces of scalp.

Slowly, she relaxed her hold on him and collapsed onto the floor. She closed her eyes, her quick, heavy breathing the only sound in the room.

She wasn't sure how long she had been lying there when she finally raised herself. Dark stains covered her sweater and she realized for the first time that her hands and clothes were covered with his blood.

Her legs nearly buckled as she pulled herself off him and stood for a moment in the silence of the apartment, steadying herself. She went into the bathroom, washed herself, took the towel and carefully wiped it over everything she could remember touching. Returning to the living room, she cleaned up, then stood over the man she had killed. There was one more thing she needed to do before leaving.

WHEN FRANK RUSSO awoke he knew it was nowhere near time to get up. He lay still with his eyes closed, hoping to drift off again. But the harder he tried, the more awake he became. He opened his eyes and looked at his watch face, glowing in the dark. Three-fifteen. He had slept only a few hours, and the prospects for more didn't look good. Images of Carla flickered across the darkened room.

He was wide awake. Sleep was out of the question. And there was no way he was going to continue lying there, playing mind fucks on himself. He got up and turned on his computer. Six weeks behind his deadline. Two phone calls last week from his publisher, telling him he was holding up the book. All the other contributors' chapters were in except his.

That was bullshit and he knew it, but this was the first time he'd missed a deadline and he didn't like it. He was nearly done and he could finish it tonight.

He put on some lights, padded into the galley kitchen, and made coffee. His stomach growled. "I'm up now, might as well make something to eat," he said aloud. Since he'd been living alone again, he'd begun talking to himself. It was when he had some of his best conversations. Actually, living alone wasn't all that bad. He was getting used to it. He could read all night if he wanted to, get up and cook at two in the morning, watch TV in bed any time of the night.

It didn't take him long to whip up an omelet with cheese, ham, peppers, onions, tomatoes, and sliced mushrooms. He gently and carefully slid it onto his plate, admiring its symmetry. The omelet was good, and so were memories connected with it. He and his father sitting in the kitchen at 6:00 A.M. when his mother was still in bed. They would talk and watch the sun come up. Silvio taught him how to fold the omelet in half before turning it so it wouldn't break.

They liked sharing the early-morning hours, getting a head start on the rest of the world. It was their time together before Frank went off to school, and his father strapped on his holster and gun and left for work. It was during one of their morning talks that he told his father he wanted to be a cop instead of a doctor.

"Frankie, you're smart enough to be the best doctor in New York," Silvio said.

He was afraid he had disappointed him and felt a twinge of guilt until his father grinned. "But you're going to be the best cop in the whole goddamn country. I have no doubt of that."

The strong coffee gave him the jolt he needed to forget about sleep and he went to work in the small study he'd created out of a corner of his bedroom. The two walls were lined with fiberboard bookcases, overflowing with books on psychiatry, psychology, psychopathology, and a section devoted to books and treatises on the mind of the serial killer. The magazines, many of which contained his own articles, ran the gamut from semipop publications like *Psychology Today* to the academic *American Journal of Psychiatry*. This was where he spent what little time he had to himself. What was left he spent in the kitchen with his other, creative passion.

At five-thirty he put the finishing touches on the third chapter, proofread and printed out the manuscript, and shut off the computer. He sat back and closed his eyes, wondering why it is when you have all night to sleep, you lie there wide awake, and when you have to get up, you feel like you could sleep forever.

After a hot shower and a shave, he brushed his teeth and gulped down the Lipitor pill he took daily to keep his cholesterol down— another thing he shared with his father. Feeling better, he wandered around the apartment, dressing in stages. First his underwear and socks, then to the kitchen to make more coffee. He was more of a morning person than ever now, since becoming an insomniac. Three, four hours of sleep was about it for him. It had been like that for six months.

He liked having the time to himself in the early-morning hours, poking around the apartment, enjoying the solitude of his own time and space. Once he hit the precinct, the world changed.

He slid a piece of bread into the toaster and pushed the lever down. It popped back up. Twice more, same result. He glanced at the note stuck on his refrigerator: *Buy toaster.* It had been there for a week.

Back in the bedroom with his coffee, he slipped into a pair of tan slacks and brown loafers. Time to call his father. Hell, seven-thirty in the morning was the middle of the day for Silvio. He'd be wound up, ready to talk all morning.

"Hello," his father's voice boomed through the small bedroom.

"Hi, Dad."

"Frankie. I had a feeling it was you. Where you been? Haven't heard from you in almost a week."

"That's why I'm calling. Starting to think about Florida?"

"Yep. We leave January second. Three months in the sun. Can't wait." There followed a pause as neither said anything for a moment. "Sorry, I meant to say *I* leave."

"Don't be sorry, Dad. Forty-five years you've been saying *we*. Mom's only been gone for three months. It's gonna take time."

"Yeah, I know, Frankie. You're right. Hey, how's the writing coming?"

"All right. Just finished the three chapters for the *Handbook of Criminal Investigations*."

"You got three chapters in this edition?"

"Yeah."

"Jesus. They must like your stuff, give you three chapters. That's the bible, Frankie."

Frank smiled. It *was* the bible, but it contained about half the knowledge his father had stashed away in his head. Thirty-five years in homicide, retired for five, Silvio Russo was a legend at the NYPD.

"And a tough cookie, your old man. Don't kid yourself," his partner, Jerry, who never pulled his punches about anything or anybody, always said. "He was no angel. He did what he had to do when he had to do it. So don't get carried away about the legend bullshit."

"Hey, when you coming over to the house, Frankie?"

"Get some Jets tickets from your buddy and let's get to a game before you leave for Florida. I've gotta run. Got a nine o'clock meeting with Jerry."

"Say hello to the old windbag for me. I'll get the tickets. Call ya."

Frank sat for a moment, thinking about his mother's death from breast cancer eight months after it was diagnosed. He'd been as close to her as to his father, but since her death, Silvio and he had grown closer than ever.

He finished dressing. Blue-and-white-striped button-down, maroon tie, and a blue blazer. It had been years since anybody at the station had given him any guff for the way he dressed. He learned his dress code from Silvio.

"Just because everybody else in the precinct looks like a slob, don't mean you have to. You're a gentleman, Frankie, and you dress and act like one. Always remember that."

He did. And he tolerated his reputation as the clothes horse of the department. Being dressed up made him feel good. He wore off-the-rack suits and jackets like they were tailor-made for his tall, slender frame.

Dark, curly hair rolled over his neck and around his shirt collar. His face had a high-cheekboned leanness, with a long elegant nose that gave a sharpness to his profile. Any suggestion of oversleekness was removed by the thick eyebrows that gave him a rugged look. Deep brown eyes flashed with an intensity that dominated a room. It was the eyes with their don't-fuck-with-me look that backed off the wiseguys in the station house that first day, when he walked in wearing the kind of pinstriped suit a cop would wear only to a funeral.

He drained the rest of the coffee and tried to focus on his meeting with Jerry, but Carla came out of nowhere. Funny how relationships end. Two people are close. Shit happens. A distance develops. And bingo! You make a 180 turn, and it's over.

JERRY BLODGETT THUMPED around the squad room. A narrow, vintage sixties tie dangled loosely from the neck of his short-sleeved shirt. The shirt curved around a massive belly, and Jerry's efforts to stuff the shirttail back under his belt met with only limited success. He shrugged and gave up. "Hey, Fraser, you seen Russo?"

Francis Fraser, a slightly built detective wearing a gray sweatshirt and jeans, looked up from the button he was sewing on his shirt. "No, try the kitchen."

"The fuck you think, I'm gonna wander around here lookin' for him without first tryin' the kitchen? He's not there."

Fraser returned to his sewing. "I don't know where he is. I ain't his keeper."

Blodgett watched Fraser for a moment. "Francis, I got a hole in my underwear shorts. I'll drop 'em off later."

Frank came out of the bathroom and moved gracefully across the room, looking out of place among the sweatshirts, jeans, sneakers, and leather jackets in the Midtown North Precinct. The high-energy adrenaline of the precinct filled the air, along with the smell of Lysol and stale coffee. Black metal desks with wood-veneer tops were scattered haphazardly throughout the long room, some empty. At others detectives sat talking loudly on the phone, writing on yellow pads, or pecking away at computers.

At one end of the room was an enclosed office belonging to the squad commander, Lieutenant Joseph Nolan. Three other adjacent offices housed the precinct sergeants, including Jerry Blodgett.

Jerry spotted Frank and motioned him over. He led Frank into his office and shut the door. "Frank, you got anything more on the Beatty case?"

Frank shook his head. "Not much." He looked through the glass walls at Fraser, who was finishing up with his button and bit the thread off. "Francis is getting to be quite a seamstress." He turned back to Jerry. "Harry and I have interviewed everybody in Beatty's building. Nobody saw or heard a thing, except for the people you talked with who live just below him.

"They heard somebody going up the stairs at about seven-fifteen, seven-thirty. Couldn't say if it was more than one person, because they didn't pay any attention. They were watching TV. Anyway, about ten minutes later they hear this commotion and thumping on the floor. Lasted for just a minute or two but long enough to annoy the guy. Says he was about to pound on the ceiling with his broom when it stopped. They could still hear somebody moving around up there, but more softly, not as heavy or noisy."

"Yeah. The killer was being careful. Cleaning things up and all. Pretty cool customer."

"Uh-uh. Whoever did this wasn't a cool customer. He tried to be, but this was the work of an amateur. OK, fingerprints wiped off, but two books were still there on the sofa with prints on them. The killer tried to pick up all the pieces of a broken glass, but he missed three. He left everything in the victim's pockets, so no effort to make it look like a robbery. This was the work of somebody who tried to cover his tracks but was sloppy.

"The hairs found on the body come from long, brown, untreated natural hair. Can't determine the sex."

Jerry took a sip from the Styrofoam coffee cup he'd been holding, made a face, and dumped in two more envelopes of sugar.

"Two books by the same author still on the sofa," Frank continued. "I figure Beatty brought someone back with him. They sat on the sofa and had a drink. Maybe they were discussing the books."

"Yeah, looks like things started out OK."

"Had to be somebody he knew, Jerry. Beatty was a highly educated guy, working in an upscale field. Look at the books in his apartment. He's got more money in books than furnishings. Whoever it was up there with him most likely came from a similar background."

"How can you be sure?"

"I'm not sure, for Christ sake. But those two books by McPhee were there for a reason. Beatty wasn't reading them both at once. We've got two sets of prints on both books. He and his guest were probably discussing them. Two wineglasses, a couple of books. These were two people having a discussion and something went wrong. I think we're looking for an educated person, somebody not unlike Beatty."

"What do you think went wrong?"

"I don't know, but this guy was really worked over. It's one thing to get whacked with a wine bottle, but that's not what killed him. He was hit on the front of his head with the bottle. The back of it was

bashed over and over on the floor. He died of a subdural hemor-
rhage. Christ, the floor's all splintered from his head. Look at the way
the back of it was split open. Somebody was very angry."

"What do you make of the wine bottle up his ass?"

"It's a statement, Jerry. It's not just a random act."

"You think the killer was a homosexual?" Jerry asked. "Came on
to Beatty and Beatty didn't like it? Called him a faggot or worse?
'Course, maybe Beatty was a fag and they had a lovers' quarrel."

"Jerry, when are you going to start being politically correct?"

Jerry started to say something, but Frank talked over him. "Anyway, all of the people who knew him said there's no way this guy was
gay. Nobody ever saw any sign of it. We know of at least two women
he dated. They said he was a good guy. Drank a little too much. The
autopsy showed a high level of alcohol in his blood. Intoxication
level. He was drunk at the time he was killed. Also still had pasta and
red sauce in his stomach, so he'd only recently eaten. Probably no
more than an hour before he was killed."

"Yeah," Jerry said. He pulled a half empty box of sugar doughnuts
from his desk drawer, took a bite out of one, and dunked the remain-
der in his coffee. Little pieces of powdered sugar floated on top for a
moment, then disappeared.

"There's no sign of anybody having cooked," Frank said. "No
pasta packages around. No empty cans. No dirty pots or dishes. A
few items from breakfast still in the sink. Coffee cup, plate with dried
egg and toast crusts, but no sign that anybody ate dinner there." He
shook his head as Jerry pointed toward the doughnut box.

"So he got the pasta in a restaurant," Jerry said.

"Yeah, and on this guy's income, you can bet it wasn't an expensive
one. Beatty was not what you'd call a mover. Look at his wardrobe.
One sport coat, an old suit, and a few pairs of chinos. I doubt he
strayed far from the neighborhood. We'll check out all the cheap Italian restaurants first and go from there."

"Maybe he ate at a friend's apartment?"

"Not likely. If he ate at a friend's place, why would they come back to his for drinks? They'd have just stayed there."

"Does look like it was somebody he knew," Jerry said. "I think you're right there."

"Anyway, we're making our way through everybody he worked with. I've had a good first session with his family on the phone. Nothing concrete yet, though. He was very well liked, by the way."

"Yeah, well, somebody didn't like him. Frank, I'm already takin' shit from Nolan on this. He doesn't want any waves to screw up his promotion. That lawyer wife of his is pushing him all the time. She's a social climber, married to a cop! What do you call that, Frank? There's a word for it. Oxie somethin'."

"Oxymoron."

"Yeah, that's it. Anyway, Nolan's gonna be all over my ass till we find the guy who did this. I agree with you. Had to be somebody he knew. He let him in, they had a nice friendly drink, and the guy kills him."

"What makes you so sure it's a guy?"

Jerry sipped his coffee and nodded. "Yeah, could be a woman. But I don't know. All that physical violence is sure not the profile of a female."

"Jerry, you ever hear of a case where the killer jams a bottle up the victim's rectum?"

"No."

"I'll run this through the state homicide- and lead-tracking program and put it through VICAP. Maybe we'll find a similar MO somewhere around the country. I'd say this one's a tad unique."

"Yeah, well, I got an appointment downtown. Talk to you later." As he walked past Frank, he patted him on the stomach. "Hey, gettin' a little pot? You better start workin' out."

"Look who's calling the kettle black. You got nerve, I'll say that for you."

And with that Jerry left for his appointment, and Frank headed over to East Fifty-first Street to talk with a publisher for whom Beatty had done some freelancing. Beatty didn't move in a very wide circle. Shouldn't be too hard to get a handle on the people he saw professionally and socially. The killer was somebody he knew, somebody he felt comfortable with. Somebody like him.

He thought about Jerry's parting shot. "Gettin' a little pot?" Too much booze. He would start working out, try that little health club he'd heard about.

Frank walked the few blocks crosstown to the East Side, snaking his way under the scaffolds that were everywhere in the city. No matter where you walked, the scaffolding dominated the scene—a reminder of New York's constant renovating, restoring, rebuilding.

Still, walking in the East Fifties wasn't too hard to take. The elegant office and apartment buildings gleamed in the midday sun; attractive, well-dressed men and women talking on cell phones hurried as if they had important destinations—which they probably did. For the first time since last winter, people wore coats, buttoned up tightly. Today's midfall temperature was a harbinger of things to come.

He reached Fiftieth Street and froze in his tracks. Not fifteen yards in front of him, Carla was crossing the street.

Bile came up in his throat. "Oh, Jesus Christ," he blurted and closed his eyes. When he opened them, all that was left of her were two long legs sliding into the backseat of a cab. She closed the door and turned to look out the back window. He was sure she saw him.

4

DENISE, I NEED to pick your brain on the Mendenhall book. Can you get his file and come into my office?" Mike Peters asked over the phone as he gazed out his window at the New York skyline.

"Sure, Mike. Give me a minute and I'll be in," Denise said.

Mike's office, although not large, was comfortable, and typical of most New York editors' offices, simple and functional. Manuscripts were strewn everywhere. Both side chairs bulged under the load of millions of typed words. Papers crept out of manila folders, battened down by thick rubber bands. The small table by the window was stacked high with fat, messy-looking folders, manuscript boxes, and three-ring binders. The only thing resembling neatness was a file of computer discs.

"Mendenhall giving you trouble again, Mike?"

Mike turned from the window and watched his associate editor come toward him. Although they had been working together for ten months, he was still in awe of Denise's beautiful body: nearly six feet tall, broad shoulders, and a waist you could put your hands around.

She was also very smart, and he planned to promote her to a full editorship at the end of the year. He knew she would do well in the college textbook business. "Yeah, how'd you know?"

Denise tapped the side of her head. "Sixth sense." She threw her head back, her light brown hair flying away from her eyes for the moment.

He wished she wouldn't do that. She was one of the best editors he'd ever worked with, and he was not about to do anything to screw things up. Anyway, he was happily married. Still, he wished she wouldn't do that. "He's pissed about the reviews I sent him on his manuscript."

"What are you going to do?" Denise set the file and reviews on his desk. She stood over him, totally oblivious, he was sure, of the effect she had on him.

"I don't know yet. The professors who've reviewed it are all at great schools, and their suggestions make a lot of sense."

"Why don't you get them all together with him and set up a focus group?"

Mike put his hands to his forehead. "That's a great idea, Denise. Let's do it. I'm sure I can get Mendenhall to come and at least listen. What would I do without you?" He smiled warmly at her.

"You'd hire somebody else and forget all about me pretty fast." She said it matter-of-factly, without humor, without irony. It simply reflected her view of things.

Mike watched her walk toward the door, her hips swaying. He called after her. "Denise, the Bookbuilders Association is having its monthly cocktails and dinner get-together on Thursday. I've got some tickets, and a bunch of us are going over. Do you want to come?"

"Oh, Mike, you know I work out every night at my health club. After that I want to finish up a project I'm working on at home. Thanks anyway."

"OK, just thought I'd ask . . . again."

At five-thirty, Denise turned off her computer and organized her to-do list for the morning. Mike was so sweet, but he just didn't get it. She didn't want to go to those publishing dinners. Her coworkers were all nice people but she just wasn't into those monthly mob scenes of drinking and schmoozing. She really wished he would back off.

"Is that you, Denise? Are you still here?" Gina Ponte's voice floated across the room.

"Yes, it's me. I'm still here."

Denise looked up and Gina was standing in the doorway. She hadn't entered yet but she seemed to fill the entire area. Long black hair curled undisciplined around her neck and over her shoulders. Hoop earrings fought their way through the mane of hair, struggling to be seen. A fresh coat of lipstick covered her lips, giving them a puckered, waiting-to-be kissed look. She was nearly as tall as Denise, and her ethnic, Mediterranean good looks stood in contrast to Denise's more subtle beauty. Her coat was draped over one arm, a briefcase in the other hand. She came in and slumped heavily onto Denise's chair.

"What a day! One of my authors, Paul Donlan, has been giving me a bad time all day. He's called me three times, bitching about one thing after another, snapping at me, growling. Fun day."

"Sounds like a day like any other," Denise said.

"I tell you, Denise. One of these days, when he gets on me like he did today, I'm going to smile sweetly and tell him to go fuck himself."

Denise laughed, the first time all day. "No, you won't, Gina. You thrive on the pressure and the give-and-take between you and Donlan. You're as tough as he is."

Gina shrugged. "You're probably right. Anyway, how was your day?"

Denise leaned back in her chair and stretched her long legs. Even though she was about to leave and wanted to get to her health club, she was glad that Gina had stopped by. "It was OK. Mike's having his usual problems with Mendenhall, but we'll deal with him. His books always wind up being worth the trouble."

"Yeah. He may be a pain in the ass, but he's a doll, that Mendenhall. I almost flipped when I saw him in the office a few months ago. I wish he was one of my authors. I'd figure out a way to soften him up. On second thought, maybe I'd just keep him hard." Gina's laugh, phlegmy and watery, erupted.

"He's married, Gina."

"So what. I'd just give him a little R and R while he was away from home. That's all. Well, see ya. I've got to go." She was up and gone, leaving Denise with a smile on her face.

It was time to leave if she wanted to be working out by six. She snapped off the light and was soon outside. The brisk October air felt good, and she enjoyed the seven-block walk to the club, absorbing the sounds of the city—horns beeping, cabbies screaming in Arabic at jaywalkers, the hissing and farting of bus brakes, and the roar of subway trains beneath the sidewalk. People bustled past her, each moving as if ten minutes late for an appointment, often turning sideways to avoid hitting her.

Club Fitness was nothing more than a second-floor room about the size of a large living room. The place was well equipped with free weights, Nautilus machines, cardiovascular bikes, and treadmills. A small reception desk stood to the right of the front door, and there were two small locker rooms and showers for men and women. That was it. No frills, the closest thing being a juice machine. But its main advantage was its location, exactly halfway between her office and apartment.

Inside the locker room she changed into her Lycra tights and tank top, hooked up her iPod, and was ready to face the machines.

Tonight, she worked on her back and shoulders. First, the back. Three sets of twelve hyperextensions. Four sets of ten rowing half seated, half at the T-bar. Four sets of ten pull-downs to back, and four sets of ten pull-downs to front.

Next she focused on her shoulders, working with the free weights. First, a behind-the-neck press, four sets of ten. Then the rest of her shoulders routine.

After she finished, she closed out her session with fifty push-ups and lay on her stomach, resting. The club had filled up during her workout. She headed for the locker room, weaving her way through the sweating, grunting men and women.

She showered and dressed, and looked forward to the walk home. She pushed through the doors as a tall, dark-haired man entered.

"Hi! Bye," they said simultaneously, laughing.

The cool air felt good. It was dinnertime and the street was crowded with chattering couples. The pace had slowed from the frenzy of people rushing from work to whatever means they used to get home.

The thought of sitting in a comfortable restaurant and having dinner with a friend crossed her mind. Gina was fun and she made Denise laugh, but sometimes she could be a little crude.

She'd been busy all week, never seeming to relax and unwind, grabbing a take-out salad in a neighborhood store run by the Korean couple, standing at the sink, eating tuna fish out of the can. Tonight she decided to treat herself.

Inside her apartment she busied herself about the kitchenette: poached a fresh salmon steak, mixed some mustard sauce, microwaved a few asparagus spears, and sliced a tomato. When everything was ready, she poured some Sauvignon Blanc into one of her new crystal wineglasses, set the table with her linen place mat, and lit two candles. She dimmed the lights and slipped in a Sarah Brightman CD, sipped her wine, and ate slowly and deliberately in the flickering candlelight. It was so nice, everything so pretty. And no one to share it with.

5

CRYSTAL WILCOX STOOD on the corner of Forty-fourth and Seventh Avenue. It had been a beautiful sunny day, but with typical fall-weather treachery, the night had turned cold. It was now late and she wasn't dressed for it. She had about decided to go home when her friend Vickie Torrez came around the corner.

"Crystal, honey, what you doin' out here? It's cold."

"Same thing you are, Vickie," Crystal replied. "It is chilly, though. Come on. I'll buy you a drink."

They headed along Forty-fourth Street, Mutt and Jeff, Crystal at five feet-eleven towering nearly a foot over Vickie's five-one. Inside the bar they sat warming themselves over some wine.

"I swear, Crystal, I'll never understand you. You got some of the richest big-shot johns in the city after your body any time you snap your fingers. You got that gorgeous apartment that you ain't never got to leave if you don't want to, and you come down here messing with scumbags looking for a little cheap pussy or a quick blow job. Why?"

Crystal snickered, drained her glass, and ordered another wine. "Sweetie, why do you waste your time wondering about me? You got enough to do keeping your own butt humping, taking care of that loser you live with."

Vickie bristled. Raoul *was* a loser and he treated her like dirt, but that didn't give Crystal the right to talk like that. Still, she didn't want no trouble with Crystal. She was mean and everybody knew it wasn't healthy to argue with her or piss her off.

"I didn't mean nothin', Crystal. It's just that I got to put up with this crap. I got no choice. But you, you're beautiful, you're smart, and everybody knows you make ten times as much as the rest of us with all your high-class clientele. And then when I see you down here . . . well, it just don't make sense." Vickie quickly put her hands up, afraid she'd gone too far. "But, hey, that's cool with me. I like seein' you. We get along OK, right?"

Crystal played with her hair and smiled. "Let's just say I get off on being down and dirty once in a while. Reminds me of my roots, OK? Come on, let's get out of here. Walk me down the corner while I get a cab."

It was nearly midnight when they started along Forty-fourth Street. A man came out of a small bar and headed toward them. He walked unsteadily, slowly, in no hurry to get anywhere.

"Well, lookie here," Crystal whispered, looking around the otherwise empty street. She grabbed Vickie by the arm and they stepped into a doorway.

The man reached them, humming quietly to himself. He was clearly drunk.

"Hi, honey. You want to party?" Crystal whispered.

The man stopped and looked at the two women standing in the

doorway. He stood weaving, looking them up and down, and moved into the doorway with them.

Vickie gave him a big smile and rubbed him a little. "You want some fun, honey?"

He studied her, trying to focus. A sneer crossed his face. "Sheeit. I don't go with spics." He turned toward Crystal. "Maybe I wouldn't mind a little white meat."

Crystal's hand found his crotch and began rubbing him. "Hmm. You feel like a real man, honey. I want some a that, eat you right up. How 'bout a nice little blow job? Send you home happy." Now she was into it, working him over. His eyes closed and little gurgling sounds came from him.

"Oh, Jesus. Yes, yes, where?"

"Come on, honey, I got a good spot. You got a hundred dollars? That's all it's going to cost you."

The man nodded and walked along with Crystal. Vickie followed behind. Halfway down the block Crystal turned the man into an alley. "Vickie, honey, would you kinda keep an eye out while we do our thing? Won't be long."

Vickie nodded and stepped into another doorway and waited. She was used to being called names, especially spic. But she still didn't like it. If she had Crystal's looks and brains she sure wouldn't be walking the streets blowing guys in alleyways.

"You son of a bitch." Crystal's voice came out of the alley. "What're you trying to pull?"

More yelling from Crystal. A man and woman rounded the corner about a hundred yards away and slowly headed toward them. Vickie decided it was time to retrieve Crystal and get the hell out of there. She headed down the alley.

HEY, FRANK, LET'S go over to Rumours and get a beer." Jerry stood over Frank's desk and grabbed him by the shoulder. "Come on, pal. Enough's enough. It's six-thirty."

Frank looked up from his computer and waved him off. "Give me a few minutes."

"Hurry up. I'm going to the head. See you downstairs." Jerry shambled across the squad room and out the door.

Frank liked Rumours. It was where he went to unwind, often by himself. It was dark and low-key and they played his kind of music, like Kenny Rogers and Dolly Parton singing "Islands in the Stream." He liked it a little too much. His monthly bar tab was killing him. He hoped the health club would take up some of the slack. But everybody needed a haven from all the bullshit and Rumours was his.

Jerry liked the place because even though smoking was banned they never gave him a hard time about at least holding a cigar in his mouth. Most of the other places wouldn't even allow that.

They settled into two of the high ladder-back chairs at the long polished oak bar. On the wall to the bar's left hung a whimsical caricature of Frank Sinatra, Dean Martin, and Sammy Davis, Jr. Four flat-screen television sets hung in strategic spots over the bar. The place was nearly empty, the after-work crowd having left and the evening patrons yet to arrive.

Jerry ordered them a couple of beers. The barmaid slid Jerry's to him and set Frank's carefully in front of him as if presenting a magic potion.

"How you doin', Frank?"

"I'm OK, how about you, Cathy?"

"I'm better . . . now." She squeezed his hand and wiggled to the other side of the bar.

Jerry took it all in and shook his head in disgust. "Whatsa matter with you, Russo? She's been throwin' herself at you for almost a year now. And all you do is give her that silly-ass grin and act like a wimp." He drained his beer and nodded his head toward Cathy. "I'll tell you one thing. She come on to me like that, she'd a been taken care of a long time ago."

"Sheeit." Frank laughed. "You'd have a heart attack with something like that. Anyway, Betty'd find out and kick your ass."

"You're probably right on both counts. What's new on the Beatty case?"

"We don't have a whole lot. I ran a check on the prints through AFIS. Neither set of prints we found on the books belongs to anybody who's been arrested since 1985. So . . . we know the killer hasn't been arrested after that."

Jerry motioned for two more beers.

"No luck on the restaurants yet," Frank said as Cathy poured his beer for him. "He had a Visa card in his wallet but no restaurant

receipt in his pocket. We checked with Visa but no charges have
come in yet. We'll follow up later in the week, but he probably paid
cash."

"Or the other person could've paid," Jerry said.

Frank nodded. "There's something else that bothers me about this
one, Jerry."

"What?"

"This could be the beginning of more to come."

"I know what you're gonna say."

"You've got a signature here with that bottle in the rectum. This
kind of behavior goes beyond the actions needed to commit the
crime."

"Yeah, go on." Jerry knew he wasn't going to like what was coming.

"Well, you get an offender with fantasies, he's going to brood and
daydream until he finally expresses and acts out the violent fantasies.
However, just commiting the crime doesn't satisfy all of his needs.
He needs to go beyond it and perform a ritual . . . a calling card."

"And the bottle is the calling card here."

Frank gave him a double take. "Uh, yeah." He grinned and tapped
the side of his head with his finger. "Now, what we have to worry
about is that the signature aspect stays with the killer as an ongoing
part of his fantasies. He's got to keep acting it out now, right?"

"Yeah," Jerry said softly.

"These creeps all start out with their fantasies and begin to live
them. Ed Kemper, John Wayne Gacy, Wayne Williams, our own Son
of Sam, Ted Bundy, Jeffrey Dahmer—"

"All right! All right," Jerry growled.

Frank watched his friend, a year away from retirement and trying
to coast home. He felt Jerry's angst and hoped he was wrong about
Beatty being the beginning of more to come. "Hey, let's talk about
something else for a change. How's Betty?"

"She's fine. Listen, kid, there is something else I want to talk to you about." He clamped his arm around Frank's neck. "Come on. Let's go sit down at a table."

They settled in at a round table under a large Guinness Light mirrored sign. Frank poured more beer and watched Jerry pull out a cigar. He knew the routine. He watched his partner take his time unwrapping the cigar, suck on it, bite off the end, take a deep fake puff, look up, close his eyes, and blow out the invisible smoke. Weird, but it seemed to give Jerry pleasure.

"Frank," Jerry began. "You know you're the best and smartest detective in the precinct, next to me, that is. I don't mind telling you that, 'cause you already know it. You're one of the best in the whole NYPD. Lotta people have their eye on you. You been doing Silvio proud. Shit, even I learn something from you every once in a while."

"Gee, thanks, Jerry."

"Don't be a wiseass. I'm telling you this because I'm worried about you. You got a great future ahead of you, kid, but you haven't been yourself these last six months since you and Carla split. You ever see her?"

"No. When she moved out and got her own place, that was it. We lost touch. I don't even know where she lives."

"Well, start seeing some women. Have some fun."

He wasn't in the mood for this. He took a long pull on his beer and looked around the bar, his eyes now adjusted to the darkness. A young hooker sat across from them, looking nervous, ill at ease, and yet hopeful. She didn't even look old enough to drink. At the bar, a fiftyish man in a three-piece suit sat alone, staring into space, not having much luck fighting back tears.

The city was full of people like that, sad people trying to cope with life, playing as best they could the hands they'd been dealt. He turned back to Jerry and saw the anguish in his face. He slid his arm up and hugged his friend. "Thanks, Jerry. I appreciate what you're saying.

I'm going to be fine." He let go of Jerry and grinned. "Tell you what. I'll go out and get laid tonight."

The joke fell flat. "You know, Frank, now that you two have been split for a while, I guess I can tell you, I think in the long run you're going to be better off. So does Betty, by the way."

Oh, Jesus, Frank thought. Jerry's wound up, probably been saving up his speech and rehearsing it. "What do you mean?"

"I mean I think you were so nuts about Carla you didn't see some of the things we did."

"Like what?"

"Well, she was moody as hell, for one thing."

"She's a model, Jerry. They're all like that. Anyway, I know what you're saying, but a lot of it was my fault. Even with the career, what she really wanted more than anything was a guy who was there for her, a lover she could count on for the emotional security she needed. I wasn't there."

"Yeah, but you shouldn't be bashing yourself, Frank. Takes two, you know. And hell, I may be way off base for saying this, but I just never felt like you had a real handle on her, you know? Hey, you know me, I'm just nosy, but whenever I'd ask you things about her, you never had much to say."

Frank pushed his beer away. "For Christ sake, Jerry, she moved in three weeks after we met, and we split three months later.

"And even during those three months we didn't see a whole lot of each other, with my crazy schedule and her modeling demands. She was off on shoots half the time. Hell, she was in Italy alone for two weeks. Anyway . . . you are a nosy son of a bitch, aren't you?"

"Yeah, well, I'm a cop. I'm supposed to be."

"Anyway, let's have another beer and get off it, OK?"

Jerry nodded. He knew his friend and it was time to drop it.

7

PAUL GALE SAT outside the warden's office of the Massachusetts State Prison at Norfolk. Today was the day for which he'd waited twenty-one years. He fidgeted nervously and his heart pounded. Through the room's two windows he could see the faded late-autumn colors of the trees and the blue October sky. He glanced at the guard sitting next to him. I won't miss seeing you anymore, asshole, he thought, resisting the temptation to say it aloud.

The guard looked back malevolently at Gale, seeming to read his mind. "You'll be back, Gale. We'll keep your cell warm for you."

The phone on the secretary's desk buzzed. "Yes, sir, I'll send him in." She hung up the phone, and without looking at the guard indicated that the warden was ready to see Paul Gale.

"All right. On your feet, Gale." The guard's voice had the tone of one accustomed to telling people what to do.

Gale struggled to his feet. The guard held one elbow as Paul shuffled across the room toward the warden's office.

When they entered the office, John Bulger slid his desk chair back and stood. A slender, scholarly-looking man, he appeared more like an academic than a warden. He spoke softly. "That's all right, Quigley. You can wait outside but leave the door open." Bulger walked around to the front of his desk and leaned against it, facing Gale. He did not offer him a chair.

Gale shifted from one foot to the other, clearing his throat, the only sound in the room.

The warden studied Gale, his face hard and unfeeling.

Gale's discomfort mounted.

"Well, congratulations, Gale. You're finally going to be leaving the system. All I can do now is wish you luck out there."

Gale shifted position again. "Thank you, Warden."

"Gale, I like to think the system has helped you. You had your troubles in Walpole but you eventually managed to keep your nose clean and get transferred here to Norfolk. You've kept out of trouble here, and hopefully you can find a place in normal society.

"But the prison psychologist tells me that you still have a lot of anger inside you, the kind that got you into trouble in Walpole. At least you've managed to suppress, or should I say contain, it in here.

"Anyway, you're free to go now, and if you want to have a decent life on the outside and stay out of trouble, try to remember what I've said. I only wish I had a better handle on you so I could feel more comfortable about your release."

Gale's face twitched. "Sorry you feel that way, sir. I did my time, and like you said, stayed outta trouble, and the parole board says I'm ready to leave." He couldn't resist a slight smile.

Warden Bulger studied him for a moment before replying. "I hope so, Gale. I truly hope so."

Gale stood silent, his eyes upon the floor until the guard entered and led him out.

The cab carrying Gale angled onto Route 1 and headed toward Boston. He sat back, enjoying the fresh air blowing through the open windows. A million thoughts raced through his mind. But for the moment, he reflected on the session with the warden. It had taken him a long time to learn. Fights and other troubles kept him at Walpole way beyond the norm. Each time he came up for his parole hearing, he was denied.

He finally got smart and learned how to go with the flow and put up with all the shit. It paid off. First the transfer to Norfolk. Medium security. Piece of cake after the tough maximum security at Walpole. And now, here he was paroled and cruising along Route 1 to Boston, a free man.

He focused on the fading but still colorful foliage on the trees and the deep blue sky he had seen precious little of for so many years.

After a while he leaned back, lit a cigarette, enjoying the scenery and reveling in his freedom.

The cabdriver turned around. "I'm sorry, sir, did you notice the no smoking sign in the back? I'm allergic to cigarette smoke and I ask my passengers to please not smoke."

Gale studied the driver for a moment, took a deep drag on the cigarette, and blew the smoke into the front seat before flicking the cigarette out the window. They rode in silence the rest of the way.

The cabbie dropped him at the Park Plaza Hotel in Park Square. His eyes darted about, absorbing everything. But he was tired, and all he wanted now was to sleep. There would be plenty of time to explore and enjoy his new freedom. When Gale reached his room, he lay back on the queen-size bed, the first real bed he had been on in years. He closed his eyes and fell into a deep sleep.

FRANK FINISHED HIS lecture at NYU and the students filed out in clusters, talking on their cell phones. As usual, Frank was quickly surrounded by them. Once a week he spoke for an hour on the violent offender to graduate students in criminal justice as part of the guest lecture program.

He had mixed feelings about it. He enjoyed teaching students and loved the intellectual give and take. Since this was his second year, it no longer required a lot of preparation time and the students loved it. That was part of the problem, he thought as he tried to make his way through the jam of mostly female students waiting to talk with him. Most were simply interested in having further discussion with their favorite teacher. It was the other ones who were getting to be a problem. They would call him at the precinct, even at home. He knew better than to encourage anyone and he was not about to get involved, even though some of them were tempting.

"Mr. Russo, I'm intrigued by your comments about fantasy being more than an escape, but how it becomes the focal behavior."

She was a good student, but she was also a toucher. He took a step back. "No question, Shelly. What I'm saying is that a sexual psychopath is able to maintain contact with reality. But his world of fantasy becomes as addictive as an escape into drugs."

He looked over her shoulder and saw Susan Lehman, holding a briefcase in one hand and beckoning him with the other. He managed to extricate himself with a smile. "Excuse me, I have an appointment. See you next week."

He took Susan's hand in both of his and squeezed it. "What a nice surprise."

He was still holding her hand in his when she set down her briefcase and placed her other hand on top, and they stood for a moment facing each other the way old friends do, Frank as always admiring her good looks and class.

"Come on. You look tired," she said. "I'll buy you a drink."

They settled into a bar at the edge of Washington Square. "So what's with you, Frank? Where've you been and how have you been?"

"I've been around and I'm OK." The scotch tasted good. He looked across the room and back at Susan. She was his buddy but she knew him too well, knew too much about him, and that made him just a little uncomfortable. "You teaching at night now, too?" he asked.

"No, I had some work to do in the library and then I figured you might be lecturing tonight so I thought I'd stop over. That OK?"

Frank grinned and shrugged. He held up his empty glass. "My turn to buy you a drink."

Susan sat back and watched him. He knew she wasn't just looking at him. She was studying him. The psychologist in her, always working. She wasn't exactly hard to look at herself. He especially liked her large blue eyes and the intelligent face reflecting an intriguing blend of smarts and sensuality.

"I've been seeing your articles in the journals. They're very good."

"Thanks."

"And Fahey tells me you might be doing a book in his criminal justice series. Articles, lecturing down here. And if I know you, you're putting in at least seventy hours a week for the good old NYPD. That sound about right?"

"Yeah, I guess so."

"Frank, you're pushing yourself too hard. Anything or anyone in your life besides work?"

"Ooh. That didn't take long. No small talk, no foreplay. Just get right to it, huh?"

She continued staring at him. He knew she would until he gave her a straight answer. "Anyway, the answer is no." He was about to say he didn't have any time but thought better of it.

"You know, Frank, my record as a therapist has been pretty damn good. I really do help people. Why did you call it quits just when we were starting to make some progress?"

He noticed the two little drops of perspiration on her upper lip. Not unappealing. "Yeah, well, I figured three months of fun and games every week was enough."

"Dammit it, Frank, that's how it works. Of course it's painful. She hurt you badly, but we were working through that. And then what do you do? All of a sudden cut it off like *that*." She snapped her fingers and glared at him.

Four beads on her lip now. "Sorry, Suze. I know we were making progress. And you're the best."

"Then why did you stop?"

"I told you. I'm not big on pain. And anyway, I'm doing fine now."

She shook her head and frowned. "Look at you. What a waste. You may be the best-looking cop in New York City. If I weren't your therapist and friend—"

"Ex-therapist," he broke in.

"OK, ex-therapist, but not ex-friend. I care about you, you jerk."
Five beads.
"The job going well?"
"Very well."
"Are you sleeping any better?"
"Not much. But then, I never was a big sleeper."
"When's the last time you had a date?"
"Susan, are we having a therapy session?"
"Yes, and this one's on the house."

BACK HOME IN his apartment he made himself a double scotch on the
rocks and slipped in a CD. He didn't know which one it was and he
didn't care. Last Sunday's *New York Times* sat undisturbed and un-
read on the sofa, where he'd thrown it nearly a week ago. The soft
sounds of Norah Jones drifted across the small living room. Good
choice, he thought as he sat down in his favorite and only easy chair,
put his feet up on the ottoman, and took a deep breath.

The scotch tasted good and helped him relax. It helped but it
wasn't enough. He was tired and he felt depressed. Why the hell
wouldn't he be?

Trying to do too much. And now here he was considering taking
on a whole book. *It's crazy. Susan's right.* He didn't know how to say
no. And she was still all worked up about his breakup with Carla.
Looking back, the relationship was lousy. Great sex but not much
else. And he wasn't stupid. He knew he and Carla were drifting apart,
and maybe he cared more about the NYPD than her. And maybe in
the long run he'd be better off without her. Maybe.

He went to the kitchen and poured another scotch. Back in the living room, he glanced at the picture of his father and him with the
mayor at his father's retirement. Shit, Silvio was a borough commander by the time he was forty. Hard to believe it had been eight

years now since he'd made detective. So full of piss and vinegar. He was going to be Henry the Fifth and turn every case into another fucking Agincourt.

It didn't work that way, but he'd get there. Two tours at the FBI Academy at Quantico, giving his own seminars, the writing, teaching. All adds up. He finished off the scotch and closed his eyes.

Funny, when he was a know-it-all graduate student he wrote a thesis on career police officers and their problems. Divorce rates off the charts, boozers living in drab little apartments. It was all so clinical, so easy to analyze with the condescending superiority of a college kid who didn't know shit about the real world.

Anyway, this was it, the real world, his real world. Maybe a graduate student will call him for an interview.

Yes, life was complicated. He still had bad vibes about the Beatty killing. It had been almost two weeks now. If he was right about the signature and the timing, something was going to happen again—soon.

Jerry. He'd learned so much from him, but now Jerry was just coasting, not wanting to rock the boat. Jerry would lean on him down the stretch. It was OK.

He set down the empty glass, walked the four steps into the kitchen, and checked the refrigerator. He found the remnants of a chicken breast, which he sliced on an angle, cut up the aging green pepper and a few shallots, sprinkled in some herbs, a little fresh garlic, and put it all in a frying pan with some wine. He was in his element, feeling a little better. He turned the heat down and whipped up some pasta with tomatoes, olive oil, basil, and more fresh garlic.

He ate his supper at the small table in a corner of the living room while reading the page proofs of one of his articles. At eleven o'clock, feeling groggy, bone tired, and generally screwed up, he flopped into bed, popped in a Beatles CD, and slipped off to sleep to the strains of "Hey Jude."

IT WAS 6:00 A.M. before Gale stirred. There was much to do today, and he was eager to get started. He opened his suitcase and removed an envelope. Inside was a cashier's check for $10,280. In prison he had opted for the work program, averaging just over twenty hours a week for sixteen years in the plate shop, making license plates. He earned twenty-five dollars per week, kept half the money for cigarettes and other incidentals, and the other half was deposited to his account. The check now would provide him with a nice little nest egg, until he could get back on his feet.

He stood in the center of the hotel lobby gazing at the lively, chattering people, talking among themselves and on small phones no bigger than playing cards and not much thicker. Christ, it seemed like the whole world now talked constantly on cell phones. A discomfort swept over him, an uncertainty as to how he would adjust to life on the outside after so many years.

His eyes were everywhere, but mostly, he watched the women. Two flight attendants bustled past him. He liked their tight little skirts and the scent of their perfume. It was the first time he'd smelled perfume since he'd entered prison. A young woman with her back to him leaned over to pick up a glove she had dropped, exposing part of both thighs.

"Goddamn!" he muttered, and headed for the checkout counter.

Outside, he stood for a while, examining the cars driving by, thinking how they all seemed to look alike now, and how so many of them were the SUVs that had first started coming out about the time he went to prison. He watched the people hurrying by, thinking that many of them were just children or not even born when he was locked up. And the women!

In the bank across the street, he used his certified check to buy nine thousand dollars' worth of traveler's checks and took the rest of his money in cash. He called the train station for schedules. A train was leaving for North Adams in an hour and a half, at eleven-thirty.

By the time he settled himself into his seat on the train, Gale's longing for a woman had become overpowering. The walk to South Station was particularly tantalizing. They were everywhere: big-breasted, long-legged, hip-swinging, lusty-looking women of all ages and sizes. South Station offered no reprieve.

If I don't get a piece a ass soon, I'll go nuts, he thought, hunkering deeper into his seat.

He forced himself to think of locating his daughter. He did know that she was in New York City. He had heard that from his lawyer. He also heard she'd changed her name. But to find anybody in New York, he needed more to go on. Twice from prison he had phoned her aunt in North Adams, and both times she had hung up on him. "Damn it, Janet, I'm her father. I got a right to know where my daughter is and to see her," he had pleaded.

"You have no rights, you pig, and anyway, I don't know where she is." And she had hung up.

On the second call, she hung up as soon as she heard his voice.

"Excuse me, conductor. You got a bar?"

"It's in the club car, sir. Three cars down."

Gale stood at the entrance, staring at the gleaming chrome. It had been so many years since he'd been on a train. He made his way across the room, settled into one of the small tables, ordered a beer, and lit a cigarette. A mirror directly across the way reflected his image. His once thick brown hair was now gone. He was bald except for a few stringy, gray wisps. He decided he would get rid of them and go completely bald, shave it all off like a lot of the cons in prison. It was kind of a cool look.

The gold tooth that long dominated his mouth had been replaced by an enamel crown, thanks to a prison fight. His attacker had flushed the gold one down a toilet. He still had the thyroid condition, but his eyes no longer bulged.

He had entered prison a slender, wiry young man of twenty-seven. Over the years, he'd put on nearly forty pounds, and if not fat, he was burly, heavyset. Unlike most inmates, he had spent no time developing his body. He was soft and flabby. The years of smoking had taken a further toll on his voice, giving it a guttural, raspy sound.

His appearance had changed significantly, but all in all, he was not unhappy at the image staring back at him. Not bad for a guy of forty-eight, he mused as the waiter set his beer down.

"Bring me another one now, before you get busy," he called to the waiter heading back toward the bar.

The door to the club car opened, and a woman made her way across the room. Gale's eyes shifted toward her.

She looked to be in her early forties, short, a little on the heavy side. Her longish red hair was too red to be natural, and her makeup was a bit much for the time of day and the setting. But Gale was looking only at her chest. He took a long drink of his beer and smiled at her as she came toward him. She smiled back.

The small room had only two empty tables. She sat at the one next to his and ordered a beer.

Gale watched her, trying to think of something to say to start a conversation. Nothing would come. She made it easier by pulling out a cigarette and fumbling around in her pocketbook. He leaned over and flicked his lighter. "Can I give you a light?"

She looked at him for a moment. "Thank you. I can never find anything in this thing." She nodded toward her pocketbook.

She took a deep drag on her cigarette. As she did, her breasts expanded, moving suggestively under her tight sweater.

Gale swallowed. "Uh, where you headed?" he asked.

"Oh, I'm going to Greenfield. That's where I live. I was in Boston for a couple days visiting my daughter. She's a nurse at City Hospital."

"A nurse, huh? Must be a smart girl."

"Well, she's hardworking, that's for sure. She put herself through the Fitchburg State College nursing program. I couldn't afford to send her there on what I make, so she did it pretty much on her own. Got both her BS and RN."

"What about her father? Didn't he help?"

"No. Him and I were divorced when she was only ten years old. He took off out West somewhere, and we've never heard from him since." She finished her beer and glanced over her shoulder.

"Uh, could I buy you another beer?" Gale asked, moving his chair closer to her table.

She eyed him for a moment before responding. "Well, we got at least a couple hours more to Greenfield, so sure, why not?" She lit another cigarette.

He braced himself for the first big puff. "What kinda work you do?"

"I'm a waitress at Bill's in Greenfield."

"Hey, I bet you serve a mean meal." His thick bronchial laugh filled the room. The laughter started him coughing.

She reached across the table and hit him several times on the back. "Ooh! That's a bad cough you have there. It's the cigarettes, you know."

Her touch made him rock hard. It had been so long since a woman had touched him. "Yeah," he wheezed. "Someday I'm gonna cut these things out. But hey! Today we're havin' a good time. So maybe I'll cut 'em out tomorrow, right?" He erupted again. His hacking laughter infected his companion and she joined in, laughing, wheezing, and coughing along with him.

"We're a great pair." Gale barely managed to get the words out, tears of laughter streaming down his face. "Hey, what's your name, anyway?" he asked, finally settling down.

"Lois. Lois Gentile." She drained her glass.

"How 'bout a couple more beers, Lois?" Gale was now sitting at her table. "Waiter," he yelled loudly across the car.

The waiter held his finger to his lips, his hand up, palm out, and nodded.

"You haven't told me your name yet," Lois said, leaning forward.

"Uh, oh yeah. My name is Paul. Paul Gillis," he said.

"You got any kids, Paul?"

He thought for a moment and surprised himself with his answer. "Yeah, I got a beautiful daughter. She's all grown up and pretty as they come." He said this with a pride that abruptly spilled out of him.

"Oh, she sounds like some classy young lady." She glanced at his finger. "What about her mother?"

He lowered his eyes. "Her mother passed away years ago."

"Oh, I'm sorry." She took another chug of her beer and asked, "How far are you going, Paul?"

Gale made a quick decision. "Well, actually, I'm going to Greenfield, too."

Lois Gentile's eyes lit up. "You're going to Greenfield? What a nice surprise."

"Yeah," he said. "I'm going up to visit an old buddy of mine to discuss a business deal."

By the time the train reached Greenfield, Paul and Lois had bonded. They were also drunk.

They made their way unsteadily off the train, Paul carrying their suitcases. On the platform, Lois staggered against him. He slid his arm around her to hold her steady. Her heavy breasts pressed against his chest. He started to kiss her, but she giggled and pulled away.

"Take it easy, honey. Not right here, in front of everybody. Tell you what. I'm going to take you home and make you the best lunch you ever had. How's that sound?"

"Lois, baby, you just made yourself a deal. Let's go. You got a car here?"

" 'Course I do. It's right over here in the lot. It ain't much, but it gets me where I want to go. And right now, where I want to go is home with you, honey." She giggled again, and pinched him in the stomach.

Once inside the car, Gale leaned over and kissed her hard. His hands groped her body.

"Hey, easy, honey, easy. We got all day," she said huskily. She squirmed away, hitched her skirt down, and started the motor. "Now, honey, you gotta let me drive and not be fuckin' around. Oops, excuse me, Paul. That just kinda slipped out. I don't usually talk like that, you know."

Gale's wheezy laugh erupted. "Oh, baby, I love it when you talk dirty to me. You can say *fuck* all you want."

"Well, anyway, Paul, we have to be careful driving. They're tough on drunk drivers in this town, so let's just cool it till I can get us home."

On the way to Lois's house, he noticed a Greyhound bus station at the end of the main street. Lois turned right at the bus station, and after less than a mile, she turned onto a dirt road and stopped in front of a small cottage, one of only two houses on the road.

"Well, this is my little haven from the world. It's close to town, but nice and private."

Gale set his bag down in the little entry hall and looked around. The house was a dump but he wasn't there for the ambience. The kitchen and combination living-dining room were all cramped together. Looking down the narrow hallway, he could see the bedroom. That was the only room he was interested in. The house smelled of cigarettes and cheap perfume. There were so many butts in the ashtray, he had to throw his in the sink.

"Sit down, Paul. I'll get some lunch started. How 'bout a nice big western omelet, some toast and coffee? But first we're gonna have a couple Bloody Marys, OK?"

She turned, and Gale was leaning against her. He kissed her. Her arms went around him, squeezing, her pelvis undulating against his. Her tongue filled his mouth.

"Oh, Jesus, Paul. It's been so long."

"Me, too, baby," he whispered, years of suffering without sex welling within him. He grabbed her by the hair and pulled her head back. She moaned and clawed at him and found his crotch.

"Ooh, baby." He moved her toward the bedroom.

They fell heavily onto the bed and he had her clothes off in seconds. He buried his head between the tits he had longed for all day.

"Oh! Jesus Christ," he muttered. "Baby, baby."

Lois sobbed, then took one of her breasts into her hands and guided it into his mouth. He took it hungrily, sucking, rubbing his tongue over it. Lois moaned and grabbed at him.

"Oh! Fuck me, honey. Fuck me."

He rolled over on top and entered her. Like two savage animals, they clawed and bit, and humped and sucked until they lay still, panting, satiated.

They both drifted off to sleep. After about thirty minutes, Gale awoke, ready for more. He reached out for Lois and began fondling her. She moaned and stirred and turned her back. Gale grabbed her and tried to turn her around. She resisted.

"Honey, not now. I'm tired. Let me sleep for a while." She moved away.

"Goddamn it. C'mere," he snarled, turning her around.

"No," she said thickly, and without opening her eyes, put her hand up to push him away. Her finger accidentally scratched his eye.

"You bitch!" he yelled and slammed his open hand across her face.

Her eyes opened wide in surprise and fear. She reached out instinctively, her nails raking his face. He roared and hit her again. Grunting and panting, he pulled her off the bed and threw her on the floor. She screamed, and he was on her, his hand clamped over her mouth. With his hand still covering her mouth, he mounted and entered her again. She managed to get his hand off her mouth.

"You're crazy, you bastard," she screamed.

He climaxed and went limp—spent. She rolled him off her and went into the bathroom.

He staggered into the kitchen, rummaged through the cabinets, and found a bottle of vodka. Three shots of the vodka calmed him, and he walked back into the bedroom and dressed.

Lois came out of the bathroom, watching him warily. "I think you'd better go, Paul," she said, hugging her robe around her.

His eyes moved up and down her body. She instinctively backed away. He stood, eyeing her for a moment before replying. "Sure, sorry I was a little rough."

He finished his drink and left. It was a few minutes to five when he reached the bus station. He was in luck. There was a bus leaving for North Adams at 5:35.

10

FRANK SAT ALONE at a small table in a corner of Rumours, eating a corned beef sandwich and enjoying a cold Heineken. A man with jowls that rippled like a water bed whenever he moved sat at the bar surrounded by plates of food. He sipped a highball while shoveling in the food.

The wine bottle thing rattled around in Frank's head. This wasn't your run-of-the-mill thug. Somebody really got off on this.

He'd talked with his contacts in the gay community, checked every gay bar within twenty blocks. Nothing.

"Frankie, if this boy was gay and looking for action, believe me, I'd have known about him," Bruce Dion, Frank's most reliable connection, had assured him. "If he was as adorable as these pictures, he would have had all he could handle. He was cute, wasn't he?"

Beatty seemed to fit the profile of being straight, but Frank had to check every possible angle. Everyone they'd talked with at his workplace confirmed his interest in women, although he hadn't seemed to have much success with them. He dated a few and asked at least four others out and was turned down. Nothing in his apartment or personal effects indicated any gay activity. Switch-hitter? Not likely, but they had to consider all possibilities.

There was no evidence of seminal fluid on, near, or in the body. No sign of robbery. This could be a random act, but there had to be a motive.

He remembered almost verbatim the words of Dr. James Brussel, a criminal psychiatrist from whose works he had studied so much. *The motivations behind perverted acts possess their own logic. The psychotic doesn't act wholly irrationally. There's a logic, a rationale hidden behind what he or she does, however bizarre and without reason it appears to be.*

He thought about how much time he'd spent over the past eight years checking out people's sex history. He'd become a voyeur, digging into their perversions, jealousies, infidelities, and lust. People die for bad reasons all the time, and if you dig deep enough, chances are there was a sex angle somewhere. What is it on this one?

PAUL GALE STOOD on the front porch and rang the bell. A small, gray-looking woman appeared behind the screen door. Gale recognized his sister-in-law.

"Yes?" The woman looked tentative, nervous.

"Hello, Janet," Gale said quietly.

She stared at him. Something in the voice tried to jog her memory. "Do I know you?"

Gale smiled. "You don't recognize me?"

"Not in the slightest. Now what is it that you want?"

"It's Paul," he said softly.

Janet continued staring for a moment. Recognition lit her eyes. Her mouth fell open, and she whispered, "Paul? Paul Gale?"

"Yes. Can I come in?"

Her mouth was still open, but she said nothing, shaking her head slowly.

Gale remained smiling, trying to appear friendly.

Janet regained her composure. "What do you want with me?"

"Janet, except for my girl, you're the only living relative I got. I was released from prison yesterday. I don't know a single soul in the outside world. I wanted at least to start out by thanking you for bringing her up, and maybe just talk a little, that's all."

"I have nothing to say to you. I told you that on the phone."

"Janet, please. It's been a long time. I've changed. I'm sorry for what I did and I've paid for it. Please, can I just talk to you, maybe a cup of coffee? I'm tired. I come a long way."

She softened. "How did you get here?"

"I took a bus from Boston."

"Are you planning on staying in North Adams?"

"I don't think so. I come up here to see you, talk with you a little."

The two of them stood facing each other for a long moment. Finally, Janet broke the silence. "All right. You can come in for a few minutes. It's against my better judgment, but I don't guess it'll do any harm to talk for a few minutes."

She opened the screen door.

Gale smiled and stepped inside, directly into the living room. Although it was still late afternoon, the darkness of the room was broken only by a small table lamp. Venetian blinds were drawn, giving the room a cavelike appearance.

She led him into the kitchen. "You want some tea?" she asked without looking at him.

"I'd love some. Thanks."

The small, spotless kitchen was as dark as the living room. The beige walls were bare except for a calendar hanging on a wall near the sink. The room showed no sign of having been lived in or used, except for the pungent smell of sauerkraut and stale coffee.

Gale looked around the house as if expecting someone.

Janet noticed. "No, I never got married, if that's what you're wondering. I've lived here alone for twenty-four years, and that's the way I like it. What's on your mind? I don't have a lot of time."

Over tea at the kitchen table they made some small talk about North Adams, her job, and some mutual acquaintances before Gale finally got around to his reason for being there.

"Janet, tell me about my daughter. What's she look like? Is she married? Kids?"

"There's not much I can tell you. She was a good kid but very shy. Kept to herself pretty much. Her and I never really talked much. She went through high school with good grades, mostly all A's, a few B's. Smart girl."

"She go to college?"

"She got a scholarship to go to UMass. After that, I never really saw all that much of her. She hardly ever came home, except for the big holidays. In the summers she had different jobs, working day and night, mostly waitressing. Ate most all her meals wherever she worked. Pretty much only slept here. Like I said, her and I had trouble communicating, so we never really talked much. To tell you the truth, I never felt like I really knew her."

"I understand she changed her name."

Janet looked at him for a moment, lowered her eyes, and said nothing.

"Come on, Janet. I want to know all about my girl."

Janet hesitated. "I don't know, Paul. I didn't like the idea and tried to talk her out of it, but she was eighteen, so there was nothing I could do about it. Said she didn't want any part of any North Adams family names. She wanted a new one."

"Don't worry about it. Tell me some more about her."

"Well, after she graduated, she went to live in Boston for a while. Then we gradually lost touch. She called a couple times when she first went to Boston. I tried to ask her about her personal life. She got huffy, we had a few words, and that was it. She never called again. I tried calling her about five or six weeks later, but the number was disconnected and there was no other listing for her in the Boston area."

Gale stared at her. She looked away, and he wondered if she was telling the truth. "What's she look like?"

"Well, like I said, I haven't seen her in about five years. But she's very attractive, tall, nice figure. Pretty girl."

"You mean to tell me, Janet, that after you brought that girl up, you just lost touch with her, and you and her haven't had any contact in five years? I find that hard to believe." His voice had taken on a less friendly tone.

"Look, Paul, that's just what I'm telling you."

"Do you have any idea where she is today?"

"No, I don't."

His voice rose. "Boston, New York, Chicago, Denver, California? I mean, no idea at all? Come on, Janet. I don't buy that."

Her eyes darted toward the door. She stood up warily. Gale still frightened her and she wanted him out of her home.

"She has some very ugly memories of you, Paul. I don't have anything more to say to you. I think you'd better leave." She pointed toward the door.

Gale remained seated. "Look, Janet. I want to see my girl. I'm her father, and if you know where she is, you tell me. Now sit down. I'm not through talking to you."

His eyes had locked onto Janet's. She tried to look away, but they held her fast. The silence in the room was now a crushing vacuum of stillness.

Gale reached across the table, grasped Janet's wrist, and guided her back to her chair. "Where is she, Janet?" He began caressing her wrist, slowly running his forefinger across it.

Janet grimaced, and started making little whimpering sounds. But she said nothing.

He leaned in close to her, rubbing his finger along her hand and slowly up her arm. "Listen to me, Janet," he half whispered. "You know what I'm capable of, don't you?"

She went quiet for a minute and then slowly nodded.

"Are you going to tell me where I can find my daughter and what she changed her name to?" His eyes remained fixed on hers. He asked her again.

It was sometime later that she whispered, "Yes."

JANET KATELEY HAD always been afraid of Paul Gale. She remembered the first time she visited her sister and Gale at their Hathaway Street house. Gale flew into a rage because his dinner was cold and wound up throwing it at Sarah. Janet never forgot the hatred in his eyes. Over nothing.

She knew of the fury Paul felt toward his daughter after the murder. She'd been standing next to her in the courtroom when Gale whispered his threat. His visit convinced her that the man hadn't changed.

Calling the police would be futile. Paul had done nothing. And, if she did and word somehow got back to him, there was no telling what he might do.

It hadn't been five years since she talked to her niece. It had been only a year. She'd wanted to lie about the phone number and address.

She'd tried but he frightened her. Now she wished she hadn't known either.

She had tried so hard to keep in touch with Lucky, but it got more difficult over the years. Janet smiled as she thought of the birthday and Christmas cards that her niece never forgot. Every once in a while she would even get a little money with a nice note. She thought of their last phone conversation and even now, it broke her heart.

"Aunt Janet, it's getting so hard even talking with you lately. It just brings back so many bad memories that I thought I had pushed away. Try and understand. It's not you. I'm trying to work some things through here and I'm just not doing very well at it right now. I'm having trouble sleeping, and when I do sleep I have these awful nightmares—and it's just not going to be good for me to talk with you for a while. Please try and respect that." And she hung up.

Janet did reluctantly respect Lucky's request. In spite of her sadness she smiled as she thought of the nickname Lucky, the name only she and Sarah used. She felt so helpless. She remembered the years of counseling, her niece leaving the doctor's office in tears, hurrying home and burying herself in Janet's arms, sobbing.

For the first few years while under the state psychologist's care, Lucky would talk about her mother's death. "Oh, Aunt Janet, if only I had done something. If I had called the police when I heard what was happening to Mommy." By the time she was twelve, she no longer talked about it. Her niece would spend hours in her room looking out the window, doing nothing, saying nothing.

Eventually Janet canceled any further sessions with the psychologist, feeling they weren't helping. And she could no longer afford them.

But Lucky's rage was at times frightening. Janet ran her hand over the long crack in the coffee table, thinking back years ago to the night Lucky had flared up over something—Janet could no longer remember what—and had grabbed her aunt by the shoulders and flung her onto the table. She then rushed to her aunt, cradled her in her arms, and cried uncontrollably. Even now, Janet could feel the intensity of her anger, so out of proportion with the incident.

Janet nervously dialed the number, and within seconds a vaguely familiar voice answered.

"Hello."

Janet took a deep breath. "Hello, sweetheart. This is Aunt Janet."

Nothing.

"Hello, honey. Are you there?"

Finally, "Yes, I'm here. How are you, Aunt Janet?"

"I'm fine. How have you been? Are things OK? Are you doing all right?" Suddenly, Janet wanted to know everything about her.

"I'm fine. I hope things are well with you."

"Oh, yes, I'm fine. The roof still leaks. I still hate my job, and I'm getting fat. But other than that, I'm doing fine. Uh, you sound like you're busy?"

"I am."

"Uh, sweetie, the main reason I called is to tell you that your father is out of prison."

Janet waited. Silence.

"Are you there?"

Silence.

"Hello! Hello! Hello!"

"Yes." The voice a deep whisper.

"Lucky, did you hear what I said?"

Her mother's nickname for her. It had been so long. "Yes."

"Well, please listen carefully. He came to my house yesterday. At first I didn't know who he was, and then when I did, I refused to let him in. He gave me a long sob story and I felt a little sorry for him. So like a fool, I said he could come in for a minute. You know me. I couldn't turn away a rabid dog if I felt sorry for him. I did feel a little pity for your father, in spite of what he did.

"Well, once he got in he started pressing me for information about you. I wouldn't tell him anything, but he frightened me to the point where I had to give him your address and phone number. Oh, God! I'm so sorry. I never, ever should have let him in.

"He took the only two photographs I had of you. He knows what you look like. Please be careful, please. . . ."

LUCKY DRIFTED AWAY to another time, a little girl sitting in a car with her mother and a handsome man, a little girl standing in a doorway staring at a handsome man in a leather jacket. "My father did it."

"Honey, what did you say?" Her aunt's voice jolted her. A headache pounded in her head.

"Nothing, Aunt Janet."

"I'm sure he's heading for New York. Please be careful. Maybe you should call the police."

She tried to focus on what her aunt was saying. "Did he say he was coming to New York?"

"No, but he was determined to know where you are. He's going to go to New York. I know he is."

Her throat was dry and she wanted a glass of water. "Aunt Janet, what does he look like?"

"Well, he's put on a lot of weight and he's lost most of his hair. He's almost totally bald. His face no longer has that lean look. He looks completely different; even his voice is different. I didn't recognize him at all. He had to tell me who he was."

"All right, Aunt Janet. Please don't say anything to anyone else. If he threatened you, you know he's capable of following through, so just keep it to yourself and say nothing, OK?"

"All right, if you think that's best."

"I do, and again, thanks for calling and telling me."

"Oh, honey, please be careful. I still do think about you a lot.

Maybe we could talk once in a while? Just keep in touch a little? I remember those nice cards you used to send me."

"I have to go now, Aunt Janet. Good-bye."

She sat by the phone in the kitchen for several minutes, staring, her
breath coming in short, loud gasps. She tried to swallow, but her
tongue was too dry. Moisture gathered under her arms and began
trickling down her ribs. The hateful words uttered in the courtroom
so many years ago echoed in her head.

12

"HEY, DENISE, LET'S go have some lunch at the Blue Wave."

Denise looked up from her computer and saw Gina Ponte standing in the doorway. She checked her watch. Twelve-fifteen. "OK."

The Blue Wave on West Fiftieth Street had only been open for a month, and it was already a big hit. California trendy, bright, sunny, and loaded with green plants and brass. The large room buzzed with conversation and energy.

The waiter took their orders. Gina also ordered a glass of Chianti, Denise a Diet Coke.

"You can bring my wine now," Gina told the waiter.

"You bet." His smile lit up the table. He turned to Denise and graced her with another. "How about you, miss. Would you like your Coke now?"

Denise looked away and nodded. "Yes, thank you."

"Jesus. How'd you like to take him home with you?" Gina watched the waiter walk away. "Look at the tight little buns on him."

"Gina, you've got a one-track mind, I swear." She looked at her watch. "I do have to get back soon. I've got a ton of work on my desk."

The waiter set Denise's salad in front of her, along with another of his dazzling smiles. Gina ordered another glass of wine

"Uh, how do you like working here?" Gina asked. "It must be fun."

He turned away from Denise and cast the smile in Gina's direction. "Yes. It's OK." A customer at another table motioned to him and he moved away.

"Dennie, this is fun, isn't it?" Gina said. "We should do this more often, maybe have dinner some night. You're not so wrapped up with some guy, are you, that you couldn't spare a night on the town with me?"

"No, but what about you? From what I hear, you've got a different guy every night."

Gina took a long sip of her wine and leaned forward. She beckoned Denise toward her. "Let me tell you a little secret. That is strictly bull. But it's good PR." She leaned back and reached for more bread. "Now, that's not to say that I don't get my share."

Denise nodded, not sure what to say.

"What about you, Dennie? I know you don't like to talk much about yourself, but hey, I'm nosy. Is there anybody special in your life?"

Denise tugged at her hair. "Anybody special? The answer to your question is no! There's nobody special in my life."

"Well, that's pretty emphatic. But anyway, I bet you get a lot of attention. They're out there. And if they are for me, then they sure must be there in droves for a lady like you." Gina sighed and looked out the window. "Yes, men are wonderful, aren't they? They're just— they're—men are assholes!"

"Gina!"

"Oops! Sorry, honey. Guess I got a little carried away there. Must be the wine."

Denise studied her friend, surprised by the abrupt change in her, even the expression on her face. "Well, I really do have to get back. But this has been fun, Gina. Let's do it again."

They paid the check and left, Denise still puzzling over Gina's comment.

AT THE END of her workday, Gina Ponte entered her apartment and sprawled on her living room couch and closed her eyes. She thought of her lunch with Denise and how she would like to get to know her better.

Restless, she sat up and flicked on the TV. *Law & Order,* something about a young girl who killed her mother for having an affair with the girl's fifteen-year-old boyfriend. She channel surfed, but found nothing of interest.

She pulled out her cell phone and punched in the numbers. "Hi, Cathy, how about meeting me at Patrick's for a drink and a bite to eat? Oh, gonna take a hot bath and relax with a video? Sounds good, maybe that's what I should do. OK, talk to you soon."

She punched in another number. "Hi, Andrea." Same question, same result. One more call. No answer.

She went into the bathroom and combed her hair. It was getting so wonderfully long. She loved the look it gave her, especially with the big hoop earrings, dramatic eye shadow, and matte lipstick.

She decided she looked too good to waste it, sitting alone, watching television and eating junk food all evening. It was a nice evening, a little chilly, but just right for a walk—work off the big lunch and the wine.

She strolled along the avenue, enjoying the crisp, clear fall evening, stopping occasionally for some window shopping. A fruit vendor shivering in the cold smiled at her and held out an apple. She shook her head and hurried past him. After another eight blocks, she headed over one block east and turned toward home.

Within a few blocks of her apartment, she slowed down and peeked into Jenny's Place. The candlelight flickering across the picture window looked warm and cozy. She opened the door and walked in.

Several young women sat at the bar, talking quietly. One of them greeted her. "Hey, Gina, where've you been? Haven't seen you in a while."

"Working hard, and I need a drink." She slid onto a stool at the end of the bar and ordered a glass of Sauvignon Blanc. She had taken a few sips when a voice behind her asked softly, "Mind if I join you?"

She turned and saw a small blond woman of about thirty smiling at her. She looked her over for a moment before returning her smile. "Sure, have a seat."

13

AFTER A LONG day and the unsettling lunch with Gina, Denise welcomed the haven of her health club. It was a little more crowded than usual, and by the time she had changed, there were already several men working out. Her eyes were drawn immediately to one, puffing along on the treadmill. He was a tall, handsome man with longish dark hair. She dismissed him, and headed for the Nautilus. On the way he noticed her and nodded with a friendly smile. She recognized him as the guy who was coming in as she was going out a week or so ago, and she nodded back.

Her workout was long and satisfying. She concluded with fifty push-ups, and when she finished, she felt as if she could do another fifty. Her body vibrated with energy. She headed for the showers and saw the stranger walking toward the men's locker room.

She showered and dressed quickly. Feeling pleasantly tired and hungry, she looked forward to dinner and turning in early for a good night's sleep.

As she headed through the club and toward the door, she noticed the new guy wearing a leather jacket and jeans walking toward Charlie, the club manager. He moved with a graceful elegance, but there was also a macho vitality about him, a study in contrasts that she found intriguing. Was he a construction worker or a college professor? She figured he could be either.

He stood talking with Charlie as she hurried by them and down the stairs into the bustle of the city at night. The temperature had dropped and it was now very cold. Steam rose from the subway grates and a brisk wind sent pieces of paper skittering along the street.

She had worked out longer than usual and Seventh Avenue was now crowded with people heading for home, dinner, or the theater, vainly searching for cabs. The cold weather had them moving quickly, coat collars up, bending into the wind.

She pulled up her own collar and tugged her gloves on, bracing herself for the long walk. She had gone about a block and was approaching the intersection when a car shot out of Forty-second Street, jumped the curb, and bore down on her. She stood transfixed, unable to move. The large black machine, so close she could see the wide eyes of the terrified man behind the wheel, was about to hit her. She closed her eyes and waited for the impact.

She was hit about waist high and felt herself moved off the ground and through the air. The impact was hard and sudden, but it was not what she expected. She felt the hot breath of a human being across her face, as she lay somewhere, uncertain where. Her eyes were still closed, but she knew she was alive. She opened her eyes and rolled over, disentangling herself from another set of arms and legs.

"Are you all right?"

She looked up and saw a man staggering to his feet, holding his hands out to her. Just to the left and behind her, she saw the black car, embedded in the window of a convenience store.

"Are you OK?" her rescuer asked as he helped her up.

Her legs felt like rubber, and she was shaking badly. "I—I don't know. I think so," she said, her voice quivering. She staggered and leaned against him. His arm slid around her waist, holding her steady. Her head began to clear, and she saw that he was the stranger from the club. "What happened?" she asked, moving slightly away and standing on her own.

"Well, I came out and headed down Seventh Avenue; all of a sudden this car shot out of nowhere and jumped the light and I saw you about to get zonked. I just hit you with an old-fashioned body block." He rubbed his shoulder and smiled. "By the way, your workouts are paying off."

At the mention of the car, they both turned toward the convenience store. An Asian couple stood in front, wailing and shaking fists at the car. A crowd had gathered, and the driver, an elderly man, was being helped out of the vehicle. He looked bewildered and frightened, but appeared to be unhurt.

The man was mumbling to a man and woman ministering to him, "The brake. Meant to put my foot on the brake. Hit the goddamn gas pedal."

A police car pulled up, and two officers jumped out and took charge. An ambulance arrived and the old man was gently moved into it. A man stepped out of the crowd and said, "Officer, I saw the whole thing. I can tell you what happened."

The crowd of people that had gathered drifted away. Frank was satisfied that the young man would give the officers a report and saw no need to get involved. He was more interested in the woman and her well-being at the moment. They walked slowly along Seventh Avenue.

"You sure you're OK? You look a little green."

"Oh, God. I think so, but I've got to sit down somewhere."

"Here, let's go in here." He opened the door to a coffee shop and led her to a booth and slipped her coat off. "I'll get you some black coffee and some water." He went over to the nearest waitress and returned with her in tow.

"Here, honey, you drink this good strong coffee and let me get you some water," the waitress said. She poured them both coffee, and returned with a large glass of water for Denise.

Denise held the mug with trembling hands and sipped the coffee, pausing for a deep breath after each sip.

He handed her the glass of water. "Here, try to drink all of this."

She took the glass, again with both hands, and took long, deep gulps of the water. It seemed to restore her, at least enough to manage a brittle smile.

"Well, I think I'm going to live," she said, slowly guiding the glass to rest on the table. She looked quizzically at him.

"You're going to be fine. My name is Frank, by the way." He held out his hand, and she feebly shook it.

"I'm Denise Johnson. Thank you, Frank. I think you just saved my life." Her eyes flicked to his for an instant and dropped to the table.

He moved his head downward, trying to find her eyes. "You're looking better already."

"Oh, well, thank you." Her hand darted up and brushed her hair back. It fell again, and again the hand went up. She glanced at him but again quickly looked away.

Up close she was even more beautiful than when he'd noticed her at the club. His first reaction was that she reminded him of Carla. Not a good thought and he dismissed it. He wondered if she had noticed him.

He got his answer. "I've seen you at the health club," she said.

"Yeah, I've seen you, too." He grinned. "I'm afraid I'm not in your league up there."

"You just have to be patient and stay with it." She finished her coffee.

They sat for a moment, neither saying anything. Frank broke the silence. "I noticed that you go through a pretty strenuous routine. Been doing this for a while?"

She peered into the coffee cup, studying it. "Yes. I—I'm kind of a jock, I guess."

He smiled at that. "Whatever you're doing, it's working."

She looked up and smiled back. "Thank you." She closed her eyes and a little shiver went through her.

"You OK?"

"Yes, I was just thinking about what happened out there. I'd be mashed between the car and the store right now if it hadn't been for you. Thank you again."

"You're welcome. I'm glad for the chance to meet you, even under these circumstances. Actually, I staged the whole thing." Her smile came more easily this time. He liked the way she smiled and the nervous shyness about her.

Denise rubbed her shoulder and made a face. "You sure you weren't a linebacker in college?"

"I guess I did hit you pretty hard. You'll probably be sore tomorrow."

"At least I'll be here tomorrow," she said. Her stomach suddenly rolled an audible gurgle. She put her hand to her mouth and giggled. "Oh, God! Excuse me, I'm so embarrassed. That's my stomach telling me it's time to go home."

"No, that's your stomach telling you you're hungry. How about some dinner?"

"No, I don't think so. I really do have to get home. But thank you again. It's been a pleasure meeting you." She reached for her coat, and he moved quickly around to help her with it.

"I wish I could've picked a better way, but I've enjoyed meeting you," he said.

He left the money for the coffee on the table, and they walked out and stood on the sidewalk for a moment. A cab cruised by, the driver eyeing them hopefully. People rushed by in both directions, everyone, as always, in a hurry. A group of young tourists emerged from a small hotel, giggling with excitement. A car horn tooted and Denise instinctively jumped and staggered. Frank held her. She smelled good, and he liked standing there holding her in his arms.

She moved away and gave him the shy smile he liked so much in the restaurant. She staggered again, but recovered quickly. "Oh, God, I'm sorry. I guess I'm still jumpy and a little dizzy. Must be from sitting all that time and suddenly getting up."

"You sure you're going to be all right?"

"Yes, I'll be fine, really."

"Well, let me put you in a cab."

"No, I'd rather walk. I need the fresh air. It's not far."

"I'll walk along with you just in case."

She started to protest, but was hit with another wave of nausea and dizziness. He braced her again. "Thank you," she said.

They walked slowly at first, but Denise gradually began to pick up the pace, and they were soon at her building, a nondescript prewar structure on West Thirty-sixth Street.

"Well, I think you're going to survive," Frank said. The wind had picked up and it was getting colder, but he didn't want her to go in.

"Yes, I'm going to be fine. The walk helped. Good night, Frank." The wonderful little smile flickered. "And thanks again."

"Good night, Denise. Hope to see you soon at the club. By the way, we're almost neighbors. I live on West Twenty-eighth."

She nodded, smiled, said good night, and went inside.

RELAXING IN HER apartment, the full impact of her brush with death hit her, and she felt exhausted. It had not been a good day. No longer hungry, she decided to go to bed.

She sat on the bed, slowly taking off her clothes. Her stomach gurgled again and Frank Russo's invitation to dinner came back to her. *He's nice. Very sexy.*

FRANK HAD BEEN walking for several blocks when he realized he'd been thinking about nothing but Denise. None of the usual crap that rattled around in his head. Just a good feeling from the hour or so that he had spent with her. He decided that if an hour with her could make him feel this good, he'd have to give it another shot.

14

AFTER LEAVING JANET Kateley's house, Paul Gale spent a few days in Boston at a small hotel. It wasn't much, but the price was better compared with the sticker shock he got from the Park Plaza. He knew his money wouldn't last long without a job.

After a good night's sleep he awoke at seven and picked up the phone. He stared at it for a moment, took a deep breath, and began punching out the numbers.

His hand shook and perspiration rolled off his face onto the phone as he waited. Finally a woman's voice answered.

"Hello."

Gale's temples pounded. His stomach began to cramp.

"Hello." The voice sounded irritated. "Hello."

He hung up the phone, his hand still shaking. He waited a few minutes to calm down before making another call, this one to his ex-cell mate Larry Cardillo, now living in New York.

"Paul, how you gonna go live in New York? You know you can't even leave Massachusetts to visit New York, let alone live there. You'll violate your parole!"

"I know. I know, Larry. That's where you come in. I need your help. You said your cousin, the guy that owns the restaurant in New York, owes you some favors, right?"

"Come on, Gale," said Cardillo. "I can't ask him to give you a job."

"Why not? I can go to New York if I have a job, a place to live, and most of all, somebody to sponsor me. You know that, Larry. Now, can you get your cousin to do this for you?"

"I dunno, Paul."

Gale waited through the long silence before Cardillo finally spoke.

"Paul, I ain't the kinda guy who forgets. I know I'd be a dead man today if you hadn't pulled those goons off me in the laundry. I'll talk to Tony and see what I can do. He does owe me one. I'll see what I can work out for you."

It did work out. Three days later Cardillo's cousin not only hired Gale but also got him a room in a friend's boardinghouse. The room was pretty raunchy but it was better than his last accommodations. He settled in, took a shower in the bath down the hall, and dressed for a night on the town.

He had always wanted to see Times Square. Plenty of action there, he'd heard, and a guy could find just about anything he wanted. Might just go find himself a little pussy.

He enjoyed the walk, taking his time, stopping to look in store windows along the way. He continued to be shocked at the price of things. Wonder how much a piece a ass costs today? he pondered.

It was a little after ten when he reached the Times Square area. He turned on Forty-second Street and stopped. Instead of the sex shops, dirty movies, and massage parlors he'd heard about in prison, it looked more like Disney World. "The hell's this?" he muttered.

The glistening new buildings and yuppie crowd were not what he'd expected. He felt out of place among the well-dressed men and women hurrying by, and the gawking tourists looked like a bunch of yokels. Where the hell were all the hookers?

He started walking west until he hit Eighth Avenue and turned uptown. This looks a little more like it, he thought, passing several small bars that looked like his kind of joint.

After a few blocks, he was about to enter a bar when he stopped. "Uh-oh. Lookee here."

A shapely black woman headed his way. He watched her approach: spike heels, short, tight skirt rolling around her hips as she swayed toward him. "Come on, baby," he whispered.

He could see her face now, mouth open, smiling. He liked the way she licked her upper lip with her tongue. A sweater a size too small highlighted a pair of tits aimed straight at him. She slowed down as she approached him.

"Want to go out, honey?" she whispered.

He was already hard. "Sure." He barely got the word out.

She continued past him. "Follow me," she said without breaking stride.

She led him along Eighth Avenue for a block before stepping into a narrow doorway. Gale quickly caught up to her in the doorway. She faced him, leaned against him, and slid her hand down to his crotch.

"Ooh, honey. You are ready, aren't you?" She gave him a little squeeze. "You ready to go out, honey?" She smiled, still holding him.

"Yeah."

"OK. What you wanna do? We can go to my place. You gotta use a condom, and it'll cost you a hundred fifty. But I'll show you a real good time, honey." She was rubbing him now, working him over.

"Yeah. Let's go to your place. Where is it?" he whispered, reaching for her.

She stepped away and out of the doorway. "It's just down Eighth

Avenue a few blocks. Follow me, but make sure you stay behind me. We don't want no shit from the cops, you know?"

"Yeah, yeah. Let's go."

He fell in behind her and watched her walk. He liked the way the curved outline of her ass strained against the tight skirt. That ass would be his in a few minutes.

She turned into the hallway of an old building and held the door open for him. "I keep a place right here on the first floor," she said.

He stepped into the small room. It wasn't much, an unmade double bed, a wooden chair, and a small, stained sink.

She set her sweater on the chair and stood facing him. "OK, honey. Let's get our business out of the way first." She held out her hand.

"Oh, yeah, sure," he said, and pulled out three fifty-dollar bills.

"Thanks, honey."

He watched her stuff the bills into her purse.

"OK. Take your clothes off, and let's get to it." Her tone was different from the one on the street. She was now all business.

She unzipped her skirt and let it drop to the floor. Gale watched her sit on the bed in her panties. He dropped the last of his clothes on the floor and moved toward her. She threw him a condom.

"Here. Put that on."

He scowled.

"You want to fuck me, put that on," she said

She knew many ways to please a man and expertly employed them all. Gale grunted, moaned, and bellowed as she worked him to a frenzied peak. It didn't take long for him to climax, after which she immediately rolled him off her and began dressing. He lay for a moment with his eyes closed, panting, slowly catching his breath. When he opened his eyes she was already dressed.

"Hey, what're you doin'?" he demanded.

"I'm gettin' dressed, honey. We done our thing. You had fun, didn't you?" She picked up her purse.

Gale bounded off the bed and grabbed her arm. "Yeah, I had fun, but we ain't finished. For a hundred fifty bucks, I want more'n a few minutes. Now take your clothes back off." He threw her hard on the bed.

She glared at him, her eyes blazing. "I don't know who you think you're fuckin' with, but I don't want none a your shit. We finished. I gave you a good time. That's what you paid for, and that's what you got."

She got off the bed, and Gale moved toward her. "Come on, honey, just one more go at it."

In a second, she had a knife out of her purse, opened and pointed at him. She moved it back and forth in front of her, clearly no stranger to handling it.

"Now you better get out of my way, mister, or you gonna get yourself cut up bad," she hissed.

Gale stepped back and went into a little crouch. He would have to be careful, but he was enjoying this. She moved around the bed and backed toward the door. He stood, naked, watching her.

She reached her free hand in back of her, groping for the doorknob. As she did, her head turned slightly to the left. Gale lunged first to her right, toward the knife, then quickly moved left. She slashed in the direction of his first move. His open left hand chopped hard at her extended arm, and the knife fell to the floor. He was on her, throwing her across the room, and picking up the knife in one movement.

She sat cowering on the floor, fear and fury in her eyes. Gale held the knife and looked down on her. "Now, who do you think you're fuckin' with, honey?" he asked, taunting her. "Get up and take your clothes off. I told you we're not finished."

She got up slowly, never taking her eyes from him.

"I said get undressed. You gonna show me a good time, honey."

She balanced herself against the chair as she took off first one shoe and then the other. She continued to glare at him, hatred in her eyes.

"Now, let's just get this knife outta the way, so nobody gets any ideas, and nobody gets hurt. I'm not such a bad guy. I didn't come here to hurt you. Just one more good fuck for my hundred and fifty bucks, that's all. And then we can both be on our way."

It was many hours later before Paul Gale continued on his way.

15

CRYSTAL WILCOX SAT on the couch in her living room reading Hemingway's *The Sun Also Rises*. Of all his books, this was her favorite. She'd read it several times but never tired of Lady Brett Ashley, with whom she liked to identify—intelligent, beautiful, oversexed, and self-destructive. There's no past or future, only the present. She liked that. It suited her. "We do what we do," she said aloud as she got up to pour herself a glass of wine.

The phone rang. "Hello, Crystal. How are you?" There was no need to identify himself. She recognized the measured, cultured voice.

She went into her act. "I'm just fine, honey. Nice to hear from you. Must be you're in the mood to party."

Even his laugh had breeding. "I'm in the mood for you, Crystal. Can you come over?"

She gave him the dirty laugh he liked. "Well, I was just reading a good book and relaxing with some wine. The wine's getting me a little mellow, if you know what I mean."

"I know what you mean, Crystal. Now how about grabbing a cab, and I'll see you in twenty minutes."

"See you soon, sweetie." She hung up the phone and stared at it for a moment, smiled, and went into the bedroom to change.

THE PHOTO SHOOT was finally over, and Carla couldn't wait to get outside into the fresh air. The studio was hot and oppressive and everyone had become cranky.

"Come on, Carla. Let's get out of here. I'll buy you a drink." Melissa Slade was as beautiful as Carla. Tall, pencil thin, teal-colored eyes, and honey blond hair. Carla liked Melissa and enjoyed working with her. She was a real pro and a good person.

"Sounds good to me. Let's go." They loped along Fifth Avenue, two thoroughbreds gliding gracefully through the crowds.

It was still early when they slipped into the cocktail lounge of the Pierre Hotel. The Pierre was Carla's favorite, with its understated charm and warm gold and burgundy colors. Whenever she felt like winding down, alone or with friends, that was where she went. The bartenders knew her and made sure nobody hassled her. She could relax and not be bothered by jerks trying to hit on her.

They sat at one of the small round glass-top tables. Fluted crystal glasses on each table held two dewy red rosebuds. The tables faced floor-to-ceiling mirrors between two large candelabras with the bar just to the left. Pure elegance. Each woman ordered a glass of white wine.

"Carla, this is the first chance in ages I've had to sit down and talk with you," said Melissa.

"Yes." Carla sighed. "Life is hectic, isn't it?"

"Must be," Melissa said. "If you have to turn down an opportunity to do a movie in Italy."

Carla smiled. "You've been talking to Randy."

"Yes, I was flabbergasted. I think Randy still is. Sounded like a fabulous break. I mean, that's what we pay people like Randy for, isn't it? Movie offers don't grow on trees, Carla."

"I know. And I know that Randy's still pissed, too. I don't blame him, but I've just got too much going on here right now. I can't afford to be away from New York when my career is about to take off big-time. This movie is not a big-budget film and it could bomb. Then where am I? Maybe I'm stupid and overconfident, but I feel sure there'll be other and better chances, particularly when I get the exposure I expect to be getting this year."

"I understand what you're saying but this is a bird in the hand. And as Randy said, you could always buzz back here for a day or so when necessary. It's not that big a deal."

"I know me and I just couldn't stand that kind of crazy commuting. Anyway, I told you I don't want to be away from New York right now." Her voice took on an edge that told Melissa it was time to change the subject.

"How's your social life? Had time for any?"

"A little. I've been to some parties, met some interesting men. Some dates here and there. Nothing serious."

Melissa looked pensive for a moment. "Carla, do you ever see or hear from or talk to Frank?"

Carla smiled. "Someone else asked me that the other night."

"Must have been a woman. He's a beautiful man."

"Anyway, the answer is yes, and no and no. I did happen to see him on the street just the other day as I was getting into a cab. Actually, I'd been thinking about him these past few days since I saw him. Maybe that's one of the reasons why I don't want to leave New York for a while."

"Well, I was just curious. The few times I met him I envied you."

"Yes." Carla sighed again. "I wish it could have worked, but it didn't and life goes on, right? Then again, who knows?" She toyed with her cigarette pack and pushed it away. "He is a beautiful man."

Melissa studied her, watching her eyes dart about the room. "Carla, you know how much I like you. I've enjoyed the few times we've gotten together. I think we could become very good friends. So take this as said from the heart—from your friend."

Carla turned and looked curiously at her.

"I've been with you twice now in the past week. You've been nervous and edgy as hell. I know the signs. I've been at this business longer than you, and I know what it can do to you. Take a few days off. Get some sun and relax. Nothing's going to go away. It'll all be here when you get back."

Carla smiled and touched Melissa's hand. "Thanks. I appreciate your concern. I have to run now. Thanks for the drink."

Melissa nodded, looking at the wine Carla hadn't touched.

PAUL GALE HAD settled into a routine in New York, alternately working days one week and nights the next. The restaurant where he got a job was one of the more popular places on the East Side in Midtown. And whether lunch or dinner, Gale was constantly buried under mountains of dirty dishes, glasses, and pans, scraping and rinsing before loading them into the dishwashers. Gale certainly did need the job. Living in New York was expensive beyond anything he had expected. He'd never developed any discipline or savvy when it came to spending money, and he knew that without the job, his money would be quickly gone.

His day ended at 4:00 P.M., when smelling of garlic, perspiration, and a variety of kitchen odors that clung to him and his greasy clothes, he trudged wearily back to his room.

The encounter with the hooker had excited him. However, it was his daughter that he was focused on. Since leaving prison, he thought of little else, and after hearing her voice on the phone the first time, his mind was a mass of confusion. What was she like today? How would she react to him?

He clearly remembered the last words he spoke to her in the courtroom: *I'll kill you for this someday.* He hoped that time had healed the thoughts that he carried with him to prison. But he still had the fantasies about her. They never went away.

He knew where she lived and what she looked like. She couldn't have changed much from the pictures he got from Janet. They were only a few years old. He had been to her apartment building. Should he approach her, tell her who he was, tell her he wanted to get to know her—to be a father?

But the anger was still there. And worst of all, the fantasies. All those years in prison, they were still with him—sexual and violent. But now that he was out, enjoying freedom after so long, the hatred didn't seem as strong. It was all such a long time ago.

16

THE EARLY NOVEMBER evening was damp and chilly, causing her to shiver as she stepped out of her apartment building. She pulled up the collar of her coat and began walking. Not a good night to be outside. But she'd been restless all evening.

The wind picked up and rain began to fall, but she continued, oblivious to it. No feeling. Only the vague sense of her life whirling apart. Memories of long ago began appearing in magnified close-ups. She was aware of things happening to her, a new sense of purpose, a way to bring about a thawing of her hurts until the day when all the memories could be erased and the hurts would disappear forever.

She was somewhere on the West Side, standing in the rain waiting for the light. The streets were deserted except for the lone figure of a man a block behind her, walking slowly in her direction. The light changed but she didn't move. She was in her other world, an actor in the close-ups of distant memories.

"Hey, you better come in out of the rain."

She felt something touch her arm and saw a man holding her, beckoning her toward the door of a small bar. She stared at him, turned, and saw the man who had been behind her change direction and walk away.

"Hey, you all right? Jesus, you're soaked. Come on. Let's get you dried out." The man led her inside, where the acrid smell of stale beer and sweat hit her.

"You're catching cold, baby. Come over here and sit down and let me get something warm in you." He led her to a table in a corner of the bar and took off her coat. "You sit right here. I'll bring you some whiskey. Warm you right up. That sound good?" He took off his own coat.

Her eyes focused on him, seeing him for the first time. He was a small man, wearing a New York Mets T-shirt and jeans. He rolled his pack of cigarettes into the left arm of his shirt and headed for the bar.

The place was dark and empty except for a man and woman sitting quietly at the bar drinking beer from their respective bottles. They stared straight ahead, ignoring each other.

"Hey, Billy," Joey yelled to the bartender, "gimme a coupla rye and sodas and hurry it up, will ya?" Joey motioned toward the woman at the table.

He brought the drinks over to the table, sat down, and slid her drink closer to her. "Come on, sweetie, drink up. Make you feel better." He lit a cigarette. The bartender shot him a look but said nothing.

The woman hesitated. He picked up the drink, handed it to her, and guided it up to her mouth.

"That's it." The glass touched her lips. "Atta girl, drink up."

She took a sip, letting it warm her. Then another.

He laughed and a hacking cough erupted. "Goddamned cigarettes," he rasped.

Her expression changed.

"Hey, what're you lookin' at me so mean for? You OK? I mean, can you talk? You ain't said a word since I first seen ya."

She continued studying him and when she finally spoke, the voice was deep, purring. "Where am I? What's the name of this place? Who are you?"

"Hey! She can talk. Ooh! What a voice. You're in Barney's and my name is Joey. I saw you standing outside in the rain and brought ya in here to dry off. Seemed like you were lost or somethin'. What's yer name?"

"Lucky," she said, still examining him.

The door to the bar opened again and two men walked in, looked around, and headed straight for Joey.

Joey was looking at his woman and didn't see the men approach him. He turned just as the larger of the two grabbed him by the hair and spun him around.

She started to get up from her chair, but the other man stood so close he blocked her.

"Hello, Joey, you little creep. Did you forget your debt today?" He pulled Joey's head down flat onto the table and stood over him.

Only half of Joey's face showed. The other half was flattened against the table. "Tomorrow, Sal, tomorrow," Joey's half face whispered. "I'll have it for ya tomorrow at noon."

Sal held him fast. "You better have it tomorrow or you're history, Joey."

The woman grabbed her coat and managed to squeeze her chair away from the other man. "Excuse me." She looked at Billy and edged her way past the two men.

Billy bounded over to the group. "OK, Sal, give it a break. That's enough."

The woman went out the door and stood on the corner. The rain had stopped. She started to cross but stopped and returned, stood for a moment, and began walking slowly along Seventh Avenue.

"Hey! I thought I lost you, Lucky."

She turned and saw the ugly little man standing on the sidewalk, grinning at her. Disgusting vermin. But she was strangely pleased to have him back.

"Lucky? Come over here where I can talk to ya." He went to her and put his arm around her waist. "Ooh! You're a lotta woman, ain'tcha?"

He steered her back onto the sidewalk and started walking her downtown. "Come on, baby. Let's go back to my place and have a little drink. Come on, I'll show you the way. It ain't too far."

He led her along Seventh Avenue. She endured his stupid prattling, but she neither cared nor heard what he was saying. "What do you like to drink, Lucky?"

"Whatever. Maybe some wine, if you have any."

His eyes brightened. "How about I get us a couple bottles. There's a store in the next block."

She stood outside the liquor store, waiting. She hugged her body to ward off the damp chill of the night and watched the little fool inside buying his wine.

They reached Joey's place on Eighth Avenue and entered through a small doorway between a coin-operated laundry and a pawnshop.

"Here we are. See, that didn't take long, did it?"

Joey pulled out a chain laden with keys and unlocked the door. He led the way up the stairs. "I got a nice deal here. I'm the super of the joint. Get my pad for nothin' plus a few bucks besides. I have to take care of the five apartments and kinda keep an eye on things, but it ain't hard. It's a good deal."

They reached Joey's place on the second floor over the Laundromat. She noticed that Joey's was the only apartment on the second floor.

He opened the door and snapped on the light switch. She coughed and turned away as a small rat ran past them and out the door. Joey laughed. "Don't worry, Lucky, he's gone. He ain't gonna hurtcha."

The apartment turned her stomach as much as Joey did. It wasn't really an apartment, just one room with a bed, a small table, two straight-back chairs, and a TV set. The sink had a hot plate on it, surrounded by dirty dishes. A refrigerator stood to the left of the sink, and to the right was a bureau. A clothes bar, jammed between the refrigerator and the wall, held two pairs of pants and a few shirts. She looked around for the bathroom.

Joey read her mind. "Uh, if you have to go to the toilet, it's out in the hall."

She nodded.

"Christ, you're a quiet one, sweetie. But that's OK, I like 'em quiet. Sexy and quiet, my kinda woman."

He pulled a bottle of whiskey from the cupboard under the sink. "Hey, what's your name anyway?" He stuck his head back in the cabinet.

"I told you. It's Lucky," she said, watching his every move. "Lucky, you little scumbag," she whispered to herself.

"You say somethin', Lucky?" he asked, pulling out two glasses and wiping them off with a dirty towel sitting on the sink.

"No, just humming." She was still smiling, not taking her eyes off him. She tried to figure out his age, but it was impossible. He could have been anywhere from thirty to fifty. No matter. She moved closer to him.

"Oh, you must be havin' a good time, huh? Well, I'm goin' to show ya an even better time, honey." He poured himself a large drink of whiskey and poured her wine into a water glass.

Joey handed her the glass of wine. At the same time, he slid his arm around her waist and squeezed her buttocks. "Oh, baby, what a beautiful ass. You gonna give Joey some a that ass, ain't ya, honey?"

"Easy does it. We don't want to rush this." A deep voice. Different.

Joey looked surprised, pleased. "Hey! I like your style, Lucky. OK. OK." He drained his glass and poured some more. "Yeah, you're right. We got all night and we're goin' to enjoy this, ain't we?"

"Yes." She smiled. "We're going to enjoy this."

17

FRANK SLEPT LATE for a change. It was the first decent night's sleep he'd had in months. He rolled over and felt a sharp pain in his shoulder. The shoulder still hurt from the body block he'd thrown at Denise. He'd been thinking about her a lot since the brief time they'd spent together. Maybe that's why he slept well.

She was still on his mind as he dressed. He thought of her on two levels. Her wholesome good looks were unique. No question about that. There was also that shyness about her, a gentleness.

He walked through the living room on the way to the kitchen. That's all his living room was, a passageway between the bedroom and kitchen. He never used it. The sofa and chair he'd bought at Pier 1 on the way back from lunch one day still had the plastic covers on them. Should have saved his money and got his car fixed instead. But then he never used that, either. It'd been sitting in his parents' garage in Jersey for nearly a year.

He made some coffee and eyed the brandy bottle that stood next to the cups. Not a good idea to start sucking up booze in the morning. What the hell. He splashed in a little. The brandy warmed him more than the coffee. He didn't guess there was any harm giving himself a little extra jolt before going out to deal with the dickheads of the world.

"Russo. Jerry's been callin' all morning for you," Ben Thiel, the duty officer, greeted him. "Guy was knocked off in his apartment on Eighth Avenue a couple nights ago. Jerry and Harry Leonard are in the stiff's apartment. Better get over there."

"Relax, Ben. How about if I first get myself a little cup of coffee. That OK with you? You can go back to playing with yourself soon as I leave." He liked to tweak Thiel, who was an officious little prick with peers and obsequious around authority. An ass kisser.

"Anyway, here's the address. They're waiting for you." Thiel handed Frank a piece of paper and went back to his magazine.

The small room was crowded when Frank arrived. The body was on the floor and the medical examiner was still with him. A photographer took pictures while an officer dusted the place for fingerprints. Jerry talked with a man at the kitchen table.

"Where the hell have you been?" Jerry growled at Frank.

"I had some things to do this morning, like catch up on some sleep. Where are we?"

"OK, thanks for your help on this, Mr. Quinn. I may want to talk with you later, but that's all for now. You can go." Jerry dismissed the man and turned to Frank.

"Poor little shit was really roughed up, Frank. Same MO as Beatty."

"Wine bottle?"

Jerry nodded. "Head bashed in with a wine bottle still full a wine when it hit him. Then it looks like whoever did it just grabbed his head and pounded it over and over on the floor. Looks like he was then dragged over by the radiator, where they really did a number on his head. Medical examiner says he died somewhere between ten and midnight night before last." He nodded again, anticipating Frank's next question. "Yep, same deal with the wine bottle."

"Who found him?"

"The victim was the super of the building. The neighbors tell us that he was around every day, kind of on call. Nobody could reach him yesterday or last night, so this guy that just left called the owner of the building this morning. The owner sent somebody over with a key a little later, about nine-thirty. The guy found him and called us. Harry's been talking with the man who found him and a couple of other people in the building. I think we got a pretty good fix on where he hung out. From what they tell us, we shouldn't have too much trouble tracking down where he was two nights ago."

"Hi, Frank." Harry Leonard came over and joined them. Harry was about Frank's age, two inches taller, and twenty-five pounds lighter. He looked like an adolescent, still trying to grow into his body, all gangly arms and legs. His slightly hunched shoulders and droopy eyes gave him a hang-dog appearance. In the rumpled sport coat that he wore every day, he reminded Frank of a crane in tweeds.

"What've you got, Harry?"

"We got some hairs on the body and on the bed, but they look like brown natural-looking hair. They also picked up some fiber material off the victim and off the bed. We got prints on the kitchen sink and the table."

Jerry broke in. "Joey Brewer, that's the victim's name, by the way, didn't stray very far from home base. Didn't have a real versatile social life. He was pretty predictable. Hung out in three joints, all within a few blocks from here. You won't see 'em mentioned in the society columns. The Mohawk Bar at Forty-third and Eighth, Barney's Pub on Seventh near Forty-fifth, and Sully's on Seventh between Forty-sixth and Forty-seventh. Chances are he was in one or all of them the night he got whacked. Frank, you and Harry check out these joints this afternoon. See what you come up with. I gotta get back to the station. Talk to you guys later."

Frank went over to the body lying next to a radiator about eight feet from the bed. His pants and underwear were pulled down around his ankles and a wine bottle protruded from his rectum.

Vincent Craven, the medical examiner, looked up at Frank. "I'm about to remove this, uh, appendage, Frank. Anything you want to check before I do?"

"How far up is it?" Frank asked.

"Pretty deep, maybe three or four inches."

"That took some doing."

"Absolutely," Craven said, standing and flexing his knees until they cracked.

Frank knelt and examined the bottle. "Like somebody was real angry."

Craven shrugged. "Yes, I'd say somebody was very determined to get it up there and stay. As you said, it took some doing."

Frank walked back over to the bed. The sheet and blanket were sprawled across the bed, half on and half off, partly on the floor. He didn't figure Joey as a great housekeeper, but this bed was messed up big-time. Somebody had been flailing around on it. No question that's where the fight began. Was Joey on the bed with someone to begin with?

He checked the rest of the room. Same scene as Beatty. Bottle of whiskey on the table, a glass with some whiskey still in it. Glass of wine with the bottle standing next to it. Joey and his guest were having a friendly drink, or so Joey thought, when bingo! He got zapped. He didn't figure he was in any danger. Same as Beatty. Whoever it was came into these guys' apartments only to kill them.

On the way to the Mohawk Bar, Frank and Harry stopped in a coffee shop for lunch. Harry ordered a cheeseburger, double order of French fries, a piece of apple pie, and two glasses of milk.

"How long you been eating like this?" Frank asked.

"About a week," Harry replied, a hint of pride in his voice.

Frank shrugged. "Well, maybe you'll put some weight on. You are a skinny bastard."

"That's what I'm trying to do. I've got a new girlfriend, tells me she wants more meat on my bones. Says it'll improve my stamina. You know what I mean?"

"Yeah, you'd put on a hundred pounds if it would help you get laid."

Harry started to reply when Frank cut him off. "Harry, you think it's a woman doing these guys?"

Their lunch arrived, Harry's taking up most of the table. He took a couple of bites of his cheeseburger before responding, nodding and chewing the way people do when they're trying to say something but need to get rid of some food first. "Could be," he mumbled through the cheeseburger. "The wine bottle's a sexual thing, so it's either a woman or a homosexual. From what we've heard about Joey so far, it's hard to imagine either wanting to be with the guy for sex unless he paid for it.

"But then, why kill him? No, I think with both this guy and Beatty, the person's mission was to kill them. Man or woman? Dunno. We'll maybe get a better fix from the joints he hung in."

"Yeah," Frank said, watching Harry tear into his cheeseburger, ketchup dripping down his chin. He made a note to avoid dining with Harry while he was on his weight-gaining kick.

THE BARTENDER IN the Mohawk, a short, squat man with a crew cut and small blue eyes that nearly closed when he squinted, had the ruddy, vein-streaked face of a man who probably sampled his wares often. He was predictably shocked to hear of Joey's murder. "Geez, I'm really sorry to hear that," he said. "I'm not surprised, though, in a way.

I mean, he was an obnoxious little shit when he drank a lot, which was most of the time."

"Were you working the night before last?" Frank asked.

"Yeah. I work twelve, thirteen hours a day in this joint."

"Was Joey in that night?" asked Harry.

"No, I ain't seen him in over a week. I'd remember if Joey was in here. He wasn't."

"You're sure?"

"Yeah, 'course I'm sure. You're talkin' only two nights ago, and I ain't seen him in over a week."

"Can you think of anyone who might have wanted to kill him?" Frank asked.

The bartender shook his head. "No, nobody that I ever saw. I mean, he was just a little zero. Nobody got worked up about him one way or the other."

"Did you ever see him with a woman?"

"Joey?" the bartender said, raising his voice in disbelief. "Shit no. He was always sniffing around any broad that came in but they wouldn't give him the time of day."

"Did he seem like the type to take up with a homosexual?" Harry asked.

"I don't know," the bartender said. "I never really paid that much attention to him, to tell the truth. I never saw him with any fags. But then I don't know everybody who comes in here, you know?"

Like the Mohawk Bar, Barney's was a long, narrow rectangle with a bar running along one side and a few tables and booths opposite. Dark and dreary and nearly empty. The bartender was washing glasses and placing them upside down on a dirty cloth stretched out on the sink. One patron sat at the bar, a half-empty shot of whiskey and a glass of beer in front of him. The smell of disinfectant permeated the place. The customer belched.

"Come on. Let's get to it and get out of here," Frank said.

They sat at the bar in front of the bartender. He continued washing the glasses without looking up. Frank cleared his throat. "Be with you in a minute," he said, still not looking at them.

"How about being with us now," Frank said, as he reached over and held his badge under the bartender's nose.

The man gave a little twitch and tugged at his Prince Valiant–style hair hanging just above his shirt collar. His wispy goatee was inconsistent with the thick mane of hair on his head. "What the hell do you guys want?"

"We're looking for some information about a guy who comes in here a lot," Harry said. "Might've been in here a couple nights ago. What's your name, by the way?" Harry took out a pad and set it on the bar.

"Uh, Billy," he said.

"You got a last name, Billy?"

"Oh, yeah, sorry. Burnash. Billy Burnash."

Harry wrote in his notebook. "Billy, do you know a little guy named Joey? Joey Brewer. About forty. Got a couple tattoos on his arms, about here." Harry pointed to his arm just above the elbow. "One arm says *Born to* and the other has the word *Lose* on it. We're told he was a regular in here."

Billy was nodding before Harry finished talking. "Joey. Sure, I know Joey. He's in here all the time. I ain't seen him in a couple days or so, but I'd say you could call him a regular. What's he done? He in trouble?"

Russo leaned in. "Do you work nights, too, or just days?"

"Yeah. I work nights and days. I work two nights six to closing and then two days eleven to six. I alternate, ya know. Two days, then two nights, then two days, then—"

"I get the picture," Frank interrupted. "Were you on two nights ago?"

"Yeah. I worked last night and the night before."

"Was Joey in two nights ago?" Frank asked.

Billy frowned and put his fingers to his chin. "Hmm. Lemme see. He wasn't in last night," he said slowly, thinking his way along. "Now, when was he last in? Oh, yeah. Sure. He was in two nights ago. How could I forget? We had a little problem that night. I thought for a minute Joey was gonna get roughed up real bad."

"What do you mean?" Harry asked.

"Well, Joey's sittin' at that table over there with this woman. The door opens and in come these two guys. They head straight for Joey, and they start workin' him over a little bit. Nothin' real heavy, you know, but I can tell they mean business."

"Do you know who the guys were?" Frank asked.

"Well, they— Hey, wait a minute. You wanna tell me what this is all about?"

Frank leaned forward and spoke softly. "Joey Brewer was murdered two nights ago, the night he was here in your bar, the night we are now discussing. We are investigating a homicide, and we expect full cooperation from you. We expect you to answer all of our questions and to help us in every way that you can. That's what this is all about."

Billy turned white. His hand slipped off the bar, hitting one of the glasses drying on the sink and knocking it to the floor. "Holy shit!" He barely got the words out. "Jesus. Joey was such a nothin' little guy. Who'd want to kill him?" Billy asked, shaking his head. "I mean, he could be a pain in the ass sometime, but he was harmless. I mean, when you think of it, who'd want to take the trouble to kill the little nitwit?"

"Well, now that you're through grieving over Joey, do you think you'd like to answer some questions, Billy?" Frank asked.

"What about these two guys? Tell us what happened," Harry broke in.

Billy poured himself a shot of whiskey and downed it. "Well, like I said, Joey is sittin' at that table over there with this woman he walked in with a few minutes before. These two guys come in and start workin' Joey over. They were givin' him some shit about some money they said he owed 'em. I was at the end of the bar when they first came in, but when they grabbed him and slammed his head on the table, I shot over there. They weren't talking very loud, but I was close enough to hear what they were saying. They said Joey didn't pay 'em that day, like he was supposed to. Joey said he'd pay 'em the next day, and they let him up and said he'd better, or he's history. Jesus, I guess they meant it."

"Do you know these men, Billy?" Harry was off his stool and leaning over the bar, his face close to Billy's.

"Well, yeah, in a way. I mean, I know their first names, and I know they're loan sharks, but that's about it." Billy looked around the bar, and his face twitched.

Frank asked Billy for a drink of water and when he brought it, Frank touched his arm. "Look, Billy. Don't worry about those two. Just tell us everything you saw and everything you know about them. We'll take it from there, and you're out of it. So you've got nothing to fear, OK?" Frank smiled, probably the first time a cop ever smiled at Billy.

"One's name is Ron. The other is Sal. They're loan sharks, and they operate in this neighborhood. They come here once in a while for a couple drinks, but they never stay long. They hang around a joint called the Alcazar mostly. It's a few blocks from here over on Eighth Avenue. Everybody knows 'em over there."

"How long did they stay here, after they roughed up Joey?" Frank asked.

"Well, Joey took off pretty quick, after they let him up off the table. They stayed and had a couple drinks each, and I heard 'em say they were going over to the Alcazar. Then they left. That's it."

"Do you remember what time it was, when all this was happening?" Frank asked, holding up his empty glass and nodding for more water.

"Yeah. I remember it was still early. Maybe nine, nine-thirty," Billy replied, as he handed Frank his water.

"Tell us about the woman," Frank said.

18

YEAH, THE WOMAN," Billy said, rubbing his chin. "She seemed like spacey, you know. I mean, Joey was kinda leading her in like she didn't know where she was. I noticed for a couple of reasons. First, I'm surprised to see Joey with such a good-lookin' woman. I mean, even the usual pigs who come in this joint ignore him. And then second, she's pretty tall. Shit, she towered over Joey."

"She have heels on?" Frank asked.

"You mean like high heels, spike heels?"

"Yeah."

"I dunno. I couldn't tell."

"Joey wasn't very big," Frank said. "Most women would look big next to him. How tall would you say she was?"

"Ah, shit. I don't know. I didn't really get that good a look at her. I just know she was a lot taller than Joey. I'd say maybe five-nine, five-ten, up to maybe six feet."

Harry was writing while Frank continued. "What'd you mean when you said she seemed spacey?"

"Well, she just sorta stared straight ahead. I mean, she wasn't lookin' at Joey. 'Course, I can't blame her for that. He was an ugly little shit. She wasn't really lookin' at anything. I dunno. She just seemed out of it."

"Drunk?"

"No. I can tell a drunk. She wasn't drunk. Just actin' funny."

"Did she seem like she was on drugs?"

Billy shrugged and shook his head. "I dunno. I'm no expert on that. Anyway, you gotta remember I was over at the bar and I never really got close to her." Billy looked around the bar, hoping he might be needed elsewhere. He was running out of gas with the two cops.

Frank sensed it. "Billy, you're doing great. You've got a hell of a memory. Keep it up. Just a few more questions. Did Joey and the woman come in together or did they meet here?"

"They came in together," Billy said. "I remember doing kind of a double take when I saw them."

"Tell us some more what she looked like," Frank continued. "What color hair? Long? Short? How old? Was she pretty?"

Billy exhaled with a frown. "Yeah, she was a great-lookin' chick. That's why I noticed her. Especially bein' with Joey. I'd say maybe late twenties, early thirties. Hair? Hard to say. Her coat collar was up when she came in and her hair was kind of tucked into it. I think she took her coat off later at the table but tell you the truth, I didn't even notice her hair."

"You couldn't tell if it was long or short?"

"Nooo." He dragged the word out, thinking along with it. "Yeah, I remember it was wet and it seemed like it was pinned up, you know?" He held out his hands, exasperated. "I just couldn't tell if it was long or short. I couldn't tell the color either, except it wasn't blond. I guess it was brown or black."

Frank noticed that Billy would be a great witness in a trial. He had remembered and answered all of his questions in reverse order. "Was she with Joey when Sal and Ron came in?"

"Yeah. But then when things got rough, she got up and left."

Frank frowned. "How long after she left did Joey leave?"

"Shit, I don't know." Billy looked around the bar again. "I mean, I had other customers, you know? Once things quieted down over in Joey's corner, I didn't pay much attention."

Frank persisted. "Was it a long time? Did he leave right after her? Think, Billy!"

"Naw. It wasn't a long time. Maybe just a couple of minutes. Not long."

"Was that the last time you saw him or did he come back?" Frank asked.

"No. That's the last I seen of him."

"Did you ever see Joey leave with a woman before?" Frank asked.

"Nope. Not even the hookers who come in here would go out with him. Like I said, that's why I was surprised to see him with such a good-looking woman."

"Did she look like she might have been a prostitute?"

"No, that's what I'm sayin'. You know, working in this joint, I can spot a hooker a mile away. This woman did not look the type, not at all."

"Ever see him with a fag?" asked Harry.

"Naw. I think Joey was pretty straight. 'Course, you never know. I mean, that was just my impression of him."

"Did Joey have any enemies that you know of?" Frank asked. "Other than the loan sharks."

Billy shook his head. "Naw. Joey was such a cipher, nobody could get worked up enough about him one way or another." He nodded toward a new customer sitting at the bar. "Excuse me. I gotta go wait on that guy."

Frank touched his arm. "Last question. Who else was in the bar?"

"Jackie Fleming and his girlfriend were at the bar. They come in almost every night, sit there and drink. Don't say much."

"Anybody else?"

Billy thought for a moment. "No, nobody else. That it? I gotta go wait on that guy who just came in."

Frank nodded and thanked him. "It doesn't sound like we're going to have a lot of trouble finding Sal and Ron," he said to Harry. "We'll go over to the Alcazar and talk to some people. If Billy knows what he's talking about, and we get lucky, they might even show up while we're there."

"I guess you could say they had a motive, huh?"

"You could say that," Frank said. He took out his cell phone. "Jerry's all worked up. I've got to call him. He filled in the lieutenant on Joey, and Nolan's paranoid. He's bent out of shape about similarities between this one and the Beatty killing, and he wants a report this afternoon, before he leaves. You go in and write the report on what we've got so far. I'll check the Alcazar and Sully's. I'll be in later. Nolan wants to see Jerry and me at four-thirty in his office."

"OK, Frank."

Frank headed for the Alcazar, avoiding the black plastic trash bags that were fixtures along the sidewalks. He was encouraged by what they had learned from Billy, but the thing with the two loan sharks was just too pat, too easy. Guys like that just don't go around advertising that they're going to kill someone, and then turn around and do it a few hours later. On the other hand, fear and intimidation were the stock and trade of loan sharks, and maybe they wanted to send a message to the rest of the neighborhood. Maybe they really were that tough and that stupid.

He couldn't get the woman out of his mind. What would a woman like that be doing with a creep like Joey Brewer? Spaced out but not drunk. She came in with him. An unlikely pair for a date. So she's spaced, high on drugs. Maybe came from a party and little Joey spots her and sees she's out of it. Decides to take advantage and hauls her in here to work on her.

He remembered it was raining that night. And Billy said her hair was wet. Joey probably ran into her on the street outside and hustled her in out of the rain. Could she have done him? Billy said Joey left very shortly after she did. Did he catch up to her outside? Could there be a connection between Joey and Beatty and the loan sharks? Were they into Beatty, too? He reached the Alcazar and walked in.

19

THE ALCAZAR, TWO blocks from the Mohawk, had the rancid smell and feel that bars have in the daytime. The place was dark, and it took a minute for Frank's eyes to adjust. A circular bar stood in the center of the room, with small tables clustered around to one side. Opposite were a dance floor and a bandstand. Against another wall to the left of the entrance were several booths covered in green vinyl. He made a mental note to tell Harry about the sign at the entrance advertising Tuesdays and Thursdays as "LADIES NIGHTS. ALL DRINKS HALF PRICE FOR UNESCORTED LADIES."

The place was a mess of dirty glasses and empty beer bottles. Frank approached the bartender, who was sitting on a stool behind the bar picking his teeth, and asked him about the two loan sharks.

The man, about Frank's height, wore a sweat-stained T-shirt that barely contained biceps looking like they had been carved out of oak. The top of his head was tightly wrapped with a red bandanna and a dirty blond pigtail trailed down his back. He responded without looking at Frank. "Who wants to know?"

Frank showed him his credentials, which did nothing to change the bartender's attitude.

"Big fucking deal. What do you want from me?"

He really was tired of having to deal with creeps like this. Phony tough guys who liked to flaunt their dislike of cops. He leaned on the bar and swept his arm across it, sending the dirty bottles and glasses clattering onto the floor. Shards of broken glass exploded around the bartender's stool. "Sorry about that," he said. "I'm such a klutz."

The bartender leaped off the stool, broken glass crunching under his feet. His eyes burned with hatred, a look Frank had seen many times.

"Anyway, the big fucking deal is I'd like you to answer a few questions about Sal and Ron."

The man hesitated, as if debating what to do next. And then he looked toward the door. "Well, I guess today's your lucky day, because your two guys just walked in."

Frank turned and saw two men heading toward the bar.

"How's it goin', Russ?" the smaller of the two greeted the bartender.

Russ looked toward Frank, who introduced himself and showed them his badge. "I wonder if I could speak with you guys over in a booth?" Frank asked.

They stood next to Frank and looked him up and down. The bigger of the two towered over Frank, standing six-four or -five. He studied Frank's credentials and badge, and dropped them on the bar. "Yeah, sure. Russ, give us a couple of beers first. You want one?" he asked Frank.

"No, thanks."

Russ, still glaring at Frank, delivered the beers, and they settled into a booth.

"Well, what can we do for you?" Sal, the big one, asked.

"I want to talk with you about a little guy named Joey Brewer. Name ring a bell?"

Sal and Ron looked at each other for a moment before Sal replied, "Yeah, we know Joey. What's the problem?"

"What makes you think there's a problem?"

"What, are you just coming in here for the atmosphere and shoot the shit with us about Joey Brewer?" Sal asked, lighting a cigarette.

"When's the last time you saw Joey?"

Sal shrugged and turned to Ron. "Ronnie, when's the last time we saw Joey?"

Ron was short and stocky and had a stubble of beard, which about matched the amount of hair he had on his head. He wore a blue shiny vinyl jacket over a gray sweatshirt. "Geez, I don't know. We see a lotta people. It's hard to keep track of who we see when." He gave a little smile, showing teeth that resembled corn kernels. Frank was glad he'd had the jolt of brandy before leaving the apartment.

"You remember where you were the night before last?"

"Night before last. Night before last. Tuesday. Yeah, we had a few beers in a couple a joints, then had a bite to eat and went home. I was feelin' kinda sick, so we went home early. Right, Sal?"

Sal nodded. "Yeah, I remember now."

"You two live together?" Frank asked.

"Yeah," Ron replied. "What's this all about, anyway?" he asked.

"Did you guys go to Barney's Tuesday night?" Frank asked, ignoring the question.

"Barney's," Sal thought out loud. He turned to Ron, who nodded.

Sal hesitated for a moment. "Yeah, we were in Barney's for a while. In fact, now I remember. That's when we saw Joey."

"Oh, yeah?" Frank replied. "You talk to him?"

"Yeah, we talked to him."

"What about?"

Sal flared. "Hey, look, you want to tell us what the hell this is all about? You come in here and start givin' us the third degree. For what? What's goin' on?"

Frank spoke quietly. "You want me to get a warrant and take you two punks down to the station for questioning? Want me to do that? Or we can finish our little chat right here. It's up to you."

They each lit another cigarette. The booth was blue with smoke. Frank's eyes began to burn.

Sal exhaled in Frank's direction. He gave a final, last-minute poof toward Frank to make sure all the smoke reached him. That was bad enough, but it was the smirk that really did it. Frank slapped the cigarette out of his mouth and sent it skittering across the floor. Sal leaped to his feet and cocked his fist, ready to swing.

Frank was on his feet ahead of him. "Go ahead, asshole, and we'll have you in a cell before you can light another cigarette. Anyway, it's against the law to smoke in a bar. Or didn't you know that?"

Sal's eyes narrowed. He held his fist in position for another thirty seconds before he dropped it and sat down. The smirk returned, and he was Mr. Cool again.

"OK. Joey owed us a little money, and we talked to him about that. Sounds like you already been to Barney's, so yeah, we roughed him up a little. You know, just enough to let him know we want our money. That's all. Then we left. We came here and had a few beers, then stopped in the pizza joint on the corner, had some pizza, and went home, OK?"

Frank sat staring at him, then turned to Ron. Ron smiled again, showing his little yellow teeth. He squirmed and looked around the room, avoiding eye contact with Frank.

"What time was all this?" he asked. "How long did you stay here? What time did you get home?"

"Goddamn it!" Sal yelled. "What do you want from us? What's this all about?"

"Joey Brewer was killed on Tuesday night. You two were seen working him over and threatening him in Barney's. A few people noticed." Frank's eyes never left them.

"Holy shit," Ron muttered.

"Oh, I get it," Sal said. "You guys are gonna try to pin this on me and Ron, because we had a little tiff with Joey. Is that it?"

"Maybe. And maybe your telling him he's history if he doesn't pay up might get some attention."

"Well, screw you, pal. We had nothing, nothing whatsoever to do with Joey Brewer getting killed. We walked out of that bar, and never saw him again."

"Nobody's accusing you guys of anything. Lot of things could have happened, and anybody could have done this. I'm just trying to get some help, that's all. I understand Joey was sitting with a woman. Did you get a good look at her?"

"No, we didn't pay any attention to her. Anyway, she cut out pretty quick. All I remember is she was pretty good-lookin' and tall," said Sal.

Ron spoke up. "Yeah, she stood up next to me, and I was eye level with her boobs."

"She have heels on or flats?"

"Heels? Shit, I don't know. It's hard to say, you know? With those tits, I wasn't looking at her feet. Tall though, maybe close to six feet."

"How about her hair?" Frank asked. "What color?"

"Yeah, her hair." Ron looked puzzled and glanced at Sal for help.

Sal spoke up. "Hard to tell. She had it covered with some kind of scarf. The little bit I could see seemed like it was dark. You know, maybe dark brown, black."

Frank's eyes still burned. He half wished that Sal had swung on him. "How long after the woman left did Joey leave?"

"He left right after she did," Sal said. "Couldn't wait to get the hell out."

"So he was just a few seconds behind her?"

"Yeah, I'd say so."

After another twenty minutes or so Frank had pretty much the same information he'd got from Billy, including their doubts that the woman was a prostitute. He took their addresses and phone numbers and left.

Outside, a strong wind had picked up. He put his head down and walked to the precinct, where he brought Harry up to date. It was nearly four-thirty when he entered Jerry's office with the report.

"Jesus, I'm glad you're here," Jerry greeted Frank as he walked in the door. "Nolan is ranting about his goddamn intuition. Says it's telling him that Beatty and this one are connected. Give me a quick rundown before we go in to see him."

Frank went over everything. "We've finally got something to go on. It's not much but it's something."

Jerry stood up and tucked his shirt into his pants. He straightened his tie and put on his coat.

"Jerry, how long you and Nolan been working together, fifteen years? You think he doesn't know the real you by now? Why do you have to fix yourself up to look like Tom Cruise every time you go in his office?"

"I'm insecure. Let's go."

Lieutenant Joseph Nolan was a small, dapper black man of about forty-three. His dark brown hair, flecked with gray, was clipped short, his salt-and-pepper mustache neatly trimmed. He had been with the New York Police Department for nineteen years and had worked his way up from rookie patrolman to the position he now held.

Nolan's ambition was no secret. He was bucking hard for captain, borough commander, and chief, and some day even commissioner. Smart and savvy, he had a special set of antennae that went up whenever he detected a situation developing that could slow down his personal goals. More than anything else, he feared media attention or pressure. When he sensed a problem, he was quick to take action to defuse it.

"Hello, Frank. Come in. Come in." Nolan did not get up, nor did he offer Frank and Jerry a seat. There was no chitchat.

"Now, Frank, you may think I'm overreacting to the murder of this little nobody over on Eighth Avenue. And I know that you and Jerry and Harry have just gotten on it. So I'm not expecting you're going to turn over the killer to me today. However, let me tell you I have very bad vibes about this. It's a carbon copy of the Beatty case, and you don't seem to have much on that one yet. Now, what I don't want is to find ourselves in the middle of a series of killings that are going to get the wrong people's attention. Do you know what I mean, Frank?"

Frank knew what he meant. The last thing he wanted was to get on Nolan's shit list. He looked at Jerry.

"Jerry already heard my speech earlier today," Nolan said sharply. "Now tell me exactly where we are on this one, Frank. What do you have, anything?" The lieutenant leaned forward expectantly.

Frank handed Nolan a copy of the report and filled him in on what he and Harry had learned from Billy and the two loan sharks. "We've got some leads now, Lieutenant. We should have more later in the week."

"Well, I hope you do, Frank. But whatever, I expect action and re-sults on both these cases—pronto. Keep in very close touch." Nolan wheeled his chair sideways and picked up the phone. They were dis-missed.

"Get the picture, Frank?" Jerry asked as they headed toward the watercooler. Jerry's shirt had managed to come out of his pants again and his tie had unloosened. They each drank two paper cups of water and sat down.

Frank nodded. "Yeah, I get the picture."

Jerry got up and headed toward his office. He turned. "This is go-ing to get worse, Frank. I can feel it."

Frank went over to his own desk and slumped, tired and tense. He knew Jerry was right. It is going to get worse. His gut feeling told him the loan sharks didn't do these guys. They're scumbags and he'd like nothing better than to nail them for something, but it won't be this. No, somebody's out there was getting their kicks, satisfying some sick need. And they're not finished. The time frame in between is going to get shorter. And Nolan is going to get nastier.

He took the three Nerf balls from his drawer and shot a few hoops in the basket he'd rigged up. Three in a row. Not bad, he thought, for a guy with a bum shoulder. He felt the shoulder, smiled, and decided to go to the health club.

20

PAUL GALE WAS increasingly stressed out. His work at the restaurant had become unbearable.

And now that he had been a free man for several weeks, he'd begun focusing on a part of life he had never known. Occasionally, when momentarily caught up on his work in the kitchen, he would peek out and observe the upscale, happy-looking people in the restaurant, the nice clothes the men wore, the beautiful women.

One night he watched a man take off his coat and pull a bouquet of flowers from under it and present it to the woman with him. It was a simple thing, but it was the expression on the woman's face that stayed with him.

But he hated the goddamn job and wasn't even sure he would stay in New York. Everything about his life was up in the air. He was here because of his daughter, but he was beginning to struggle with uncertainty. He thought back to the woman on the train—how he'd bragged about his daughter, about whom he knew nothing at the time.

He'd begun to realize he said things he only hoped were true. And now he knew there was even more to her than he had bragged about. He took out his wallet and admired the photo of her he'd taken from Janet. A smile softened his face.

He could shake the hatred that had been burning inside him for so long. Maybe if they met, talked. Maybe.

GINA PONTE POPPED her head into Denise's doorway. Her perfume preceded her and Denise turned and spotted her friend.

"My. Don't we look sexy tonight," Denise said.

"Come on, Dennie. Give me a break. It's Friday night. Everybody's going over to the Splendido. Get your coat and let's go." She was in Denise's office, playfully tugging at her. "Come on. Kiss your computer good night and let's go."

Denise looked her up and down and couldn't help smiling. The black pants and sweater Gina wore fit as if they'd been painted on her. "You look like you're ready to howl," Denise said with a smile.

"Bet your sweet life, honey. Let's go."

"No, I can't. I'm going to the health club for a while and then I'm going to work on the curtains and duvet I've been making. I want to finish the curtains tonight and I'm coming down the home stretch on the duvet."

Gina shook her head. "I swear, Dennie. You are so talented. You're the only person I know who can sew like that."

"I guess you don't know many people," Denise said. "Anyway, thanks for the invite. But have a good time. I'm sure you will, knowing you."

Gina shrugged and left. Denise sat for a moment, half wishing she had gone with her. Gina was fun, one of the few people able to make her laugh. But all those phonies posturing and preening, all trying to impress each other. Who needed it?

Anyway, she'd been thinking a lot about Frank Russo. Surprising. Most of the men she'd met in New York weren't worth much. But Frank was so nice and God, was he good-looking! He had mentioned that Fridays were probably going to be the best nights for him to get to the health club on a regular basis. It might be kind of nice to bump into him again. She smiled at her choice of words.

And then, she really was looking forward to working on her home-decorating projects. The material had set her back almost a week's pay, but it was gorgeous and worth it. Now she couldn't wait to finish everything and get her bedroom looking just like the one she'd seen in *Elle Décor*.

THE CLUB WAS crowded as usual on Fridays, but she was disappointed not to see Frank. He's probably got a date, she thought, and headed for the locker room.

But when she came out she spotted him pumping away on the stationary bike. A warm rush of well-being swept over her.

Frank saw her and motioned her over. His wave was so friendly that walking over to him seemed perfectly natural.

"Hi, Denise. How are you?" He wore a pair of gym shorts and no shirt. Sweat glistened on his body. Standing there, looking down on his nearly naked body, she felt an odd intimacy in spite of all the people around them.

"Hi. Looks like you've really been attacking that thing."

"Yeah, well, I'm not sure who's winning. Right now I'd say the bike is."

She laughed and started to move away toward a Nautilus machine.

"How long do you usually work out?" he asked.

She stopped and drifted back a couple of steps. "About forty-five minutes or so tonight."

"That sounds good for me, too." He beckoned toward the juice machine. "Can I buy you a drink when we finish?"

"Sure."

Frank went back to his bike. She looked even better than he remembered. It had been a tough week. Nolan was pressing Jerry hard. They had never liked each other and Nolan seemed to get off on riding Jerry if he was bothered. He had good reason to be bothered now, and he was turning the screws. Everybody on the Beatty–Joey Brewer cases was snapping at everybody else.

He watched Denise lying on her back, pumping the Nautilus contraption up and down, her beautiful, muscular body moving in an easy rhythm. She sat up and glanced over and caught him looking at her. He jerked his head down and fumbled with the tension control on the bike.

After about forty-five minutes they rendezvoused at the juice machine and sat together on a mat in the corner of the room. He liked sitting next to her and the slightly musky female smell she gave off. Little ringlets of sweat formed on her forehead and occasionally dropped into the cleavage provided by the tank top she wore. He watched with some envy as they rolled down and disappeared into her breasts.

He looked up sharply, wondering if she'd caught him, and was relieved to see her leaning back with her eyes closed. "Penny for your thoughts."

Her eyes opened and moved in his direction. "No thoughts. Just resting and relaxing."

She lied. Her head was filled with thoughts—thoughts put there by Frank and how natural and comfortable she felt sitting next to him, their half-naked bodies nearly touching. She wondered what it would be like to make love to him.

"I love these workouts, don't you, Frank?"

He thought about his aching thighs and shortness of breath. No way could he say he loved what he had just suffered through. "Uh, to be honest—not yet. But maybe it'll grow on me. I can tell you do by the expression on your face."

When she turned and looked at him, her eyes luminous and sparkling under the soft lights, he realized all the more what a beautiful young woman she was. He also wondered if she knew—or cared—how goddamned sexy she looked sitting here.

Denise felt a stirring that had lain dormant for a long time, and wished she could tell him the expression on her face had less to do with her workout than sitting here with him. She knew she was being foolish, but still . . .

They sat with their backs against the wall, making small talk, or at least he was trying to. She definitely was shy and he didn't feel like he was having much luck drawing her out. Over the past few months, he had been the one with the monosyllabic responses and indifference. Now, here he was acting like a school kid.

She finished her juice and set the can down. "I've got to go. I've really enjoyed seeing you again, Frank."

"OK," he said and started to get up. He groaned and held his back. "Maybe I'm too old for this stuff."

"No, you're not." She laughed. "And don't you dare give up on it. I expect to see you here at least every Friday."

That was encouraging. "Tell you what," he said. "It only takes me a few minutes to grab a quick shower and change. I'll probably be out before you. I'll wait and walk you out, if you don't mind."

"OK," she said without hesitating.

He stood by the door for about ten minutes before she appeared. Her long dark brown hair gleamed, and the brown eyes were even more lustrous—like polished stones, only filled with warmth. The big bag she carried looked like the kind Carla toted around. He felt a twinge. Denise spotted him and broke out in a smile that made him weak in the knees. The Carla twinge disappeared.

She reached him in three long strides. "Hope I didn't keep you waiting too long."

"No," he said, his eyes playing across her. "But if you did, it would've been worth it." Her face flushed. She was actually blushing. He couldn't remember the last time he'd seen a woman blush.

The night was almost balmy, with clear sky and a nearly full moon. October, his favorite month, was over now, and he hated November. It was always damp and cold, trees turned into gaunt, leafless spindles against a gray sky, a harbinger of the long winter ahead. But tonight was a rare treat. "Beautiful night," he said, as they stood somewhat awkwardly on the sidewalk.

A young man and woman shot by on Rollerblades. Well-dressed professional women wearing sneakers, carrying their dress shoes in bags over their shoulders, hurried by.

"Denise, you haven't had dinner yet, have you?" Frank asked.

She hesitated. "Well, no, but I'm just going to make something light when I get home. I'm working on a project tonight."

"Oh. Well, all that exercise has me hungry all of a sudden, and I don't have any strength left to cook anything myself. Too dehydrated and weak. If I don't eat soon, I'll probably get sick."

She started to giggle. "I think you'd better get yourself to a restaurant, fast."

"Can't," he said. "I get indigestion if I eat in a restaurant alone. Always have. I've got a solution, though."

She was already shaking her head. "I can't, Frank. I really have some work to do tonight."

He looked at his watch. "Come on. It's only six-thirty. I know a great little spot just a couple of blocks from here. I also know the owner. We'll be in and out in an hour, you'll have performed a humanitarian act, and you'll be working on your project by eight-thirty. You like Thai food?"

"It's my favorite."

"See? Come on. OK?" He reached out for her.

She stood her ground, watching him. He had made her laugh, the way Gina could, and there was a quality about him that made her feel safe, comfortable. Why not?

The restaurant was small and filled with delicious smells. Cozy booths lined one wall, which held vivid paintings of Oriental scenes. Delicate wood carvings on teak shelves adorned the other walls, covered with coordinated fabric.

Two petite Asian women, wearing colorful, authentic Thai dresses, bustled about serving customers. The owner, a Thai woman of indeterminate age, greeted Frank with a hug and a kiss. "I miss you, handsome. Where you been?"

"Awful busy, Mai Lee. Say hello to Denise."

She greeted Denise and seated them in one of the booths with benches upholstered in a Thai fabric. "We take good care of you, Frankie." She hugged him again and scurried toward the kitchen.

Denise watched her go and smiled. "Something tells me you have that effect on most women."

Frank's eyes twinkled. "You, too?"

She blushed again. "Guess I walked into that one."

They both ordered pad thai with shrimp and some Thai beer.

"This is wonderful," Denise said. "I'm glad you suggested it."

He smiled. "Me, too." She was easy to be with. None of the edge that most women in New York had. No BS. Just . . . nice. "How about another beer?"

She looked at her watch. "It's twenty after seven. Remember your promise?"

"Oh, yeah. What's your project?"

"Just some sewing I'm doing."

"Sewing? Like darning holes in your socks?"

"No." She laughed. "I'm making curtains and a duvet."

"You're making a duvet?" Frank wondered what that was, but didn't ask.

"Yes, it's sort of my thing. I like designing and decorating things, mostly for my apartment. It's relaxing and I think I'm pretty good at it. Guess you'd call me a poor woman's Martha Stewart."

He nodded like he knew she'd be pretty good at it. "You mentioned you work for a publisher. What do you do there?"

"Yes, we publish college textbooks, and I'm an associate editor. I work for the editor in chief. Sometimes he can be a pain, but I've learned a lot from him. What do you do, by the way?"

He took a deep hit on his beer and gave a little laugh. "You don't want to know."

"Yes, I do. Now you've got me curious."

"I'm a cop."

"A . . . cop," she stammered.

"Did I say a dirty word? Come on, it could be worse. I could be a lawyer."

She touched his arm. "No, no. I didn't mean to hurt your feelings. I'm sorry. I guess I just never thought of you as a policeman, that's all."

"Why not?"

"I don't know. I guess I thought all policemen wore white socks."

"What did you think of me as?"

She shrugged. "I guess I never really thought about it." She studied him. He sure was easy to look at. "A business executive, advertising, TV, a lawyer. Oops, sorry. What kind of a policeman are you?"

"I'm a detective, a homicide detective."

"Homicide?"

He watched the expression on her face and was sorry the whole thing came up. It really got tiresome, watching people react to his job. It's like everybody knows there are cops who investigate and solve murders, but nobody ever wants to know such a creature personally. It's OK in the abstract.

"Yeah," he said flatly. "Homicide. You know, like in murder?" Something about her attitude now was different and he didn't like it.

She picked up on the change in him, too. "Sorry, Frank. I just never met a real live homicide detective."

No kidding, he thought. What a surprise. Usually, if people reacted in a funny way to his job, he liked to tweak them. With Denise, he felt a need to justify himself. "It's something I always wanted to do." He resisted the urge to add, *OK?* "My father and two uncles were police officers. I've been a cop for twelve years and, it may sound corny, but I happen to believe in what I do."

Denise stared at him. "I'm sure you're a very good detective," she said softly.

He grinned. "Sorry for getting carried away. Didn't mean to jump on a soapbox."

"That's OK. Your job must be fascinating. What are you working on now?"

He looked at his watch. "I'll tell you another time. I promise. But right now, I'm going to keep tonight's promise, much as I hate to."

"Oh," she said, looking at her own watch. "That's right. I do have to go."

Frank paid the check and they left, after another hug from Mai Lee, this time for both of them.

"I'm going to catch a cab," Denise said. "But let's just walk along for a minute. It's such a nice night."

"Perfect," he said, glad for the chance to enjoy her a little longer. He lived his life like he was always running late, but she had a way of slowing him down, even relaxing.

They walked for a few blocks, neither saying much. It was a

comfortable silence, the kind that people have when neither feels any pressure to keep conversation going, but somehow there is communication.

People hurried by carrying colorful shopping bags, getting a head start on the Christmas season. The wind had picked up, carrying pieces of paper that skittered along beside them. Winter was beginning to elbow its way in.

A bus pulled up next to them, dropped off two teenagers, and muscled its way back into traffic, spewing its fumes. The driver of a car behind it jammed on his brakes, blew his horn, and flipped the finger toward the bus.

Denise spotted a cab cruising down the street and hailed it. "I'm going to catch this cab, but I hope I'll see you again . . . soon?"

He grinned and touched her face. "Count on it," he said, opening the door for her. He slipped the driver a ten-dollar bill and turned back to Denise, who had the window down, her head partially out of it.

"Thanks again, Frank. I really enjoyed it."

"Me, too." He leaned in and gently kissed her on the lips.

The cab pulled away. He watched and waited to see if she would turn and wave. She did.

21

I**T WAS SUNDAY** and Frank was up early. Beautiful day for a football game. Jets and Patriots tied for the division lead. He smiled as the phone rang. "Hi, Dad."

"Frankie!" His father's unmistakable New York accent. "You wanna come by the house first or just meet at the park?"

Another smile. Football and baseball games were still played at "the park" to Silvio Russo. He called Madison Square Garden "the gym." "Meet you at the park, Dad. It's another hour for me to get to the house and back to the park. Meet you at gate eighteen at eleven-thirty and we'll have a bite to eat at Conlins. OK?"

"OK, kid. See ya then."

Over coffee Frank read some FBI memoranda on profiling serial killers. He reflected on his most recent three weeks at the academy in Quantico. Great stuff, and he'd learned a lot about serial killers—all male. There was actually very little on female serial killers. It just isn't something that's received much attention. But they're out there.

The violence of Beatty's and Joey's murders didn't jell, though. Women still don't like to get their hands dirty. Poison is their weapon of choice, followed by gunshots. Nice and impersonal. These two didn't fit the pattern.

His stomach growled. Nothing in the refrigerator and no bread for toast. It was still only eight-thirty and there was no way he could wait until eleven-thirty, so he went down to the corner store for some bagels and orange juice.

On the way back to his apartment, someone called his name as he was about to enter the building. He turned and saw a tall man with thinning hair and a thick dark mustache smiling broadly and shaking his head.

"I don't believe it, Frank Russo. For Christ sake. How are you?" The man approached him, grabbed his hand, and pumped it warmly.

Frank stared for a minute, trying to jog his memory. No luck.

"It's David. David Bernstein." The man's outstretched arms, palms up, telling Frank he should have recognized him.

"David!" Frank grabbed him and hugged him.

"That's better," David said. "Thought you forgot your old buddy there for a minute. I haven't changed that much, have I?"

"Well, uh, let me see. Last time I saw you was at that graduation party at Northeastern. You had hair then and no mustache and you were hanging all over Ginny Freeling. Ever get in her pants?"

David's hands went up to his head. "I still have hair." He looked at his reflection in the glass door and brushed back the strands he had left. "Yeah, I got into Ginny's pants. I married her. We got divorced a few years later. Haven't seen her since. How about you?"

"Nope, still single."

They compared notes the way old friends do who haven't seen each other in almost fifteen years.

"You're a homicide detective. I'm impressed."

"You're a television producer. I'm impressed—I think," Frank responded.

"Hey, Frank. I'm having a little shindig tonight at my place. How about coming? Be lots of good-looking unattached women there. They'll be all over you. I'm up on East Seventy-second. What do you say?"

"Hmm. I'm going to the Jets game. I—"

"So?" David interrupted. "The game's over by four. Party won't get going till eight-thirty or nine." He gave Frank a card with his address and made him promise to come.

"FRANKIE. YOU'RE RIGHT on time." Silvio Russo stood in front of their appointed meeting spot. With his brown leather jacket, thick mane of silver-gray hair, and aviator sunglasses, he looked like an older, heavier version of Frank.

They hugged each other, and Silvio stepped back to look at his son. "Frankie, I don't see you enough anymore. Goddamn, I miss ya, kid."

"Hey, come on. You're seeing me now, so what's to miss?" Frank pulled a five-dollar bill out of his wallet. "I'll give you three points and take the Patriots for five."

"Shit," Silvio said. "Make it ten and you're on."

They found a small table in the bar at Conlins, ordered two beers and a couple of hamburgers. "I'm telling you, Dad, Brady is the best quarterback since Marino. He'll pick these guys apart."

"Yeah, dream on, kid. I just hope you can afford the ten. So, what're you doing? How's the writing coming?"

"Good. I just went over the proofs for the crime scene article and I've got a contract sitting on my desk for a book of my own. I sent you the article in *Crimes and Punishment* a couple of months ago. So— I'm keeping busy."

His father nodded and pursed his lips. "You gonna do the book?"

"I don't know. Haven't made up my mind yet."

"They offer you a big advance?" Silvio was eating this up.

"An advance? Yeah. Big? No."

"How much?"

"Seventy-five hundred."

"Hey, that's not bad, Frankie. You do this one and they'll give you twenty for the next one."

"Oh. That's how it works, huh? What're you, a book agent now?"

"No. I just know what a great writer you are. Look at all the letters you get from your articles and all. You think your old man doesn't puff up his chest when I read those letters about you in the magazines? By the way, I had dinner with the chief the other night. He was down here for a meeting and called. We talked about the old days. I told him if I hadn't retired I'da been chief today instead of him."

"What'd he say?"

"Told me I was full of it but that he wouldn't be surprised if the real cop in the Russo family became chief one day."

"Swell. You still milking him for compliments about me?"

Silvio chuckled and motioned for two more beers. "No. I didn't have to milk him. They poured out of him. You're a fair-haired boy, Frankie." He grabbed his son around the neck and pulled him roughly to him. "You're going places and you know it. I'm proud of you, kid. You're a chip off the old block." Silvio lowered his voice and leaned forward. "Chief's worried about these wine bottle killings. Sounds like you may have a serial killer on your hands. You got anything?"

Frank frowned and shook his head. "Not much. Same MO in both. Same fury, no forced entry. Robbery doesn't seem to be involved. More like a killing of anger, rage. The victims most likely knew the killer."

"Why do you say that?"

Frank explained their rationale with the Beatty case. "Could be a woman."

"Oh?"

"The second victim was seen with a woman the night he was killed. Tall, good-looking, not the type this guy would've been with. No indications in either victim's background of any contact with homosexuals. 'Course, you never know, but people who knew them rule it out."

"What else?"

"The description of the woman with this Joey Brewer fits the type you might expect the first guy, Beatty, would've had in his apartment."

"Go on."

"There's no connection between these two guys. Their murders are random acts. Dad, we both know that homicide usually involves a killer and a victim who know each other or are related. The data doesn't hold up when it comes to serial killers."

"Yeah, but not with women. They don't usually kill strangers," Silvio said.

Frank shook his head. "That's not so anymore, Dad. Over half the female serial killers reported having killed strangers only."

Silvio arched his eyebrows and nodded once slowly, his way of saying, *OK, I didn't know that.*

Frank continued. "Female serial killers usually kill because of abuse they've suffered in the past. So we could be looking for a woman who's been abused."

"Payback, huh?"

"Could be."

"What else?"

"The wine bottle thing. It's a sexual act. Perverted but definitely sexual. Not likely the act of a heterosexual man. And I'm not buying homosexual—at least not at this point."

"Prints?"

"Looks like our killer's learning from experience. We've got two sets of prints on a couple of books in Beatty's place."

"Nothing from the last one?"

"Yeah, we got some prints off the kitchen sink and table. Everything else was wiped clean."

"You check the prints from Beatty through AFIS?"

"Yeah. Nobody arrested in the state since 1985 with these prints. It only goes—"

"Hey, we gotta go. Game starts in fifteen minutes."

The Patriots won by a touchdown and Frank collected his ten dollars. "You know, Silvio, I commit a felony every time I bet on a game with you. It's stealing. What'd I tell you about Brady? Four touchdown passes convince you?"

He walked his father to his car before heading for his bus stop. "Take care, Dad. I'll call you this week."

"OK, kid. Frankie?"

"What?"

"Sign the book contract."

Frank was back in his apartment by six o'clock, made himself a martini on the rocks with a twist, and sat down with Eric Hickey's *Serial Murderers and Their Victims*: "The prime marks of the serial murderer are a sense of rage and nagging revenge carried over from early childhood." He smiled. He'd read a hundred of these books. Learned more from the old man than from all of them together.

22

DAVID BERNSTEIN'S APARTMENT building was one of those opulent, pretentious Upper East Side structures with a glass facade and marble-covered lobby, designed to intimidate the hoi polloi. Frank rode up in the elevator with a man and woman who had to be heading for David's party. Her hair, down to her waist, was the color of a ripe banana and looked like it had just been pressed at the dry cleaner's. His was slightly shorter and he wore a diamond earring in each ear. His silk shirt was unbuttoned halfway down his chest, baring a tattoo of a reptile. They were both in expensive black leather. The elevator smelled like a tannery.

Frank stood in the apartment's entryway, wearing a tweed sports coat, black turtleneck, and gray slacks. His thick hair curled and snaked its way around his neck and his dark eyes sparkled with curiosity.

David greeted him with the same enthusiasm as when they met earlier. "Frank, you made it."

Frank looked around at the beautiful people being served drinks and hors d'oeuvres by a battery of tuxedoed waiters. "Was I supposed to bring something? A six-pack? Chips?"

David, pumping Frank's hand, greeting other guests, and warding off the caresses of a theatrical-looking blonde, didn't hear a word he said. "Come in. Come in. Make yourself at home. Relax. Have a drink. Circulate." He disappeared into the crowd.

Frank grabbed some champagne off one of the trays and turned into the outstretched hand of a woman who was a dead ringer for Barbra Streisand and about the same age.

"Hi, I'm Leslie Gordon."

Frank was startled by her voice. It was as deep as his. He shook her hand. "Hi. Frank Russo."

She held his hand, looking at him the way a mackerel eyes a minnow. "I didn't know David had such gorgeous friends."

The woman's perfume hit his nose like a laser. He felt a sneeze coming on. His hand remained firmly in her grip while the champagne glass balanced precariously in the other. "Excuse me," he said, extricating his hand from Leslie just in time to reach his handkerchief and get it up to his nose a second before the sneeze exploded. "Sorry," he said. "Just a little cold. Nice meeting you, Leslie."

He was into his second glass of champagne when an unmistakable voice from behind him whispered, "Excuse me, I think I used to live with you."

He wasn't sure whether to turn around or head for the door. He turned and stood eyeball to eyeball with the woman he hadn't talked with since the day they split.

She wore a black cocktail dress that fit her model's body like it had been made for her. And then he realized it probably was. A gold choker necklace circled her long, slender neck, and her dangling earrings looked to him to be real diamonds. Her dark brown hair, rolling softly over her shoulders, gave her a sultry, exotic look. In her heels she was as tall as he.

"Hello, Frank." She offered her hand.

He stared helplessly at her, ignoring her hand. Déjà vu. He knew what she would say next, repeating the scene when they first met.

"You do shake hands, don't you?" The same teasing, friendly tone.

The ice was broken and they both laughed. He took her hand. "I'd say that was a familiar scene."

"I'd say," she said. "How are you?"

"How am I? I don't know. I guess I was OK until a minute ago. Now I'm not so sure."

Her eyes inspected him. He wished she wouldn't look at him like she did.

"You look elegantly handsome as always," she said.

"Thanks. No point in expressing the obvious about you. I'm sure you hear it every day."

Her eyes hardened for a moment, but regained their luster when she smiled. "It would be nice to hear it from you. It has been a while."

"You look very beautiful. How's that?"

The smile disappeared. "I forgot how direct you are, Frank."

"What'd you expect, small talk and bonbons?"

"Frank, I actually felt a shiver when I spotted you. I can understand how you feel. But what's done is done. If you don't want to talk, then I'll leave. No hard feelings."

"No hard feelings. Gee, aren't we magnanimous and forgiving." He didn't like what he was saying, but it just kept coming and he knew he'd pushed her too far.

"Go to hell, Frank," she said and started to walk away.

"Carla."

She stopped and turned.

At that moment, she looked more beautiful and desirable than he had ever seen her.

"Sorry. You want some champagne?"

She hesitated before smiling. "Sure."

23

BERNSTEIN'S PARTY WAS a haphazard affair with people coming and going all evening. The drinks flowed freely without interruption. Most people just grazed from the buffet, while others took time out to sit and consume a whole meal. There was no set pattern or order to things, you just winged it as you went along.

Carla and Frank found a quiet corner, where they sat with plates of shrimp, little medallions of beef, and a bottle of champagne Carla had liberated from the bar.

"David's kind of a wild man and so are his parties. People kill to come, though. He's very popular and you never know who you're going to see here," Carla said between bites of shrimp.

"Yeah. I met Barbra Streisand earlier," Frank said. She looked surprised and started to speak, but he continued. "So—you're getting close to the big time in your career—very close from what I see and read in the magazines. And there's no Mr. Perfect in your life right now?"

"There is no Mr. Perfect period," she said.

Frank held out his hands. *"C'est moi."*

"Close, but no cigar," she said. "You already have a mistress, re-member? She's called NYPD."

"Thanks. I need to hear that."

"And speaking of your mistress, I gather she's keeping you busier than ever. I see your name in the papers, too, you know. They say you may have a serial killer on your hands now?"

"Oh, Jesus. You, too? Why can't I just eat shrimp and drink champagne and talk about sex and residuals like everybody else here?"

"Because this is more interesting. Are you making any progress? The media's giving you a bad time. Says you're not. That doesn't sound like you, Frank."

"The media's a crock of shit. You of all people must know that by now. Anyway, look at those two over there. I don't think they're talk-ing about serial killers. And they're definitely having more fun."

Carla looked over at a man and woman standing on the terrace, wrapped around each other, kissing and dry humping. "They may be having more fun, but I'll tell you what they don't have and that's class. Kind of a stupid display, if you ask me."

"Ooh, Miss Prissy."

"No, I'm not prissy, Frank. I just get disgusted with vulgarity when I see it, that's all."

"Me, too. That why I hang out with cops."

"Very funny. Are you seeing anyone these days?"

"I see a lot of people."

"You know what I mean. Anyone special in your life?"

"No." Funny how Denise slipped into his mind at that question. Maybe no wasn't quite the right answer. But at the moment, it was hard to imagine anything better than sitting in a quiet corner drinking champagne with the beautiful woman who had once been his lover.

He hadn't expected this and was troubled at how quickly and easily he slid into it.

"Hard to believe," she said, moving in close.

She smelled delicious and the urge to grab her and kiss her everywhere was making him dizzy. She sat looking at him, as if waiting for him to do just that.

The moment passed. She took a drink of champagne and glanced around the room. A young man stood near the bar, smiling and nodding at her. Her eyes lit up and she jerked forward. She turned quickly to Frank. "Frank, I'm sorry. There's someone over there I must see. Excuse me." She pecked him on the cheek and hurried toward the theatrical-looking young man with the simpering smile.

"Nice going, stupid," Frank growled to himself and left.

AT SEVEN O'CLOCK that night Gale left his room and hailed a cab. The cab dropped him three blocks from his daughter's apartment. He stepped into the darkened doorway of a jewelry store to collect his thoughts before continuing.

His mind was a jumble, filled with uncertainty and indecision. He knew he wanted to see her, but he didn't know how to go about it. How would she react to him? Was her hatred as deep as the hatred he had felt for so many years—hatred that might still be inside him?

How would he react if she cursed and screamed at him? He knew from his experience with the woman from the train that he was unpredictable. What if she turned out to be different from the image he was building of her? All questions with no answers.

She must know he's in New York. He was sure Janet had contacted her. If he called her and she blew him off, that would be the end of it, and he would never get to see her, sit down with her.

For all those years, he'd fantasized over what he was going to do when he got out. Now he was confused, uncertain. He thought of her on different levels.

Maybe if he could just get inside her apartment, let her see that he means no harm, that he's changed, that he wants to be someone in her life. Once he got with her, he was confident she would come around. And then he had an idea.

GALE REACHED THE apartment building, opened the door, and entered the small vestibule. Twelve mailboxes lined one side of the wall. Opposite them were the names and apartment numbers of the tenants.

He stood alone in the dim hallway, the sound of his own breathing deafening in the small, silent space. He could barely focus on the tenants' names. Then, there it was. He smiled and rang the bell. No answer. Again he rang and again no answer. Finally, on the third ring, a response. The voice sounded impatient. "Yes, what is it?"

"UPS, ma'am. I got a package for you. Need your signature."

No response for a moment and then the voice, again impatient. "Oh, for God's sake. I was in the bathtub. What's the package? Who's it from?"

"Don't know, ma'am. It's just a small package." Gale shifted from one foot to the other and glanced nervously over his shoulder.

"Well—I can't come down. I'm all wet, and I'm not feeling well. Please come back tomorrow and ring the super's bell. I'll authorize him to sign for it."

Sweat trickled off his forehead and dripped onto the item he held. He looked at the bank of names and saw SUPERINTENDENT, 1A.

"Hello?" the voice called.

"Uh, ma'am, I can't leave it for someone else to sign. I'm afraid you have to sign personally."

Gale's heart pounded. He held his breath, waiting, his hand

clutching the doorknob. Finally, the exasperated reply came. "Oh, dammit. All right. I'm on the fifth floor, but wait a minute."

He was sweating now. What would she do when she discovered he had lied? She would be angry. He knew that. But he had to take the chance. It was the only way. He was pretty smooth. He would quiet her down and make her see how sincere he is.

The buzzer sounded. Gale turned the doorknob and entered. He stood inside the hallway, wiping the sweat from his face. The building was quiet as he slowly began walking up the stairs instead of taking the elevator. Take his time, give her a chance to get ready.

The excitement began building in him. When he reached the third level, he stopped. The climb and the excitement building within him were almost too much. The sound of his breathing echoed through the empty stairwell. So close now.

He wanted this to work. Maybe when he explained she would understand, even feel some compassion for him. Maybe it would seem so crazy, they would later laugh about it. He moved the bouquet of flowers behind his back and continued up the stairs.

He stood in front of 5B. All those years of waiting and now all that stood between him and his daughter was a door and a flimsy chain lock. He had suffered and waited for so long and now in a minute he would be standing next to her. So many thoughts racing through his mind mixed with those he'd dreamed all those nights lying in the cell she had put him in. Trickles of sweat rolled down his chest, stopping at the elastic of his underwear. For the first time he realized that he had an erection. He rearranged the bulge in his crotch, trying to wish it away, and wiped his forehead. Footsteps sounded from the other side of the door, and after a deep breath and another swipe at his forehead, he rang the bell.

"Yes?" The voice came from near the door.

"UPS, ma'am."

Locks began clicking and a bolt slid. The door slowly opened about four or five inches, as far as the chain lock would allow. A partial face appeared but enough to reassure Gale that it was the face he was looking for. He stood at an angle from her line of vision, his breathing louder than ever in the silence of the hallway. He ran his fingers over his bald pate, wiping away the sweat. Before either could speak, the phone rang from inside.

"Oh, excuse me," the voice said and the door closed. Locks and bolts clicked and slid, and the footsteps moved away from the door.

"Son of a bitch," Gale murmured and leaned his back against the wall next to the door. He closed his eyes and waited. He heard her answer the phone.

"Hello."

"Hi. How are you?"

"I'm fine, but I've got a UPS man at the door, and I have to sign for a package. I can't talk to you right now. Let me call you back."

"I was just wondering if you'd like to meet for a drink."

"No, not tonight. But I do have to run and sign for the UPS package."

"OK, but you don't have to sign for UPS. Just tell him to leave it."

"Yes, I do have to sign. He said so. Now let me call you back."

"You don't have to sign for UPS packages. I get them all the time. It seems late for a UPS man, anyway, I'm not sure they deliver on Sunday. I wouldn't open the door if it were me."

The woman never took her eyes off the door. Her stomach tightened. "I've got to go." She hung up and walked slowly toward the door.

"Are you still out there?" she asked, raising her voice to a shout.

"Yes, ma'am, but I'm runnin' real late. Can you sign this so I can get going?"

She backed away from the door. "Excuse me, but just leave the package and go. My friend on the phone just told me you can do that."

"What's this shit?" Gale mumbled. He started to speak to her but she interrupted him.

"Did you hear me? If you don't leave I'm calling the police." She picked up the phone but held the button down with one finger, and walked toward the door. "Hello, police. There's a man outside my door who won't go away." In a loud voice, she gave her address and apartment number and told them to hurry.

There was no question the man had heard her. She stood just inches from the door, listening. Her stomach churned and she suddenly had to go to the bathroom but was afraid to leave the door. She could hear the slow, steady breathing outside her door, then mumbling, shuffling, and finally, footsteps moving quickly down the stairs. She went to the window and looked down on the street. After a moment, a short, heavyset man wearing a dark jacket and a baseball cap appeared, crossed the street, and moved quickly out of sight.

24

ONLY 6:00 A.M. and she'd been lying in bed wide awake for fifteen minutes. Her head felt like she'd been hit with a hammer and the dull, heavy abdominal ache that had awakened her now expanded into biting cramps. The headaches always came when she was agitated and upset.

The UPS man. She shivered and pulled the blanket up under her chin. *I'm runnin' real late. Can you sign so I can get goin'?* How could she have been so stupid? She wasn't thinking. That's how.

Could it have been him? He knew where she lived, and probably a whole lot more. She would have to be careful.

She clutched her stomach in pain and rolled into a fetal position. Tears welled and trickled down her face. She unwound and pulled herself slowly out of bed. The movement accelerated the pain in her head, but three Percodan would help. She also took a Darvon for the cramps and made her way back into bed. There was no way she could go anywhere today. Her only obligation would be to herself, to stay in bed and hope the pain in her head, her stomach, and her mind would let up.

PAUL GALE FINISHED his workday at the restaurant. Last night he had come so close and he would have been inside charming her, letting her see he held no grudges—that he wanted to get to know his daughter. He tried to picture her expression when he pulled the flowers from behind his back and presented them to her.

He had developed a reputation in prison for having a smooth line of bullshit. He thought back to the woman on the train, how he had sweet-talked her. Yes, if it hadn't been for that fucking phone call. He pulled the collar of his jacket up, tightened his baseball cap, and bent into the wind.

AT SEVEN O'CLOCK the woman got out of bed. She'd been sleeping off and on for most of the day, getting up only for more pills. The cramps were nearly gone but she took another Darvon just in case.

She was famished. The apartment was hot and stuffy and she felt fidgety, irritable, out of sorts. She needed fresh air. Without bothering to shower, she splashed on some Jean Naté and quickly dressed in black pants and sweater. The Jean Naté smelled fresh and clean, just as it did when her mother used it. Memories of her mother came back whenever she put it on.

The night was bitter cold, but no matter. She needed to walk, walk off the anger that was building again.

She walked several blocks, picking up speed as she went along. The more she focused on last night, the more foul her mood, and the faster she walked.

She was now convinced it was him. He had actually come to her home, right to her doorstep. She clenched her fists and cursed.

A man of about fifty approached her from the other direction and smiled at her. "Slow down, honey. The night's young."

She blew by him, then slowed and stopped. She turned, and so did he. She stood for a moment, looking at him, the stupid smile still on his face. He was short and overweight. The overcoat he wore, fashionably long, looked ridiculous on his stumpy body. It was also too tight around his middle.

She was about to turn and continue on when he spoke again. "You keep walking that fast, you're going to run somebody over." He took a couple of steps toward her.

She watched him approach. And waited.

He took another few steps and stood next to her. "Cold night for a pretty lady like you to be out walking alone."

She wanted to wipe the silly smile off his face. But she said nothing, just stared at him.

The smile broadened. His hand went out. "Hi. I'm Phil Chesbro."

Her hand went up slowly. He took it and squeezed it and put his other over hers, like they were old friends. That was probably what did it.

"Hi," she said.

"What's your name?" he asked.

"My friends call me Lucky."

"You always walk that fast?" He was still holding her hand.

"Yes."

He moved closer. "Well, it's pretty cold tonight. That's a good way to stay warm. I got a better idea, though, on how to beat it." He nodded his head toward the café next to where they stood. "How about if we go in here for a drink?"

She studied the man holding her hands, his jowls rippling around the obnoxious smile. "Yes," she said. "Let's do that."

25

JERRY BLODGETT HEADED across the precinct bullpen toward Frank Russo's desk. Frank saw him coming and braced himself.

"You and Harry come into my office," Jerry growled. He continued toward his office, head down, his massive body rolling from side to side. "I just left Nolan. Took another sack of shit from him. Last night's murder confirmed his worst nightmare. He's got a serial killer on his hands, he tells me," he added over his shoulder.

Frank and Harry looked at each other, then stood and followed Jerry into his office. "Smart cop," Frank said. "Must be why he's a lieutenant."

"Cut it out, Frank," Jerry snapped.

Harry had been about to add a crack of his own but thought better of it. "What'd he say, Jerry?" he asked.

"What do you think he said? He wants results. Now! He's taking this personally. This is a man feeling pressure from a lot of directions.

He's gotta let some out of the bottle and guess who's getting it? Anyway, what have you guys got?"

"I was just writing up the report on this morning's investigations when you hauled us in here," Frank said.

"You finished?"

"Pretty much."

"Go get it."

Jerry paced back and forth in the small office. Harry sat quietly, watching Jerry's shirttail flap up and down.

Frank returned, thumbing through his report. "Guy was found by his cleaning lady about eight this morning. She knocked several times, then let herself in. Found him on the floor of the living room next to the sofa. Head bashed in with a wine bottle. Hit at least three times. This time the bottle broke. Then his head was smashed up and down on the floor again. Hardwood floor covered with blood. His head was cracked maybe a dozen times on the floor."

"What've you got on him?" Jerry asked.

Frank referred to a small notebook. "Phillip Chesbro, forty-seven years old. Divorced six years. No kids. Ex-wife in St. Louis. He lived on West Thirty-fourth Street, about twelve blocks from Joey Brewer. He was an insurance salesman. Worked for Metropolitan."

"No forced entry?"

"None. Whoever did it just strolled politely through the door, sat on the couch with the late Mr. Chesbro, they had some wine together, and he got whacked," Frank said.

"You say the wine bottle broke?" Jerry asked.

"Yeah, but there was another in reserve." Jerry started to speak and Frank nodded before he could get it out. "Yep. Same as Beatty and Brewer."

Jerry nodded. "These are random picks. But why?"

"Jerry, I'm more convinced it's a woman doing this," Frank said.

"Why?"

"We've got a faint smell of perfume on the body. There's also a touch on the back of the sofa where the killer probably sat. I don't think there's enough for us to do anything with."

"Could be men's cologne?"

"No. It's more like a perfume. Anyway, we checked the victim's cologne. He had several bottles. Totally different from this."

"Could be his visitor's?"

"Could be. But I don't think it's a men's cologne." Frank looked at the picture of Jerry's wife, Betty, on his desk. Even at fifty-six she was a beautiful woman. Under the picture was a date written and circled. It was Jerry's retirement date, now less than a year away. Nolan wasn't the only one getting nervous about this case.

"Guy was single," Jerry said. "Must've had women up there from time to time. What else have we got?"

"We've got a few prints and some hair fibers again. Can't tell yet if they're natural or from a wig. We'll find out from the lab. We've also got his address book with a whole lot of names and phone numbers in it. Mostly people here in Manhattan, Queens, Brooklyn, and a few out on the Island. He was an insurance agent. Most of them are probably clients or leads. We'll have them all checked out."

"Best lead we have so far is the woman with Joey Brewer," Jerry said. "Gotta be a prostitute. Why else would a good-looking woman like that be with Brewer? Bartender said she seemed spaced out. A hooker on drugs. That's how she winds up with a loser like Brewer."

"Yeah, and so far none of the hookers know from nothin'," Harry broke in. "The ones that fit the description all have alibis."

"Yeah. They were probably all with you," Jerry said.

"Cut it out, Jerry. That's not funny."

"Wasn't supposed to be. Hell, you're our hooker specialist. You oughta be able to find out who's bullshitting us."

"We're still checking them out, Jerry," Harry said.

"The guys who roughed up Joey in Barney's don't really have an alibi for that night," Frank said. "Claim they went to the Alcazar after Barney's, then to a pizza joint and home. Alcazar and the pizza joint check out. After that they can't substantiate their whereabouts. I think they're hiding something but I don't think they did Joey. Couldn't shake anything out of them when we brought them in, but we're not ruling them out. But, Jerry, they along with everyone else we talked with who saw the woman with Brewer said she did not fit the profile of a prostitute."

Jerry nodded. "No indication that Chesbro was a client of the loan sharks?" Jerry said.

"No, not yet, but we're working on it. And there's no indication anywhere that Ron and Sal knew Beatty. He had a bank account with fifty-two hundred dollars in it. No withdrawals for almost a year. Nothing but deposits. We didn't turn up any financial problems. I'm satisfied there's no connection there."

"I'll check with the lab on the hairs," Harry said. He was still smarting from Jerry's crack about the hookers.

"OK," Jerry said. "I gotta go. Nolan wants me downtown for a meeting at the chief's office. Guess what it's about." He drummed a pencil up and down on his desk.

Harry turned and left; Frank stayed, watching the pain in his friend's face.

"Two weeks between the Beatty and Brewer murders," Jerry said. "Six days between Brewer and Chesbro." He looked up.

Frank thought how tired he looked.

"My gut tells me this isn't the last one. How often am I wrong on my hunches, Frank?"

"Not often," Frank said.

———

FRANK'S LIFE WAS getting complicated. The message on his machine from Denise was warm and friendly. No, more than friendly: "Frank, I miss you. Give me a call." Short and sweet, but for Denise practically a proposition. He smiled as her voice rattled around in his head. Nice voice.

And Carla was back in his life. The brief time he spent with her at Bernstein's party accentuated the scary fact that he still wasn't over her. Even though she had dumped on him again, leaving him almost in midsentence, she had left her mark, and he knew she knew it. And something told him she would be calling.

DENISE RETURNED TO her office after a meeting with Mike, and had just settled into her chair when she looked up and saw Frank Russo standing in her doorway.

"Hi," he said.

When he smiled her hand hit the pencil holder and sent pencils clattering along the floor. "Frank," she mumbled as her stomach turned over.

"Sorry if I startled you." He gathered up her pencils. "Can I sit down?"

"Sure. Sure. My God! What a surprise!"

His presence filled the small office. He looked like one of the editors in his tweed jacket, khaki-colored slacks, dark blue shirt, and dark tie. She also thought he looked very sexy. She wanted to touch his hair curling around his ears and collar. They both sat awkwardly looking at each other for a moment.

"I was just driving by with my partner and decided to stop in and say hello."

"Hello," she stammered, still feeling the effects of his presence. "How'd you find my office in this maze?"

He grinned. "Your receptionist. She was very helpful."

"Why am I not surprised?"

"Harry's double parked and probably given himself a ticket by now, so I have to run."

She felt the disappointment and actually made a face.

"What I wanted to ask you, though, is if you're not doing anything on Sunday, you might like to sort of make a day of it. I have a meeting at the precinct in the morning, but I'll be finished before noon. We could take a walk in the park if it's not too cold, have some lunch or dinner, a drink, shopping, movie, a trip to Havana?"

"Havana?"

"Just wanted to see if you're listening. What do you say?"

"Sounds great," she said.

"I'll call you in a day or so about the time and all."

"Hey, Dennie, can you help me with—?" Gina careened into the small room, nearly bumping into Frank. "Oh, excuse me." She eyed Frank with the same predatory look Denise had seen her give the waiter at the Blue Wave. "Sorry," she said, never taking her eyes off Frank. "Didn't know you had company."

Denise introduced them and Frank eased his way out before Gina could get into her routine.

"Nice meeting you, Gina. I'll call you, Denise."

"*Who* was that?" Gina demanded.

"A friend of mine."

"A friend of mine," Gina mocked. "There's not a woman alive who'd just be a friend of a guy who looks like that. Where've you been hiding him? What's his name?"

"Down, Fang. His name's Frank and I met him at the health club and sorry to disappoint you, but we are just friends."

"Jesus," Gina rumbled. "He's a doll. What's he do?"

"He's a cop."

"A what?"

"A cop. Actually, he's a homicide detective."

"You're kidding."

Denise shook her head.

"What's he want with you?"

"What do you mean, what's he want with me? You think he was here to arrest me?"

"No, no, I just—I mean . . ."

"Gina, you're mumbling."

"Sorry, guess I'm just jealous that you found him first."

FRANK WALKED INTO his apartment and slumped into a chair. It had been a long, miserable day, tracking down leads that led nowhere. In and out of bars, trying to talk with evasive, uncooperative hookers, and another session with Sal and Ron, the friendly loan sharks.

His father's advice came back to him. *It ain't gonna be easy, Frankie.*

Dropping in to see Denise gave him a big lift. Best part of his day. He hadn't stopped thinking about her since leaving her office. Now he felt like a kid looking forward to Sunday. The next few days would feel like a month.

The phone rang.

"Hello."

"Hello, Frank. It's Carla." The voice soft, seductive.

Something kicked his stomach.

"Hi."

"Oh. The enthusiasm of one hand clapping."

"Well, let's see. The last I saw of you, you trampled six people lunging toward some guy with an earring and too much hair. His parents bring him to the party?"

"Very funny. I know it was rude, the way I left so abruptly. I called to apologize."

He was about to zing her again but thought better of it. "It's OK," he said.

"Frank. I did enjoy seeing you. A lot. I meant it when I said I've missed you. I just thought maybe you'd like to get together, just the two of us, you know, when we both have some time with these crazy schedules."

Oh, Jesus, he thought. Don't do this. "When did you have in mind?"

"Well, I'm sure with this serial killer case you must be straight out day and night."

He waited for her to continue but she stopped. After waiting another beat, he replied, "Yeah. I'd say I've been busy."

"Any progress?"

"Not much. How about you?" he asked, wanting to change the subject. "From what you were telling me the other night, you don't have much free time either."

"I'm free this Sunday. All day. All yours." The last in a half whisper.

Why do you do this to me? he wanted to ask. It was just like her. Vintage Carla with the sixth sense, the instinct for the jugular. Sunday!

"Frank?"

"I'm thinking. I'm thinking. I had something doing Sunday and—"

"We could go out for lunch, go to the new exhibit at the Museum of Modern Art and back here later, where I'll make you dinner." Her voice sounded like her lips were resting on the phone speaker. He could almost smell her.

"Ah, well . . ." He wanted to ask her what she was wearing at that moment. He wanted to ask her if they could make love on Sunday. He wanted to ask her if she would be his girl again. Instead he thought of Denise and asked her if he could take a rain check for another time.

"Oh?" The lips were no longer resting on the speaker. "You mean you can't change your plans or you won't?"

"I guess it means both."

"Well, then, I guess I understand. Thank you. Maybe another time."

"Yeah. I'll call you."

"Sure. Bye-bye."

"Bye."

Her phone clicked and he sat holding his, staring at nothing, listening to the silence. Finally, he hung it up. Hard.

"Frankie, I'm proud of you," he said aloud.

26

SUNDAY TURNED OUT to be the kind of day Frank had been hoping for all week, sunny and warm. By the time he met Denise at Tavern on the Green in Central Park, it was an unseasonable sixty-two degrees.

"Denise, only tourists go to Tavern on the Green," he protested over the phone.

"I don't care. I've always wanted to go there and I never have. Come on, Frank. It's a famous place."

She also insisted on meeting there rather than him picking her up. "I'm going to be over that way to meet with one of our authors and drop an edited manuscript off to him so he can take it with him on a trip tomorrow. So I'll just meet you at Tavern on the Green."

After three phone calls dealing with some of the rudest people he had ever encountered, Frank finally secured a reservation in the Crystal Room. He arrived at the restaurant early, claimed their table, and ordered a beer. He had to admit the room was elegantly beautiful. An enormous mural depicted Central Park at the turn of the century and antique Baccarat chandeliers gleamed overhead. Their table overlooked the garden, with its menagerie of topiary animals, including a reindeer, elephant, and gorilla. He double-checked to make sure he had his wallet.

He sipped his beer and soon spotted Denise coming in the door. He got a kick out of watching her speak to the maître d', then look over his shoulder, scanning the room. He waved but she didn't see him. The maître d' led her toward his table and she broke out in a big grin and waved when she spotted him. He knew it was going to be a great day.

"You look fabulous," he said as she settled in. He took his time looking her over, admiring her. She wore a soft white sweater, gold hoop earrings, and dark blue pants. Her eyes and hair sparkled and her face looked like she had just washed it in milk. "You also look happy," he said. "You must have had a good week."

"It was OK. Maybe I look happy because I'm about to have lunch with you in Tavern on the Green."

"Sounds good to me."

Lunch was one of those languorous, unhurried affairs. With nowhere to go, no schedules, no appointments, they drifted through it, sharing a bottle of wine and each other.

Frank loved watching her. He liked the way she sipped her wine, never taking more than a dram at a time. She'd notice him watching her and nervously look away, then dart her eyes back to him.

Every once in a while he would catch her little half smile, her way of telling him she was enjoying herself. It was as if she wanted him to know that, but wasn't sure how to express it.

"Dennie, tell me about yourself. Where are you from? How long have you been in New York? Any family? What—?"

"Whoa. Slow down, Officer," she interrupted. "You've got to leave a woman with a little mystery."

"Hey, right now you're all mystery. I know you work for a publisher and you like decorating and working out in your health club. And you like famous restaurants. That's it."

She laughed. "Maybe that's enough for now. Actually, you've just about covered it all. I'm really pretty boring, I guess." She took one of her quick little sips of the wine. "My mother and father are both dead. I've been in New York since just after nine-eleven. I guess you'd say I'm kind of a loner. Keep pretty much to myself." She laughed again. "And yes, I do have a passion for decorating."

"OK." He waited but she was finished. It didn't seem like anything more was coming. "That ought to hold me for a while. You forgot one thing. You're even more beautiful when you laugh. You should do it more often."

After lunch they walked through Central Park. It was one of those rare late fall days, especially for November—probably the last such day before the long hard winter set in. Bright sunshine baked the brown leaves on the ground, which crunched like popcorn underfoot.

"Come on, let's catch a few rays." He led her up a small hill, where they sprawled in the grass under the warm sun.

"What about you, Frank?"

He sat up. "What do you mean?"

"Well, I don't know much about you either. For all I know you could be married. Are you?"

"No."

"Were you ever?"

"No."

"I feel like I'm playing twenty questions. Is that how your suspects answer you when you're grilling them?"

"We don't grill people. We interrogate them. Good word, though." He put his arm around her and was surprised at how quickly and easily she snuggled into him. "I lived with a woman for a while. It didn't work out."

"I'm sorry. Where is she now?"

"Here in New York."

She turned to look at him. "Do you ever see her?"

"Funny you should ask. I hadn't seen her for six months, not since we split up. The other night I went to a party and she was there. We talked for a while before she spotted some young stud she knew and sprinted away."

"Too bad," she said, some distance in her voice.

"No, it wasn't."

"Were you glad to see her?"

"No," he lied.

"Think you'll see her again?"

"Hey, this *is* twenty questions. First of all, I barely have time these days to see myself in the mirror shaving. Secondly, if and when I do get some free time, I'd much rather see you." He paused. "Than her or anybody else."

She moved in closer and when she did, he kissed her. She responded, at first tentatively, then he felt a shiver pass along her body. They kissed hungrily, the way lonely people do. Some kids walked by, giggling. Neither heard them.

She moved her lips away and whispered into his ear, "Mmm, Frank."

He maneuvered to kiss her again but she spotted the four giggling kids watching them. She slid away. "My God! Here we are necking in broad daylight in Central Park."

"Yeah. Great, huh?"

"Yes, and no," she said, getting up. "Yes, it's great and no, not here. Come on. Let's go." She pulled him to his feet.

Maneuvering around the in-line skaters, couples strolling arm in arm, and parents pushing baby carriages, they headed toward Fifth Avenue holding hands. All of New York was out enjoying the crisp air and last rays of the autumn sun. Joggers came and went, stylish in the colorful warm-ups they didn't need today. Was the weather really beautiful whenever he was with her or did it just seem that way?

They reached Fifth Avenue and strolled along slowly, like a couple of tourists. Frank watched a police car cruise by. The two uniforms inside looked bored. A siren wailed in the distance. Today he was just a citizen.

"So—what else do you do besides be a cop?" she asked.

"I do some writing, teach a little, go to an occasional football or basketball game. And I like to cook when I have the time, which isn't very often."

"What kind of writing do you do?"

"Mostly about police work, investigative techniques, things of that kind. Nothing very creative."

"That's interesting. Where does your stuff appear?"

"Oh, some really exciting places like *The Encyclopedia of American Crime*, *The Journal of Forensic Science*, *Criminal Justice Quarterly*. You know, the kind of stuff everybody has on their coffee table."

"Sounds impressive to me. How's the Wine Bottle Killer case coming?"

"It's not."

"Any progress?"

"No more than what you read in the papers. Hey, let's grab a cab."

"To where?"

"The best Italian dinner in New York."

"Where's that?"

"My place."

"I DON'T BELIEVE you, Frank," Denise said, trying to get used to the taste of the brandy she was sipping. "This dinner was a work of art. Let's see. Fettuccine with Gorgonzola sauce, Caesar salad, charcoal-broiled chicken marinated in pepper, oil, and lemon. Did I get it all?"

"Don't forget the vanilla ice cream with the little macaroons."

"Where did you learn to cook like that?"

"From my parents. Actually, my dad's the real cook. I learned mostly from him. It's been sort of one of our things together."

"Well, the whole meal was delicious. I'm stuffed."

They sat on the couch in the small living room, sipping brandy, listening to Pavarotti on CD.

"It's been a wonderful day, Frank. Just lovely."

"It's not over." He gently pulled her toward him. She slid easily into the space between his shoulder and neck. Her hair brushing against his face tickled him. As he adjusted his face downward toward her, she looked up and they kissed. This one began like the one in the park and accelerated as quickly. Their mouths opened, groping, exploring, nibbling. He felt a hollow aching begin in his throat and move through his body as he held her in his arms. He barely managed to whisper her name.

She arched her back and rolled over on top of him.

Frank caressed her breasts and moved his hand down to the two buttons of her pants. He unbuttoned them, slid his hand down, and gently touched her.

She scrambled to her feet. "No, Frank." Her voice was husky and heavy. "Not so soon. Not tonight. I've got to go. It's late, and I have a very early morning meeting tomorrow. I'm hoping we're going to see more of each other, and there'll be plenty of time for . . . you know."

Frank lay back, still catching his breath, the moment gone. "You're going to go and leave me for dead?"

She stood, her back to him, straightening her clothes. After a few moments, she turned and managed a laugh. "Sorry, Frank. I know it's cruel and unusual punishment. For me, too." She leaned over and kissed him lightly and caressed his face. "I like you a lot, Frank Russo. I'm glad we met. But let's not rush things, OK?"

He still hadn't pulled himself together. His head lolled crazily against the couch pillow. "OK, I understand . . . I think." He got up and stood next to her.

"I do have to go, Frank. And thanks again for a fabulous day. Call me. Soon?"

He was breathing normally again. "You bet I will." They kissed good night and she was halfway out the door when he called.

"Dennie?"

She turned.

He wanted to say something but he wasn't sure what. "Good night."

It had been a great day but he hadn't figured on the abrupt ending. Maybe he'd been out of practice too long. Losing his touch. No. He should have known. Denise Johnson was a class act, not a woman who hopped in the sack on the first date. He smiled, thinking of the quaint way she characterized their relationship: *There'll be plenty of time for . . . you know.*

He took a long shower, dried himself, wrapped the towel around him, and poured some more brandy. He sat on the couch and closed his eyes. Her smell was still there. Beautiful, sensitive, vulnerable—a complicated lady.

27

DENISE TOOK A long hot bubble bath when she arrived home. It had been a wonderful day, her best ever in New York. She felt comfortable and safe with Frank. He wasn't one of those wise guys, overly impressed with himself. No, he treated her with respect, like a lady should be treated. Frank Russo was a gentleman. Most men swaggered through life, demanding, insensitive. Frank was different.

She had seen the women in the restaurant looking at him. She watched their eyes follow him as they walked along Fifth Avenue. She saw them look her up and down as if wondering what it is she had to be holding hands with a man like that. She wasn't sure herself. Maybe he was just playing her along, out for one thing. It didn't take him long to get his hands into her pants.

The water had turned cold and her body felt dank and chilled. She shivered as she toweled her body and put on her pajamas. Eleven o'clock, but she wasn't tired. Thumbing through one of her decorating magazines, she saw a small living room not unlike hers and liked the arrangement. It took her only fifteen minutes to rearrange her furniture. First the couch went over to the other side under the two windows. The table lamp that had been next to her wing chair and the pharmacy lamp near the slipper chair were placed on either end of the sofa. And she knew just the lamp she would buy at Bloomingdale's to place on the table she now had between her chairs. She completed all the other little touches until she had everything just right. She loved her apartment. It was the nicest one she'd had yet in New York.

Now she did feel tired, more a physical exhaustion, and fell into bed. But the restlessness returned and she picked up the phone.

"Hello." He sounded sleepy. She pictured him lying in bed in the dark, probably in his underwear.

"Did I wake you up?"

No answer. Was he trying to decide who it was before committing himself? She wished she hadn't called.

"No."

"This is Dennie," she blurted, still not sure he knew.

He smiled. "I think I know that voice. I thought you'd be sound asleep by now."

"No. I just felt like calling you and thanking you again for a wonderful day. I loved it."

"So did I," he said. "You know what?"

"What?"

"I was just going to call you."

"Well, I'm glad I beat you to it. But you can call me, soon, I hope."

"Tomorrow soon enough?"

"Perfect. Good night."

———

CARLA SANDERS STOOD on the balcony, dressed in elegant black silk flared pants and halter top, enjoying a rare moment of solitude, a solitude she knew would be short-lived. But it was nice to reflect and recharge, no matter how briefly.

It was hard to believe this was her life. So much had happened in the past year. But now, standing on the terrace of a penthouse apartment looking out across the city, her city, maybe it had all worked out for the best.

Things had moved so quickly. She had changed and grown and moved on, swept into the fast lanes of Henry Manning's world.

"I'm going to make you one of the top models in New York, Carla," Henry had promised. And now, a year later, she was getting closer. She'd been in a couple of obscure fashion magazines that hardly anybody read, but the pace was picking up. In January she'd be in *Cosmo* and her agent was working on a cover for *Vogue.*

Henry had taken her a long way, but he had become too possessive, and he was terrible in bed. Frank had spoiled her in that department. Henry was definitely worth staying on good terms with, but the romance was over.

Tonight's party was typical of the world she'd been living in during the past year. Kenneth Amory was one of the world's leading fashion designers. His wife, Claudia, was the winner of this year's Tony Award for best actress in a musical. At first she had been thrilled and honored, being invited to such affairs. Now, standing on the penthouse's balcony, she was considered a catch.

Her reverie was abruptly shattered.

"Carla, for God's sake. I heard you were here. How are you?"

She turned and said hello to Linda Kellerman, a woman she hadn't seen in probably a year and a half, yet she greeted Carla as if she had just seen her yesterday. "Hello, Linda, nice to see you," she replied. She remembered Linda as a pain in the ass, always trying to push her way into Carla's circle of friends.

"I've been out of the country for a while but I've been hearing about you. You're doing great." She lowered her voice. "Sorry to hear about you and Frank. How's he doing?"

Stupid, intrusive question. "I don't know. I haven't seen him since we split," she said, lighting a cigarette.

"Oh! Well, he was some gorgeous guy. Is he still a cop?"

"I really don't know that, either. Why don't you call him up and ask him? Excuse me, Linda. There's someone I need to see." She swirled past Linda and into the living room.

"Well! Excuse me," Linda called.

Carla spotted her agent, Randy Stern, pushing his way through the crowd toward her. "Carla, I need to talk to you privately for a minute." He led her into a quiet corner of the room, removed his eyeglasses, and began polishing them with a white handkerchief.

"Listen, I've been talking with Bruno Mori from Milano again. He's still interested in you for a part in that movie he's putting together in Italy. If he likes you, and you test OK, he might want you for another he's going to be starting right after this one. The thing is, you'd have to be in Italy for the better part of about six months, but—"

Carla was shaking her head.

"Hey, Carla, the money would be great, and you can always zip back here from time to time as needed. I mean it's not like—"

"Randy, I really don't want to be out of New York right now. OK? The thing in Italy sounds interesting, but the timing just isn't right. If they want me now, they'll want me a lot more if I'm on the cover of *Vogue*. And I don't want to screw that up."

Randy started to speak again, but she shut him off. "No."

"OK, I hear you. I'll pass on this one, but you owe me."

Carla looked around the room. "Randy, who is that darling young man standing over there in the blue jacket?"

Randy put his glasses back on and scanned the area she directed him to. "Oh, that's Rob Sturgis. He's the big new stud on that soap *The Young Lions.*"

"Hmm. Is he gay?"

"Shit, no. Not from what I hear."

"Would you ask him to come over? I'd like to meet him."

28

AT ELEVEN O'CLOCK Monday morning, Frank called. "Dennie, I only have a minute but I just wanted to call and say hello."

She rocked back in her chair. "Hi," she said, stretching the word out.

"Listen, Dennie, I'm dying to see you again, but we're straight out on this case we're working on, and it's not getting any better. Can we play it by ear this week till I can see some daylight? Let's talk during the week and try to shoot for Friday."

He waited for a reply, but when none came, he continued. "Dennie, I hate being so vague and I don't want to screw up your plans. If something comes up for you, I'll understand. But I really am dying to see you soon. Yesterday was fabulous."

She wished she didn't feel so disappointed. But she did. Now she had to sound casual, like everything was OK. "Sure, I understand,

Frank. Call me this week and we'll hope for Friday night. What's going on? Anything you can talk about?"

"It's this Wine Bottle Killer. We're just under a lot of pressure. I gotta go. Call you soon." And he was gone.

At three o'clock Gina popped into Denise's office. "Hey, Dennie. Let's go downstairs and get some coffee. Come on, you need a break."

Gina was right. She did need a break. It had not been a good day.

The cafeteria was crowded but they got their coffee and found a small table. "Does anybody ever work in this building?" Denise asked. "No matter what time of day you come in here, it's crowded."

Gina looked around. "Yeah, that waitress over there with the cute little body probably makes more than the two of us together. Hey, I called you a few times yesterday to see if you wanted to go to the movies, but no answer. You must've been gone all day on a hot date."

Denise smiled. "I was."

"Oh? Anybody I know?"

"Frank. Remember the guy I introduced you to the other day in my office?"

"Oh, Jesus. I just saw him today. I was having lunch with a friend over by the police station on Fifty-fourth Street, and I saw him walking down the street." She leaned over and spoke in a half whisper. "Hate to tell you this, Dennie, but a beautiful woman was hanging on to his arm. I thought for a minute it was you. She looked a little like you."

Denise's stomach tightened and she put down her cup. "How nice of you to tell me."

Gina touched her hand. "I'm sorry, Dennie. I shouldn't have just blabbed that out. But you know me. I never was known for my tact. I guess I didn't know you were really interested in this guy . . . are you?"

"We're friends. I have to get back to work."

"Relax. You haven't finished your coffee. Anyway, how about that movie? You want to go tomorrow night?"

Denise pushed the cup aside and got up. "I don't think so. Maybe next week." She turned and left.

29

EDWARD NEMEROW LEFT his office at 6:30 P.M. His Jaguar XK-8 stood waiting for him as he emerged from the building. Joshua Nemerow, Edward's grandfather, was one of New York's most prominent patrons of the arts. Plaques in his honor hung in Carnegie Hall, the Metropolitan Museum of Art, and other bastions of culture throughout New York.

Joshua's son Benjamin continued in his father's philanthropic footsteps, and although lacking the humanistic orientation of his father and grandfather, Edward did inherit their talent for finance. He was acknowledged as one of the most brilliant arbitrageurs and merger specialists in the country.

He lived in Greenwich, Connecticut, with his second wife, Pamela, and also maintained an apartment on West Fifty-ninth Street, overlooking Central Park. On the rare occasions when Pamela would come into the city, the apartment was a comfortable haven. It also served Edward's other needs.

THE REFRIGERATOR WAS empty, except for some bottled water, leftover limp salad, and a withered, mushy apple. She was tired and the thought of climbing into bed with a book sounded good. But she knew the hunger would only continue gnawing at her.

She leaned against the sink and read the headlines in the *Daily News* again. NO PROGRESS IN WINE BOTTLE KILLINGS. Although she'd read the article three times, she began reading it again. "In spite of working around the clock in an effort to catch the serial killer responsible for the wine bottle murders, police yesterday admitted they have no suspects. But Lieutenant Joseph Nolan continues to be optimistic. 'We have our best people heading the investigation. I have every confidence in Sergeant Jerry Blodgett and Detective Frank Russo. Every homicide detective in our task force is assigned to this case, and I can assure you we will not rest until the killer is apprehended.' "

She smiled at the policespeak. *We will not rest until the killer is apprehended.* But it was undoubtedly true and she would have to be careful.

The hunger wouldn't go away and she thought of the French restaurant on Thirty-eighth Street that she'd been wanting to try. It wasn't far and if it was as good as she'd heard, it might be just the thing to buck up her spirits, which were low again.

PAUL GALE WAS cold, tired, and hungry. His luck had to change soon. He could see the lights on up in her apartment. But he missed her going in, and now it looked like she was settling in for the night. "Goddamn!" He flicked his cigarette high into the air and started to leave, when the door to her building opened and she appeared. She stood for a moment and began walking north. Again the door opened and two couples came out and headed in the same direction. Gale fell in behind them.

This time he would have to find a way. Maybe just walk right up to her and present himself. *Hello, Tookie. I'm your father. Could we stop somewhere, have a coffee and talk?* He frowned, not liking the sound of that. But he knew he had to do something, stop acting like some goddamned wimp. Fuck it, it's worth a try, he decided, and quickened his pace.

Finally, in a little stretch between Sixth and Seventh avenues, she was alone. He was no more than fifty feet from her, staying close to the buildings, being smart and quiet. She didn't know he was behind her. He moved forward silently on his sneakers. The street was dark, and except for some people slightly ahead of them on the other side of the street, they were alone.

He closed on her fast, twenty feet, ten feet away from her now. So close, he could almost touch her. He silently rehearsed his opening line: *Hello, Tookie, can we talk?* A couple more steps. As he reached her, she took a sharp left and disappeared into a restaurant.

He stood outside watching a guy in a tuxedo smiling at her, leading her into the kind of fancy restaurant he'd never been in. Now he couldn't see her anymore. "Well, I ain't letting her out of my sight this time. No way." He unzipped his jacket and entered the building.

"Can I help you with something, sir?"

The man in the tuxedo stood in front of him. His eyes arched and he looked as if he'd just seen a cockroach crawl across his shoes.

"Uh, yeah. I thought I might get somethin' to eat."

The tuxedo man stared at him in disbelief. "Do you have a reservation, sir?"

"No, I ain't got a reservation. Why?"

"I'm sorry. We're booked solid all evening."

"OK, I'll just get me a beer in the bar." He started toward the bar.

The tuxedo man was around in front of him. "I'm sorry, sir, but the bar is already filled over our capacity. Why don't you try us another night?" He smiled thinly and gestured toward the door.

Gale stared at him, looked into the bar and back into the face of the tuxedo. Prick was still giving him that phony smile and nodding toward the door.

He headed toward the exit, the tuxedo man right behind him. At the door Gale turned and drove his knee into the man's groin. "See ya, asshole," he said, hurrying out the door and up the street. It was the only satisfaction he'd had in weeks of frustration.

He walked a block and studied his reflection in the window of a store. Greasy poplin jacket over an old sweatshirt, baggy jeans, and sneakers, a two-day growth of beard.

The tavern a few doors away looked more like his kind of place. He entered and ordered a beer.

SHE WAS GLAD the restaurant wasn't crowded. The chilled white wine she sipped and the rich food smells of the place brightened her mood. The restaurant really was quite elegant. Soft lighting and the gentle sounds of a harp drifting across the room created an atmosphere of refinement and romance.

She settled back and tried to relax. But the room was warm and her mind refused to stop racing. She felt the twinge of a headache coming on. She also felt an aching loneliness crowding in on her. It saddened her knowing there was a side of her that could have a good life, a life like other women.

So many times in the past few weeks, she had sensed his presence. Was he watching her? He knew where she lived. What else did he know? He was here in the city. Crawling around. He would find her. Or she would find him.

IT HAD BEEN a long day for Edward Nemerow. He checked his face in the car mirror and winced at the tired-looking, bloodshot eyes staring back at him. But then last night had been such fun. He took pride in his sexual prowess. At times it seemed he was indefatigable. And last night was one of those times. Yes, she was a lusty one.

Tonight, though, he was grateful for a rare evening without commitments of any kind. He looked forward to a quiet dinner and a good night's sleep. He'd been hearing good things about Les Bois, the new French restaurant on Thirty-eighth Street.

It's small, quiet, and not frequented by any of the investment crowd. And the food is terrific, friends had told him.

That was good enough for Edward. He called himself and made the reservation under the name Charles Barton. He didn't want them recognizing his name and fawning all over him.

Nemerow entered the restaurant, glanced around, and nodded his approval. The maître d' led him to his table. On the way they passed a young woman sitting alone, sipping a drink.

One glance and Nemerow's practiced eye gave him a quick snapshot. The lustrous hair rippled softly over her shoulders onto a wine-colored cashmere sweater. A touch of eye shadow gave her eyes the sensuous, sultry look he liked. He admired her high, firm breasts.

By the time he reached her table he was no longer tired. "Hello. How are you this evening?" he said, flicking a smile at her.

She looked up quickly. "I'm sorry. Were you speaking to me?"

"Yes, but forgive me if I startled you. Enjoy your dinner." He continued along with the maître d' to his table. The man appeared to have a limp she hadn't noticed before.

She had observed the well-dressed, self-assured man heading toward her table. He was short, not more than five-eight, but he carried himself erect, with style, his tailored suit draped with a loose elegance over his slender frame. He smacked of grooming and money but there was something about him that irritated her. Maybe it was the swagger, the condescending arrogance in his voice.

She heard the maître d' ask him if the table was satisfactory. Out of the corner of her eye she watched him dismiss the maître d' with a lowering of his eyes and a curt nod. He preened for a moment and sat down.

"Well, isn't he just too, too much," she snickered to herself. She finished her drink and after a few moments glanced his way. He was looking directly at her, smiling intrusively. She turned her head and was relieved when the waiter brought her meal.

The coq au vin was superb. She ate slowly, trying to enjoy it, but something about the man's presence unnerved her. She knew he was still looking at her, waiting for her to look up, so he could favor her with his insolent smile. She decided to skip coffee and get outside into the fresh air.

"Excuse me, but since you've finished your dinner, would you like to have some brandy at my table?"

She spun around. He was standing with his hands resting on the back of her chair, ready to slide it out and assist her up. She turned her head back to her table, away from him. "No, thank you."

He slid around the chair and stood in front of her. "I'm told that the coffee here is wonderful. You do drink coffee, don't you?"

She looked up at him. The perfect teeth were bared together in a Jack Nicholson smile. His eyes moved up and down her body. Did he think he was being cute with his singsongy, "You do drink coffee, don't you?" She thought about leaving but the familiar sensations took over. Time slowed down and she saw herself as a player in a slow-motion movie. The sounds, colors, and odors of the restaurant were more vivid, more intense.

"Yes, I drink coffee," she said.

"Well, then, you must have one cup of their wonderful espresso with me." Again, his hands went to the back of her chair.

Oh, must I? She continued to watch him.

He beckoned toward his table. "Come. Brighten my evening. Join me." It wasn't a question, more like a command.

Her eyes were still fixed on him, distaste for the man intensifying by the second. A small smile crossed her lips. "All right. I'll join you."

AFTER THREE BEERS and about forty minutes, Gale left the bar and walked back in the direction of the restaurant. If he got lucky and spotted her he would walk right up and introduce himself. The beers had fortified his resolve. He would tell her how proud he was of her. Maybe her goodness and class had given him new direction, a new sense of self. Not that he had forgotten how she had put him in prison and the desire for revenge that had consumed him.

He had become racked with confusion, and he knew he was on the edge. As he neared the restaurant he saw her emerge with a man holding her arm. They were no more than three feet from him. Wondering what she was doing with such a faggy-looking little shit, he skidded to a halt, ducked into a doorway, and watched as they climbed into a Jaguar parked in front and drove away. At that moment a cab pulled up and a man and woman paid and got out.

Gale entered the cab and told the driver to follow the Jag. They followed for several blocks until the Jag stopped in front of a swanky building on West Fifty-ninth Street—Central Park West. Gale watched as the garage door slid open. The Jag drove in and disappeared as the doors went down.

"Son of a bitch," he muttered as his cab drove away.

NEMEROW'S APARTMENT WAS about what she expected—gilt, mirrors, and expensive art everywhere. Through the French doors leading to the balcony she could see the broad expanse of Central Park. She turned to the exquisite figurines and sculptures, Nemerow watching her with his phony smile.

"I can see you like beautiful things," he said, moving around behind her and sliding her coat off. "The two figurines are by Nike de Saint Phalle, the ceramics are Picasso, and the horse sculpture is a Deborah Butterfield." He laid her coat over one of the chairs. "But please, sit down and let me bring you something. I believe you said you like wine?"

She stood rigid as he sidled up to her and beckoned toward the sofa. "Please sit down and relax. I have a delicious Chardonnay or would you prefer a Cabernet?"

She studied the obnoxious little man before replying. "I would like some Chardonnay."

She watched him mince his way toward the kitchen and shuddered. The headache had settled in and her head throbbed. She took a Percodan from her purse, swallowed it dry, and sat heavily on the sofa. Beads of perspiration trickled down her body. The woolen slacks clung to her and pressed against her pelvic area. She opened and closed her legs.

"Here we are, my dear." Edward Nemerow stood in front of her, wearing a dark blue silk smoking jacket. He held a silver tray containing a bottle of Chardonnay iced in a gleaming silver bucket and two half-filled wineglasses. He handed her wine to her, set the tray down, and sat on the sofa. "I thought I'd get into something a bit more comfortable than all that wretched, heavy clothing. May I offer you the same opportunity?" he asked, caressing her face.

She ignored the question.

"You are a beautiful woman, my dear. I've had very strong feelings for you from the moment I saw you in the restaurant." He raised his glass. "Here's to you and your beauty."

She forced a smile and sipped the wine, ignoring his inane chatter. Her mind drifted. She was in another place, another time.

Nemerow downed the rest of his wine and set his glass down.

He moved in closer to her and placed his mouth next to her ear. His breath was hot and unpleasant and she choked back the impulse to gag. The Percodan made her dizzy but did nothing yet for her headache.

She pulled away and stared at the repulsive little man, who seemed to be heading out of control already. How could he possibly believe she could feel anything but revulsion for him?

Suddenly he was kissing her hungrily, his tongue licking and exploring. She tried to move away, but his strength surprised her. Then it was he who broke away and put his lips to her ears again. "I want you to do something for me." His voice was a harsh whisper. "I want you to come into the bedroom and handcuff me to the bed. And then I want you to do unspeakable things to me. Will you do that?"

She pushed him away and gazed at him with eyes that passed through him as if he were a window. After a long silence she slowly nodded. "Yes," she said. "I would like to do that."

Inside the bedroom she stood at the foot of Nemerow's bed, watching him take off his clothes. He peeled off his shirt, revealing a hairless pink chest. The rest of his shapeless body was soft and doughy, unremarkable except for the ugly erection, grotesquely out of proportion to his puny frame.

She hated looking at it and closed her eyes for a moment. When she opened them, he lay spread-eagled on the bed holding a pair of handcuffs. "Please, please, take your clothes off and come to me." He held the handcuffs out to her.

She wanted to leave this repulsive man and go home. But the dark entity that raged within her took over. Her eyes fixed him with a distant stare before she moved toward him, slipping out of her slacks along the way.

Nemerow groaned and writhed on the bed. "Oh, God, take your sweater off. Now," he commanded.

She slid off the sweater and stood over him.

"Now, I want you to put these handcuffs around my wrists and snap them around the bedposts." He barely rasped out the words.

She did as she was told and leaned close to him. "You're mine now, aren't you?" she whispered.

He tried to speak, but he was breathing so hard the words squeezed out in little gasps. "And-now—I-I . . . want-you-to-take-off-your-panties-and-sit-on-my-face."

"Yes, of course," she said. She moved onto the bed and straddled him somewhere up around his neck.

Nemerow's moans grew louder. "Oh! God! Sit on me. Sit on me, baby."

She slowly lowered herself over his head and settled the full weight of her body onto his face. "Now, there. Do you like that, Charles?"

She barely heard his muffled voice. "You still have your pants on. Take them off." He was still commanding her, still thinking he was in charge. She would enjoy this.

She moved her thighs in closer along the sides of his face. "No, I like it better like this. You like it, too, don't you? Don't you, Charles?" Her voice was soft, cooing.

She controlled the muscles of her thighs, flexing them into a tightening vise around his face and head. He thrashed like a wounded duck. His legs flailed helplessly. He mumbled and made noises; muffled screams and bits and pieces of unintelligible sound came from under her thighs. She grabbed at a bedpost and pushed up with her arms, forcing her body harder into him. After a while the squirming slowed, then stopped. There were no more sounds. Edward Nemerow lay motionless.

She slumped forward and lay her head against the wall. Her work was done. She felt satiated, at peace. She wanted to close her eyes and sleep. But not yet.

31

JERRY AND FRANK were in Jerry's squad car, heading for an appointment, when they received the call directly from Lieutenant Nolan. A prominent citizen had been murdered, and they were to get over to the scene immediately. After getting the address Jerry plunked the siren on the roof and, tires squealing, made a U-turn and took off. Twenty minutes later, they were let into the apartment by a uniformed police officer, who led them over to a man and woman sitting on the couch.

The woman got up and shook Frank's hand. "I'm Michelle Vivier, Mr. Nemerow's secretary." She nodded her head toward the man with her. "This is Mr. Byrd, the manager of the building."

Frank was impressed by the lady's composure. Byrd was agitated and fidgeted on the couch. Probably worried about the scandal in his fancy building.

"Mr. Nemerow failed to show up for an extremely important meeting this morning," Vivier reported. "It just wasn't like him. No one, including his wife, had heard from him, and he didn't answer his phone. I became worried and came over here. Mr. Byrd let me in and we found him."

Frank looked at Byrd, who was now standing. He was a tall, gaunt-looking man who reminded Frank of Ichabod Crane. Byrd nodded and explained how Nemerow took his private elevator up from the garage so no one normally saw him coming or going.

Fifteen minutes later, Lieutenant Nolan, Chief Sacco, and Commissioner John Keohane himself arrived, followed shortly by the medical examiner, a police photographer, a sketcher, two uniformed officers, a fingerprint specialist, Harry Leonard, and two reporters from the *New York Post*, who were outside in the hall.

The commissioner, a burly man with snow white hair, spoke quietly with Michelle for a few moments. He then adjourned to the hall with Jerry, the chief, and Nolan. "Gentlemen, as you know, the man lying dead in the bedroom is Edward Nemerow. And you know who Edward Nemerow is, or was. I can tell you that before this day is out, the shit is going to hit the fan in this city unlike anything you have ever seen.

"Those two reporters over there are the beginning of big trouble. I don't know how they got up here but I want them out. I expect no more leaks to the press. I also expect a visit from the Nemerows very shortly, and the pressure they're going to put on me will be passed on to you. Now, get those reporters the hell out of here, and get busy. I want a full report on your progress before I leave my office. I'll be there at least until seven tonight."

He grabbed Nolan by the arm. "Come on, Joe, I've got to get back. You and I need to talk some more. We can do it in my car."

Nolan glared for a moment at Jerry, then left with the commissioner and Chief Sacco.

Jerry went back into the apartment and found Harry. "Harry, get out in the hall and get those reporters out of here. Go down the elevator with them, and make sure they leave the building. There should be an officer down there to see that they don't get back in. Find out how the fuck they got up here in the first place. Also, find out which doorman was on duty last night and talk to him."

Jerry was now in charge. He tucked in his shirt and walked over to Frank, who was talking with the medical examiner. "Frank, check the other occupants of the floor and see if they saw or heard anything. I think we're finished with Mr. Byrd and Miss Vivier for now. They can go."

Frank grabbed Jerry by the arm. "Jerry, have you gotten real close to the body yet?"

"Depends on what you mean by real close. Why?"

"He's got a smell of perfume on him. I mean, it doesn't smell like men's cologne. It sure as hell isn't the cologne he's got in the bathroom. It smells like a woman's perfume or lotion. Check it out. Check his clothes. I'll see you in a while."

Jerry walked back to the bedroom, where Edward Nemerow lay as Byrd and Vivier had first discovered him. The photographer was still taking pictures: full-body views, general views of the body and the crime scene, close-up shots of wounds, and photos of contiguous areas, as well as of the entire apartment. The crime scene sketcher was also still at work, as were the fingerprint man and the medical examiner. A wine bottle protruded from Nemerow's rectum.

Frank walked along the long, wide hallway of the building. He had learned from the building manager that there was only one other apartment on the tenth floor. It was located around the corner of the building and faced south.

Frank rang the doorbell, and a woman's voice replied from within, "Yes, who is it, and how did you get up here?"

"Police officers, ma'am." He held his badge in front of the viewer in the door, and made certain that the uniformed police officer he had brought with him was visible to her.

The door opened as far as the thick chain on it would allow. The woman's voice was apprehensive. "Please let me see your credentials."

Frank handed them to her. She studied them carefully and handed them back to him. Her eyes darted from Frank to the patrolman. "May I ask what this is all about?"

"I'm afraid there has been a crime committed in your neighbor's apartment. I wonder if I might ask you a few questions, ma'am?"

"A crime? What kind of a crime?" She sounded frightened.

Frank spoke softly. "Mr. Nemerow has been murdered. May we come in and talk with you? You may be able to help us."

She gasped and closed the door. Frank heard the chain being unlatched, and the door opened.

A petite blonde who appeared to be in her early forties stood in the doorway. Her short hair framed deep blue eyes, with just a trace of indigo eye shadow over them. She wore no other makeup, and the news Frank had just delivered had turned her porcelain features chalk white. The blue-and-white designer warm-up suit she wore fit as if tailored for her, which he figured it probably was. Her white sneakers were spotless. He admired her, in spite of the circumstances.

"Oh, my God," she stammered. "I can't believe I heard what you just said. Please, please come in and sit down."

They sat down in the living room. The apartment was as elegant as the woman. The ceilings in the entry hall and living room had to be at least fourteen feet high. The crystal chandelier hanging over Frank was almost as big as his whole living room. The artwork alone, if it was original, and he was sure it was, might have been worth as much again as the apartment. He resisted the temptation to press his fingers into the carpet under their feet. The pile was soft and easily an inch or more deep. He wondered for a moment what it must be like to have this kind of money, and then got down to business.

Her name was Alexandra Iburg. She was a freelance casting director and her husband, Daniel, was a surgeon. They had no children and had been living in the building for nine years. They knew Nemerow, but were not friends of his.

"Let's just say we didn't approve of his lifestyle," she said.

"What do you mean?" Frank asked.

"Well, it was no secret here in the building that Mr. Nemerow was fond of entertaining women in his apartment. They came in various colors, some black, some white, and they came and went with some regularity."

"Wasn't Mr. Nemerow married?" Frank asked.

"Yes. That's what I mean about not approving of his lifestyle," she replied. "He made no effort to be discreet. My husband and I often shared the elevator with him and one of his women. I felt so sorry for his wife."

"Did you ever see him with a man?"

"No, never."

"Did you see him with the same woman more often than with others?"

She thought for a moment. "No, not really. They were pretty much a mixed bag." She looked up at Frank and smiled. "If you'll pardon the expression. Some were tall, some short."

"Any similar characteristics about them?" Frank asked.

She looked away and ran her tongue along her upper lip, then back to Frank. "They were all very attractive women." A hint of pique crept into her voice. "Now, can you please tell me what happened?"

Frank nodded. This was not a woman accustomed to being questioned. She was instinctively courteous. Good breeding. But she had an imperious quality about her that warned him she wasn't going to suffer through this very long. "We believe he was killed last night, sometime between ten P.M. and one or two in the morning. Did you see or hear anything at all?"

Mrs. Iburg stared at Frank, her eyes widening. "Oh, my God. Of course we did."

32

IT TOOK MRS. Iburg a minute to compose herself after she realized she'd probably just missed a murderer.

"What did you see?" Frank asked again.

"Well, as we were coming down the corridor heading toward the elevator, I could see it was open and I yelled for whoever was in it to hold it. But just as we got there it was closing and I caught a glimpse of someone inside."

"One person?"

"Yes."

"Do you recall what time it was?"

"Yes, as a matter of fact, I remember exactly. My mother was due to arrive at JFK at eleven-forty on a flight from Seattle. Dan and I were leaving to pick her up. I wanted to be certain to be there in plenty of time before her arrival, and I was concerned that we were running late. It was about ten-fifteen."

"Please describe for me, if you will, the person you saw on the elevator, Mrs. Iburg."

She ran her fingers through her hair, and shook her head. "Well, that's going to be difficult. We really didn't see much, I'm afraid."

"Can you describe what you did see?"

"Well, as I told you, we got to the elevator just as the door was closing. There was one person on it, and we were a little exasperated, because she could have pressed the button and reopened the door for us. There was still time. But she didn't." Iburg paused and frowned, as if remembering her annoyance.

Something about the way she frowned told him this was a lady with a short fuse. "Mrs. Iburg, are you sure it was a woman?"

"Yes. She had a hand up to her face, partly covering it, but I could see enough to tell she was female."

"What was she wearing?"

"She had on a long dark coat, black or dark blue. Dark slacks and a dark scarf covering her head."

"Shoes?"

"Yes, the shoes. They were the other reason I'm assuming the person was a female. They had a wedge heel with a moccasin front. I picked up on the shoes because they were very similar to a pair I have. Can I offer you gentlemen some coffee, a soft drink?"

"No, thank you," Frank said.

"No, thanks," the uniformed officer spoke for the first time.

"Mrs. Iburg, would you mind showing me your shoes—the ones similar to those worn by the woman on the elevator," Frank asked.

"Certainly." She left the room and returned carrying a pair of shoes.

Frank took a mental picture of them and sketched on his pad. "How tall would you say she was?" he asked.

"Gee. I don't know." She thought again, took a deep breath, and let it out. "Maybe five-nine, five-ten. She was tall."

"Would you say the build was slender or heavyset? I mean, could you tell if—"

"Mr. Russo," she interrupted. "Please remember that we caught only the most fleeting glimpse of her." A touch of impatience crept into her voice. She got up and walked over to a table, and withdrew a cigarette from a silver case. She lit it with a small silver lighter.

Frank sensed that she was getting tired and knew he'd have to wrap it up soon. "I'm sorry, Mrs. Iburg. I know this isn't easy, and I apologize for having to take so much of your time. Maybe just a few more minutes?" He smiled at her like they were old friends.

The smile bought him the time he needed. She smiled back and touched his arm. "Forgive me for snapping. I know that your questions are important and necessary. Please continue." She took another deep drag on the cigarette and inhaled in a quick gasp.

The woman had presence. Even through the warm-up suit he couldn't help but notice she had a great body. The kind of woman who took very good care of herself. "I was asking you about the woman's build," he said.

"Well, as I said she was wearing a heavy coat, and it seemed like she had fairly broad shoulders. But that could have been the coat."

"Before the door closed, was there any possible way you could determine if she was one of the women you had seen Mr. Nemerow with on the elevator? You did say that some of them were tall."

"Well, I guess it's possible. But as I said, I did not get a good look, and I really paid very little attention to her. I didn't expect to be having this conversation, you know." She gave him a little smile.

He grinned back and nodded. "I understand. Did the scarf completely cover her hair?"

"Yes."

"Did you see enough of her face to determine what color her skin was?"

"Yes, she was white."

Frank got up and held out his hand. "I think that's about it, Mrs. Iburg. Thank you for your time and for being so cooperative and helpful. Oh, by the way. Did you smell any perfume or any kind of scent coming from the elevator?"

"Hmm . . . no. I can't say that I did."

"Did the women you've seen on the elevator in the past wear perfume?"

"Yes."

"Could you identify any of it?"

"No."

"Just one last question, Mrs. Iburg. You would have to assume, wouldn't you, that since Mr. Nemerow's and yours are the only apartments on this floor, the person would have been coming from Nemerow's apartment? I mean, could there be any other explanation for her being up here?"

She shook her head vigorously. "No. We have very tight security here. We've been trying to get them to put a video camera in the entry hall. Maybe now they will."

"Yes, well, thanks again. I may be calling you."

"I would look forward to it," she said, touching his arm again as she showed them out.

Back inside Nemerow's apartment, Frank reported the results of his discussion with Alexandra Iburg. "Jerry, the person she and her husband saw is our killer," Frank said matter-of-factly. "That would put the time of the murder at maybe somewhere between nine-thirty and a little after ten. Our serial killer is a woman, Jerry. And she's also an attractive woman. You can bet on it. Nemerow was a very wealthy guy. He was not about to bring some pig up to his fancy apartment."

Jerry led Frank over to a quiet corner of the large living room, where they settled into matching Louis XIV chairs. The sight of Jerry's massive frame bulging over the delicate chair brought a smile to Frank's face.

"What's so funny?" Jerry growled.

"Don't get up quick. You'll be wearing the chair."

Jerry snorted and leaned forward. "Your thing about the perfume is right on. There's perfume on his suit coat, his shirt, the bathrobe, and you can smell it on his chest. At least it smells more like perfume than men's cologne. And you're right. It's definitely not the stuff he's got in the bathroom. We're sending the clothing over to the lab for some gas chromatography."

Frank nodded and sat quietly for a moment. "That's good, Jerry, but you know what I'm going to do? I'm going to take a piece of his clothing down to Macy's, to one of those women at the perfume counters. Those ladies are like bloodhounds. I'll bet any one of them can take a whiff of this stuff and tell us what it is."

Jerry chuckled. "You're right, Frank. They are like bloodhounds."

Frank nodded. "They pick up any prints?"

Jerry looked toward the bedroom. "Yeah. We got some in the bathroom and a couple off the bedroom door. Nothing on the wine bottle or the glasses. Probably been wiped off."

"Anything else?"

Jerry pointed to a man bent over the sofa with a flashlight and tweezers. "They've found some strands of hair, here and in the bedroom. Appears to be brownish. It's on its way to the lab now."

"Well, we know that whoever zapped him didn't exactly break the door down to get in," Frank said. "There's no sign of forced entry, unless she shinnied up the side of the building."

Jerry nodded. "Had to be one of his guests. Hey, Harry!"

Harry Leonard appeared from the bedroom. "Yeah?"

"Harry, come over here. I want you to listen to Frank's interview with the neighbor. What'd you find out about the doorman?"

"He's on his way in now. I talked to him a little on the phone. I don't think he's going to be much help. He told me the same thing

Byrd did. Nemerow always went in through the garage and took his private elevator up from there. He didn't see him at all. Didn't see any strangers leave during the time frame we're talking about. The killer probably went down and out through the garage." Harry sat and Frank filled him in on his discussion with Alexandra Iburg.

"Go down and talk to Byrd. See if he can corroborate or add anything to what Frank has."

Jerry lowered his voice. "We got something else too, Frank."

"What's that?" Frank asked.

"We got an address book out of his bureau drawer. It's full of nothing but women's names and phone numbers. Interesting annotations next to most of 'em."

"Like what?"

" 'Best blow job in New York.' 'Very kinky.' 'Likes to dominate.' 'Won't screw, but will do anything else.' 'Likes to play rough.' You know, little gems like that."

Harry stopped at the front door and started back toward them.

"Get outta here, Harry," Jerry shouted.

Harry scurried out.

"Any men in there?" asked Frank.

"None. All women."

"We'll check the names and numbers against the ones we found in Chesbro's book," Frank said. "Foreign object insertion is typically perpetrated by men on women. I've checked the computer back through 1985 for similar MOs all over the state. We've got your experience going back thirty years. I've talked with my father and retired detectives going back beyond him. Only a very few cases of foreign object insertion perpetrated on men—all homosexual related. It's not something a heterosexual man does to another. And there is no indication that any of these guys were involved with homosexuals. No, my guess is we're looking for a woman.

"We've got Jack Beatty, Joey Brewer, Phillip Chesbro, and now Nemerow all killed with the same MO. Nemerow's wallet and some jewelry were taken from him. The other guys weren't robbed. Two things could account for the difference. One, the other guys didn't have anything worth taking, and two, the killer wanted to throw us off and make this one look like robbery was the motive. Could be it's a combination of both. No big deal, as far as any change in the MO. All four are the work of the same person."

"No question," said Jerry.

The medical examiner appeared in the room. He spoke with the clipped precision of people in his profession. "Jerry, we're finished with the body, and we're ready to have him removed, unless you have anything else."

Jerry shook his head. "What have you got?"

"We've got some pieces of human hair that were on the victim and on the bed and the sofa. We'll check that out and see if we have any follicles with it. We've picked up some pieces of fabric off the victim's robe and his shirt. And his shirt and robe are in two separate paper bags for you over there on the table. Frank, I believe you said you wanted them."

Frank nodded. "Thanks, George."

"It looks like the cause of death was suffocation, but his head was also hit several times on the floor—very hard. There's blood and pieces of scalp on the floor.

"Jerry, I showed you the marks on his wrists. They're the marks handcuffs make. They were on very tight, causing pronounced lacerations."

"Handcuffs?" Frank asked.

"Yes, I'm sure that's what caused the marks, but we can confirm or deny that when we've examined him more."

Frank turned to Jerry. "That's a new twist. Any sign of the cuffs?"

"No, but the killer had another wine bottle in reserve. Yep, same deal, Frankie," Jerry said.

"Was he handcuffed to something, the bed?" Frank asked.

"Yep. You can see the marks on the bedposts," Jerry said. "But whoever killed him took off the cuffs and dragged him onto the floor so they could pound his head on it."

"I'm leaving now with the paramedics," the ME said.

"What do you think, Frank?" Jerry asked, settling back into his Louis XIV chair.

"This guy liked getting kinky with his ladies. I'm sure the cuffs bit was part of his repertoire of little games. He just picked the wrong lady this time. She probably couldn't believe her good luck. He made it easy for her."

Frank went over to the table and picked up the bag containing Nemerow's clothing. "I'm going to take this clothing down to Macy's and have some of the perfume experts there take a whiff. We'll also have the lab run some tests, but I think we'll get our answer from the perfume women."

Jerry got up and walked slowly over to Frank, his shirttail hanging from under his sport coat. "OK, Frank. I'll be here for a while. See you back at the precinct in a couple hours." He went over to the window and looked out, still thinking of the look Nolan gave him as he walked out with the commissioner.

33

MACY'S WAS CROWDED, already beginning to show the effects of the upcoming holiday season. Frank made his way to the perfume counter, approached one of the few women not busy with a customer, and identified himself. The woman, in her late thirties, wore a blue smock over a black silk blouse. Her jet black hair, too dark to be real, Frank thought, was pulled tightly back at the temples and hung in a ponytail bound with a large sequined doughnut. Dark eye shadow covered her lids.

"Well, this is a surprise. What can I do for our police department today?"

Frank set his bag on the counter. "I wonder if you could smell the garments inside this bag, and tell me if you know what the scent is?"

She gave him a quizzical look.

"Please, ma'am. It's important, and I would much appreciate it if you don't ask me any questions. I hope you understand."

She smiled at him and pointed to her name tag. "Officer, please call me Joanne. Somehow 'ma'am' makes me feel old."

Frank handed over the bag. "OK, Joanne."

She sat on the stool behind the counter, put her nose into the bag, and quickly withdrew it.

"Oh, that's too easy. Why don't you give me a tough one? I can tell you without question, it's Jean Naté."

"Can you be absolutely certain?"

"Of course I can. Most perfume scents are easy to identify. Jean Naté is one of the easiest. Listen, I've been at this stuff for nearly twenty years. Take it to the bank. This is Jean Naté."

Another perfume lady approached, this one in a green smock. Joanne called her over.

"Francine, can you do me a favor?" Joanne handed her the bag. "Smell these clothes, and tell this gentleman what the scent is."

Francine looked from Joanne to Frank and took the bag. She put her head slightly into it, sniffed, and handed back the bag.

"It's Jean Naté," she said matter-of-factly.

"Thanks, Francine. Talk to you later."

Francine shrugged and continued on her way.

"Officer, I could hand this bag to every woman on these counters, and every one will tell us the same thing, believe me. Do you want to try another?"

"No, you've made a believer out of me."

"Good. Glad to help. What else can I do for you?" Big smile.

"What type of women buy Jean Naté, Joanne?"

"Actually, we don't sell it here. You find it mostly in drugstores, Walgreens, places like that. It's an old after-bath fragrance. Been around a long time. Very common."

"Not upscale?"

"Not upscale."

"One last question and I'll let you go."

"No rush."

"It's not something men ever wear, is it?"

"No. It's a women's fragrance."

JERRY BLODGETT SAT at his desk, working on the Nemerow report, when he heard his name roar across the bullpen and through his open door. He jumped, looked up, and saw Joseph Nolan standing in the bullpen area.

"Blodgett," Nolan yelled again.

Jerry got up from his desk and grabbed his coat from the rack. He plodded across the bullpen, one arm grappling with his coat sleeve, the other vainly trying to stuff his shirttail inside his pants.

"Jerry. My office. Now," Nolan growled.

"Look at this newspaper article." He threw the *New York Post* at Jerry, who instinctively caught part of it, while other parts drifted across the room.

Jerry retrieved the paper and put it together. The front-page headline and Nemerow's photo jumped at him. WINE BOTTLE KILLER STRIKES PROMINENT FINANCIER.

"Go ahead. Sit down and read it," Nolan said.

Jerry looked at him and slumped into a chair next to him. Nolan remained standing.

" 'Edward Nemerow, nationally known and respected financier and member of one of New York's most prominent families, was brutally murdered last night. Nemerow's body was found this morning by his secretary and the manager of the posh Central Park West building where he lived.

" 'He appeared to be the victim of a serial killer, who over the past five weeks has killed at least three other men, the killer's signature being a wine bottle left in the victim's rectum. All four, including

Nemerow, were found in their apartments, brutally beaten, with a wine bottle the primary instrument.

"'Joshua Nemerow, patriarch of the Nemerow family and grandfather of the victim, expressed outrage that the police have made no progress on the activities of a vicious serial killer on the loose.'"

Jerry threw the paper down. "Fuck! I've read enough, Joe."

"Oh, there's more, Jerry." Nolan picked up the paper. "Listen to this."

"'The public has a right to know about these things,' Mr. Nemerow said. 'My family and I expect prompt and decisive action in bringing this killer to justice. We demand to know all the facts in this case, and the other three, and we want a complete accounting on what's been done to date toward apprehending this maniac.'"

Nolan threw the paper back at Jerry. "Nice, huh?"

Jerry frowned and started to speak.

Nolan interrupted. "I got the chief and the commissioner all over my ass. The Nemerows won't let up, and I'm taking nothing but shit from all directions. I don't like that, Jerry. I don't care if you guys work twenty-four hours a day. I want results." He turned his back and that was it.

Frank was back at his desk. Jerry called him into his office.

Frank told him about the perfume women's input. Jerry slumped into a chair and said, "That's the first good news I've had today."

"We can put pressure on the lab to get these other tests done right away," Frank said. "I'll have them run the gas chromatography with the scent, too, but I don't think it's going to change what we already know. We'll check the names out and compare for duplicates. We've got the hair, the prints, the fabric, the perfume. We know it's a woman we're looking for. But let's keep that little tidbit from the press."

"Absolutely!" Jerry replied. "Fuck the Nemerows. We're going to do this our way."

Frank went back to his desk and picked up the bag of clothing to run it over to the lab. As he closed the bag to tie and tag it, the lingering scent of the perfume hit him and stayed for a moment.

He pictured Edward Nemerow, lying handcuffed to his four-poster bed, all worked up over the sight and smell of the woman hovering over him, about to satisfy whatever his perverted needs were. Instead she satisfied hers.

34

SHE WAS ADDICTED to the newspaper accounts of her activities. It seemed to her that she was reading about someone else. Her activities had been so isolated, so personal, it seemed odd to be reading about them in the newspapers, odd that everyone in the city was reading about them, about her. The lead story on both the six and eleven o'clock television news was about Nemerow.

Today's paper had quotes from the mayor and the police commissioner. Even the governor had responded to a question about the killings in a press conference. He had referred to her as a monster. She wished she hadn't read that. She was not a monster. If only he knew, he would never call her that.

She read further. "Police continue to follow up on a number of leads and express confidence in apprehending the killer soon." It was the first such positive statement coming from the police. Were they bluffing? Fending off pressure from the Nemerow family?

Nemerow. She'd had a feeling that Charles Barton was a fake name. Like she was some cheap tramp he'd picked up, not worthy of knowing his real name. No question, he was an important man. Not like the others. Now she had opened a Pandora's box. *A number of leads.* Had she been careless, made a mistake?

Those people at the elevator. How much of her did they see? Of course the police must have talked with them by now. Why no mention of it? She was glad she had the presence of mind to take the handcuffs and his wallet with the American Express receipt for their dinners at Les Bois. She put the newspaper down and smiled, satisfied that she had made no mistakes.

PAUL GALE SAT on his bed sipping a whiskey highball, reading the afternoon paper about Edward Nemerow's murder. He examined Nemerow's photograph, read the address of his apartment—the murder scene—and noted the police department's estimate of the time of the murder.

Again, he studied the photo until his hands began shaking uncontrollably. He drained the rest of the whiskey, his eyes still fixed on the newspaper, trying to process what he had just read. Eventually, he closed his eyes and began slowly squeezing, tearing, and twisting the newspaper into a crumpled ball. He sat in the stillness of the dingy room, holding the ball, staring out the window into the late-afternoon darkness.

TWO DAYS AFTER Nemerow's murder, at five-thirty in the afternoon, Clark Hamilton called. "Frank, we've got some lab results for you. I'll be here until about seven-thirty," Clark said.

"Be right over," Frank said and hung up. "That's got to be a world's record for those guys, Jerry. Funny what a little heat will do, huh?"

Jerry snickered. "A lot of heat."

Frank went over to Harry's desk. He wasn't there. A hurried look around the room and Frank spotted him in a corner of the precinct talking with another cop. Even in the drab blue uniform, her breasts protruded majestically. Harry's face was inches from hers.

"Hey, Harry," Frank yelled across the precinct. "You think you could pull yourself away and come over here?"

All eyes turned on Harry and the busty cop. She turned and bolted in the other direction, while Harry sauntered toward Frank, trying to look casual. When he reached Frank, he was no longer casual. "Goddamn it, Frank. Why do you have to embarrass me like that?"

Frank shook his head. "Harry, I'm not trying to embarrass you. I just don't think the precinct is the place to be playing grab ass when we've got a serial killer on our hands. Anyway," he grinned, "she's too much woman for you."

Harry started to speak, but Frank interrupted. "Come on. Clark Hamilton just called. They've got some lab results."

The police lab was housed in a typical New York brownstone on East Twentieth Street amid rows of other turn-of-the-century brownstones. Frank and Harry went straight to Clark Hamilton's office and found him sitting at his desk, typing.

"Well, it didn't take you fellows long to get here. Nice to see you, Frank. Harry." He offered them a seat and walked over to his coffeepot. "May I offer you gentlemen some coffee?"

Harry started to sit but Frank's nudge made him stand his ground. Frank knew Clark well enough to indulge him his geniality and hospitality before they could get down to business. But he also knew that once Clark had you seated you were his, until he was ready to release you.

Clark could be ponderous but Frank liked his courtly manner and elegant bearing, definitely out of place in the police business. He never swore or even raised his voice. His silver hair and pencil-thin mustache were always neatly trimmed. A refreshing misfit.

Clark handed them their coffee and again beckoned them to sit down. They sat, knowing he wouldn't begin until they did.

"Gentlemen, I have some interesting results for you. I know how busy you are, so let me get right to it." Clark was up and pacing around his office, carrying his notebook, to which he occasionally referred. He was all business, in his lecture mode.

"We have done the gas chromatography on the perfume scent and have confirmed that it is indeed Jean Naté perfume." Clark paused to look at his small notebook and Frank seized the opportunity.

"Clark, the scent doesn't last for very long, does it? I mean, what's the longest period of time that the perfume scent would have come off onto Nemerow's garments?"

Clark's eyes widened as he stared at Frank. "Why, it had to have come in contact with him no longer ago than the evening before you found it on him," he said with the cocksure certainty that sometimes irritated Frank.

"OK, thanks. Continue."

Clark resumed pacing. "Now, unfortunately, there were no follicles in the hair we examined, so we can't say for certain whether it's from a man or woman. However, I can tell you from the pieces we found that this is natural dark brown or black hair. There are no traces of any substance to indicate this hair has been chemically treated. These pieces came from a head of long hair. That doesn't necessarily tell us that it was a woman or a man. But I can tell you that the person whose hair we examined was definitely Caucasian."

"The hair wasn't dyed?"

"Not dyed."

"Not a wig?"

"I don't think so. As you know, many wigs today are made from natural hair, so it's not possible to say with absolute certainty, but my instincts tell me that the hair samples here are natural.

"As you also know the hair found at this fellow Joey's scene also appeared to be a brown, natural-looking hair, similar to those found at the other scenes. But again, as I have said, we can't totally rule out a natural-hair wig. And Chesbro—those hairs were from a wig of dark brown hair." Clark nodded solemnly.

He resumed pacing and lecturing. "The pieces of fabric found on Mr. Nemerow and the sofa are a deep red or wine-colored cashmere. From its length and texture, I would say it's more likely from a sweater than from, say, a sport coat or topcoat. Mind you now, we can't be certain, but the consistency of the weave would tell me sweater.

"The prints we have from Beatty and Joey Brewer match. We do have several sets of prints from Chesbro's scene, but no matches with the other scenes. The glasses and the wine bottles were wiped clean.

"There were prints all over Nemerow's place, but we couldn't get a match with any of the other scenes. Again, the glasses and wine bottle were wiped clean."

With this last pronouncement, Clark fell silent, peering down at Frank and Harry over his tiny spectacles. His soliloquy was over, but his expression told them he would now take questions.

"That it, Clark?" Frank asked.

Clark nodded. "That's it." He walked over to his desk and set his pad of notes on it. "I hope we've been of some help, and please do give me a call if you need anything else." He reached toward a phalanx of pipes propped in a holder on his desk and withdrew one.

Frank backed away. Clark's pipes were known throughout the New York Police Department for the vile and foul-smelling tobacco they harbored. Clark reached into a canister and began slowly, methodically stuffing pieces of tobacco into the pipe in that familiar manner common to all pipe smokers.

"Uh, Harry, I guess we're ready to go, aren't we?"

Harry was already at the door. "Yeah. I'm ready. Thanks, Clark. Talk to you later." They were gone before Clark could light up.

"I'd say we got a pretty good profile of Mr. Nemerow's visitor the night he got killed," Frank said as they drove away. "A tall, thirtyish or younger woman with long natural dark brown or black hair, wearing Jean Naté perfume and a dark red or wine-colored cashmere sweater. She wears a long dark blue or black coat and a dark scarf. And she is one nasty lady."

35

TIME WAS RUNNING out on Paul Gale. "I have a new dishwasher, Tony," Gale overheard Peter tell Tony. "He can start in a few days this coming Wednesday. Den I get rid of the jailbird."

Wednesday. Today was Friday. Tuesday would probably be Gale's last day.

He would have to leave New York, couldn't afford to stay here long, not without a job, and who knew how long it would take him to find one. He still had some money left from his prison stake. He could go somewhere cheaper to live, get some kind of job, start a new life. But first, there was something he needed to do—something, he now realized, he always knew he would do.

FRANK STARED WEARILY at his computer. The vodka martini tasted good. On the rocks. Ice cold.

It was late and he'd been home for only fifteen minutes. Another long week. But they were making progress. Nemerow's black book was shaping up as a gold mine. Somewhere, among those pages of names, he felt certain they were going to find the woman they were looking for.

Somehow he found the mental energy to finish the article for the *Journal of Police and Criminal Psychology*. At eleven o'clock he put the finishing touches on the thirty-five-page piece he'd begun nearly a month ago. Progress on the writing was slow these days. As it was, e-mailing it tomorrow, he'd still be a few days late on his deadline. No big deal. But he wasn't built to think that way. Sometimes he wished he were.

Was it too late to call Denise? Eleven o'clock. She'd be long since conked out. He'd call her in the morning.

He turned off the computer and trudged into the bedroom. It was an effort to get out of his clothes. He let them fall on the floor, switched off the light, and fell into bed, physically and mentally exhausted but unable to sleep.

It was a confusing time. The Wine Bottle Killer had everybody jittery. Jerry was acting weird. Going through the motions, like he was tense, ready to pin the killings on anybody, just not make waves or let this thing screw up his retirement. Running scared.

Frank was still fumbling with his personal life. He'd promised to call Denise during the week and shoot for something toward the end, like Friday. Then the shit hit the fan with Nemerow.

And Carla was playing games with him again. He wished he'd never gone to Bernstein's party. He closed his eyes, and saw her standing in the doorway of the detective's bullpen, just as she had the other day.

"Uh, Frank," Steve Monahan leaned over his desk and whispered. "You've got company."

He looked up and saw her standing there, hair pulled into a knot atop her head, no makeup, wearing a baseball cap, jeans, and a wind-breaker, a bag big enough to carry Jerry hanging over her shoulder. Somehow she managed to look stunning. For a moment, typewriters stopped, the din and chatter went silent, and he thought he was going to lose it.

She moved across the room in that way that she had and stood over him. "Hi. I was in the neighborhood and thought I'd stop in and say hello." She seemed oblivious to the impact she was having on the room, but he knew she wasn't.

He was on his feet. "Nobody is just 'in' this neighborhood. What brings you here?"

"You, actually. I was five blocks away and figured it was close enough to drop by. How about taking me to lunch?"

He wished she didn't look and smell so good. "I was just heading out. I've got an appointment a few blocks from here."

"Are you walking?"

"Yeah."

"May I walk along with you? This is a rough neighborhood and I'd feel so much safer with you." She slid her arm through his.

The room was still silent. He felt like they were talking through a microphone. All he wanted to do was get the hell out of there. "Sure, let's go."

They passed the gauntlet of cops, some sitting, some standing, each ogling Carla. One of them snickered and cracked, "Bye-bye, Frank."

She continued holding his arm as they walked along West Fifty-fourth Street. It seemed so natural. Just like normal people.

"Frank, can we duck inside somewhere? I need to talk with you."

Oh, Jesus. Yes, he thought. Walking along the street with her holding on to him, with her so close, so desirable, a familiar longing took hold of him.

They went into a place called the Roasted Bean, found a booth, and ordered coffee. The booth was small and their knees touched. She placed her hands over his and gently squeezed. The physical contact was enough for him to lower his guard. His hand went up to her face.

"Nice to see you," he whispered.

"You, too." Her eyes moved up and down him.

She began to fidget, shifting her weight in the booth from one side to another, fiddling with the large pin holding her hair. She took a pack of cigarettes from her purse, started to take one out, and quickly returned it and the pack to her purse.

He raised his eyebrows, gave her a little half smile, and pointed toward the purse. "Good way to get us thrown out."

She nodded and neither said anything for several moments. Carla finally broke the silence.

"Frank, I've been thinking about you a lot since we saw each other at David's party. And then I couldn't believe how disappointed I was when I called you and you turned me down."

She was leading up to something that was going to complicate his life. *Don't do this, Carla,* he wanted to say.

She took off her cap and removed the pin holding her bun, letting her hair fall over her shoulders. "Frank, please don't think me crazy and hear me out. When I saw you on the street that day, my stomach did funny things. I didn't know what to make of it. Then, even though I was the one who cut things off at David's, I couldn't get you out of my mind. Still can't. I know this is going to sound crazy and your logical mind may not be able to process it, but please listen to me."

He nodded, trying to project a nonchalance he didn't feel.

"I've been offered a movie role in Italy. I turned it down at first, because I just couldn't leave the city at the time. That was a few weeks ago, and I still can't. But they've postponed shooting on it until February or March, and by that time I should be able to get away. So I've agreed to do it."

"Congratulations."

"Please don't take that tone of voice, Frank. I hate it when you do. Anyway, if they like my work the producer says he's going to want me for another picture he's planning when this is finished. The bottom line is I'll probably be over there for about six months, maybe more."

"Good. Sounds like a dream come true for you. Why are you telling me all this?"

"Because I know me. I'm going to want to see you and spend time with you before I go. I don't think I'm wrong in saying you might like that, too. But it wouldn't be right or fair to either of us. I'm going to be gone for at least a year and a lot can happen in that time. It could even be longer."

He beckoned to the waitress for the check.

"Frank, I know I'd be calling you in the next few days if you didn't call, and it would be very easy for me to resume things with you."

"Things?"

"Goddamn it, you know what I mean. So, what I'm saying is, I've got to head this off at the pass for my own good and yours. Now, having told you all this, if I should call, it shouldn't be hard for you to say no and hang up."

The waitress brought the check and Frank paid her. He turned back to Carla, studied her for a moment, and shook his head. "You know, you're right. I never could figure your logic. Hell, even when we lived together, I never really figured you out. So what's changed? I gotta go." He got up and left, resisting the urge to turn and look at her.

It was close to two in the morning before he finally fell off to sleep. It had been a crazy week.

36

ON SATURDAY MORNING, Denise was the first thought on Frank's mind. A good sign, but he couldn't get the bizarre conversation with Carla out of his mind. But then, she was always unpredictable.

Eight o'clock. Denise should be awake.

"Hello."

"Did I wake you up?"

"No, I—Frank?" Her voice went up an octave.

"It's your friendly wake-up call."

"How are you?" Back down two.

"Dennie, I'm sorry to take so long to call. No excuse. I've just been working constantly."

"The Wine Bottle Killer?"

"Yeah. Uh, I know this is not cool, I mean such short notice, but any chance I could see you tonight?"

She thought of his promise to call earlier in the week, his half promise to see her on Friday. She thought of Gina's comment about seeing him with another woman. Her first reaction was to tell him she was busy. "Sure."

"Great. Want to go out to dinner?"

"Tell you what. How about if I have you over here for dinner?"

"Sounds good to me."

"I'll probably suffer by comparison with you, so I'm not going to get too creative. But I do good things with fish. You like salmon?"

"Love it. I'll bring the wine. What time?"

"Seven?"

"See you then."

HARRY WAS WAITING for him when he got to the precinct. "Frank, we got a run-down on most of the women on Nemerow's list. Quite a cross section. Most of 'em are high-ticket call girls. Also got a few married ladies, couple actresses, a few models, woman who's a big shot in the garment business. He's even got a college student. Our friend Mr. Nemerow had an active sex life."

Frank nodded. A touch of envy in Harry's voice?

"Most of them have an alibi for that night. The married ones are scared shitless but the ones we've talked with so far can account for their whereabouts. Some of the hookers don't remember where they were. You recognize any of the names?"

Frank shook his head. "No, do you?"

"Er, yeah, I, uh, recognize a couple of the hookers."

"Any of them fit the description of the person the Iburgs saw on the elevator?"

"Yeah, a few of the hookers do. I mean roughly, you know? Tall, big women. Haven't been able to reach all of the women yet."

"Any of them wear Jean Naté?"

"Not so far."

"How about Chesbro's list?"

"Nothing but legitimate clients so far. We'll get to them all."

"OK," Frank said. "But I think Nemerow's list is our key. One way or the other, it's going to lead us to our killer."

When Frank arrived home late in the afternoon, there was a message on his machine to call his father.

Silvio answered on the first ring. "Frankie, you sign that book contract yet?"

"Yes, as a matter of fact, I did. Is that what you called about?"

"How much you get?"

He pictured his father, sitting on the edge of his chair, leaning forward, nodding his head. "Just what I told you. Seventy-five hundred and twelve percent royalties on the sales."

"You shoulda held out for more, Frankie. You're gonna write a hell of a book. Can I tell people?"

" 'Course you can. But I haven't written it yet. Just wrote my name on a contract."

They talked about the wine bottle case. Silvio wanted a complete update. But it was obvious to Frank that his sources had him pretty well filled in.

"Frankie, be careful you don't get sucked in too much on the hooker theory."

"Oh? Why not?"

"First of all, cashmere sweater doesn't sound like what your typical hooker wears. Even if she's making good money. Just too soft and wholesome a garment for a prostitute."

"And second of all?" Frank asked, still amazed at how much his father knew about important cases, even though retired.

"Secondly, Jean Naté is not a hooker kind of perfume or cologne. Again, not sexy enough."

Frank nodded. "Unless she figures she's already sexy enough. Maybe even wants to play it down. Anything else?"

"Yeah. The description of the woman with Joey Brewer does not strike me as a prostitute."

FRANK STOOD OUTSIDE Denise's door, holding a bouquet of roses in one hand and a bottle of wine in the other. The flowers were a last-minute impulse.

She opened the door and her eyes landed on the flowers.

"Frank! Roses! They're beautiful." She took them from him and set them on the table. "Frank, you are so sweet." She leaned forward and kissed him. Before he could react she was whirling around the apartment, setting out wineglasses, filling a vase with water, arranging the roses.

"Hey, slow down. Give me a minute to look at you."

She finished with the roses and turned toward him. The white pearls against her black sweater were one of the little simple touches he loved about her. Each time he saw her now she seemed to look more beautiful than the last time. She walked over to him, her hips rolling against the dark pants.

He slid his arms around her neck and they stood looking at each other. "I got a kiss for the roses. How about the wine?" He pulled her into him gently and they kissed, not with passion, but it was a kiss that promised more.

They made drinks and sat down in the living room. He looked around the room at the array of books and magazines on decorating and picked one up. "Your passion, right?"

"Yes, I like sewing and making things, decorating. I suppose my dream has always been to have my own home and spend all my time decorating it."

He waved his hand around the apartment. "Beautiful."

"Thanks," she said, took a sip of her drink, and flicked her hand across her hair. He liked the way she did that, too.

"How's your investigation coming with the Wine Bottle Killer?"

"Slowly." He held up his glass. "Where'd you learn to make such a good martini?"

"Frank, why is it you always change the subject when I ask you about your work? Don't you like to talk about it?"

"It's not that. I like my work. But it's with me twenty-four hours a day. When I'm with you, I like to forget it and focus on you."

"I know you like your work. That's why I ask you about it. The papers say you've got some good leads and that you expect, let's see, how did they put it? 'Expect to apprehend the killer soon.'"

He laughed. "Yeah. I wish. That's PR, to take a little pressure off. We're making some progress, but we're a long way from an arrest."

"Are you getting a lot of pressure?"

"Sure we are. Four murders in less than six weeks. And if you're reading the papers you know that the last victim came from a prominent family. That just adds to it. Anyway, I'd rather talk about you. What have you been doing all week?"

"Waiting to hear from you."

"Walked into that one."

She smiled. "Yep, you did."

"I should have warned you. You're dating an idiot who's married to his job. Causes a lot of problems. It's especially bad right now. I thought about you all week and I did mean to call you. I've been consumed with these murders and everything else just slipped away from me. I hope you know, Dennie, my not calling you has absolutely nothing to do with how I feel about you."

"You sure you didn't have other distractions?"

He looked up, studying her expression, trying to figure out the funny look on her face. And then he got it. "Care to tell me what you mean by that?"

"It's no big deal, Frank. I shouldn't have even mentioned it. Do you want another drink?"

He shook his head. "This may or may not be what you mean, but the only distraction I had other than this case was my ex-girlfriend, the one I lived with for a while, coming by the precinct. The distraction was short-lived, I might add."

"How'd you know that's what I meant?"

"I'm a cop. Let me ask you. How'd you know?"

She told him about Gina and he explained the reason for Carla coming by.

Denise sat for a moment, saying nothing. Frank got up and refilled their drinks, letting the silence hold.

It was Denise who broke it. "She must be very beautiful. I mean, a model and a movie actress."

He laughed. "Actually, she looks a lot like you. Tall, long dark hair, and if she's beautiful it's because she does look like you." He paused and touched her face. "I can tell you one thing, Dennie. She doesn't have anywhere near the inner beauty that I see in you."

Her eyes misted. "Thank you, Frank," she said and turned away.

"Hey, that's not something to cry over." He turned her face back to him and wiped away the tear.

"Sorry," she said. "It was just such a lovely thing to say. Let me get dinner going."

He put his arm around her and kissed her. "It's easy to say lovely things to you. Hey, we're always talking about my job. What about yours?"

"My job is great. I like it a lot. My boss tells me he's going to put me in for a promotion in a few months. I'm a little torn, though, about staying in college textbook publishing. Eventually, I think I'd like to get into trade publishing.

"A friend of mine is a senior editor with Little, Brown in Boston and has been after me to talk with them. What I do now is not a whole lot different from trade, but I'd be working with more interesting books."

Frank had raised his glass to take a sip of the martini, but stopped and set the glass down. "You'd move to Boston?"

She hesitated, sipped her drink, looked up and winked at him. "Leaving New York doesn't sound very appealing at the moment."

He loved the wink. It was a side to her he'd not seen before. "Oh, and why is that?"

She grinned. "You figure it out. You're the cop."

He smiled back at her. "I just did. Moving to Boston is a lousy idea." He took her in his arms and kissed her, this time with a passion that he hoped would underscore what he'd just said.

When they came up for air, Denise whispered, "Hmm, it does sound like a lousy idea."

They kissed again, and might have ignored dinner had the oven timer not gone off, signaling the potatoes were done. But the kisses had promised much more to come.

They ate by candlelight and adjourned to the small living room with coffee and brandy.

"You like the brandy? I remember you said it was your favorite."

"Courvoisier." He cupped her face in his hands. "You're a sweet-heart."

She studied him. "Frank, I'm curious about what happened to your relationship with Carla. How come you split after only three months?"

Another thing about her he liked. The blunt, straight-out-of-the-box way she had. Nothing subtle. "I told you earlier. I've been married to the job. That was part of it. But she wasn't around much either. We had separate, demanding lives. It was like neither of us had time for our relationship. Looking back, we never really had the opportunity to get to know each other in the way you would expect people living together would. Anyway, the breakup was a blessing in disguise for two reasons. One, it helped me to realize there's more to life than being a good cop."

"What's the other reason?"

"I met you."

She made a little noise of contentment and snuggled into him. "Are you happy, Frank?"

He thought for a minute. Who is ever happy? Jerry? Sweating out his last year of being a cop so he can have a few left to live like a normal human being? Harry? Married three times and still chasing any woman who'll drop her drawers for him? Carla? You gotta be kidding. Susan Lehman? Too busy trying to help dysfunctional people to pull her own life together.

He caressed the side of her face. "The simple answer to that question a month ago was no. Right now?" He moved her head from against his shoulder and held her face in both hands. "The answer is yes, very." And he meant it.

Her arms went around his neck and they kissed again hungrily, mouths open, searching, biting. Her tongue played in and out of his mouth while his explored hers.

"Denise," he whispered. "I want to make love to you."

"Yes, yes," she whispered.

He slid off the couch, took her by the hand, and led her into the bedroom.

37

ON SUNDAY MORNING Frank and Denise made love again. And again. He'd been wary and cautious for months, his guard always up. But this was a no-brainer. There was nothing about this woman he didn't like. What you see is what you get. And he loved what he saw.

Denise lay next to him, stroking his face. "Frank, you are a wonderful man, do you know that?"

He thought about her question last night. Right now he was feeling happier than he could remember being for a long time.

"What are you thinking?" she asked.

"I was just wondering if we should get up or . . . you know, fool around some more."

"Let's do both. First, I'll make you a super breakfast, and after that, we can fool around some more . . . all day if you're up to it," she said with a lascivious grin. "Go take a shower, while I get it started."

The breakfast—a western omelet, home fries, orange juice, toast, and coffee—was the first real breakfast he'd had in maybe a year. He wasn't counting the stuff he threw together at three o'clock in the morning. "You're almost as good a cook as I am," he said.

"Hmm. High praise."

"You know, last night you got me talking about a lot of things, even my ex-girlfriend. We never got around to you. Remember? You seduced me before we had a chance."

"Good."

"It was better than good."

"That's not what I meant."

"So, you've been in New York seven years. You're not a New Yorker; where are you from?"

"No, I'm not a New Yorker. I'm from Middlebury, Vermont."

"Vermont. Why does that not surprise me? And I bet you lived on a farm."

"Sort of."

"And you milked cows and drank a lot of it."

She smiled the shy smile when she knew he was complimenting her.

"You told me your mother and father are both dead. Do you have any other family?"

"No, I was it."

"Have there been any special men in your life?"

She dropped her eyes and turned her head away. He sensed a change in her mood.

"I'm sorry if the question was too personal. Didn't mean it to be."

She turned back to him and smiled. "You're not being too personal, Frank."

He placed his hands over hers and waited, wondering if he'd hit a sensitive chord.

"No, nobody really special. I guess I never met the right man. To tell the truth, it wasn't all that important to me." She shrugged and looked away.

A sadness had crept into her eyes, and the shrug struck him as a cover-up for the pain she seemed to be feeling. He was sorry he'd brought the whole thing up and was about to change the subject when she continued.

"I'm not an outgoing person, Frank. I've spent a lot of time alone and sometimes I think that's the way I've wanted it." She reached across the table and touched his cheek. "Until now."

He took her in his arms and held her.

She slid her arms around his neck and hugged him as if she would never let go.

His beeper went off. "Uh-oh." He checked the number, took out his cell phone, and went into the bedroom.

A few minutes later he reappeared. "It's one of my partners. I've got to go down to the station."

She frowned. "Why, what's up?"

"Don't know. But I have to go."

"Well, it must be pretty important to drag you out on Sunday. Is it about the Wine Bottle Killer?"

He took her in his arms and kissed her. "Hey, stop grilling me."

She smiled at his play on her word.

"Call me?"

"I'll call you." He hesitated. "Thanks for—thanks for being . . . you." He kissed her again and was gone.

HARRY WAS TALKING on the phone when Frank arrived at the precinct. Frank was not surprised that Jerry wasn't there. He couldn't remember the last time he'd seen Jerry out on a case on a weekend, either Saturday or Sunday.

"Frank, I think we're getting somewhere. Turns out that one Virginia Nichols in Chesbro's book happens to be Sandy Nichols, one of our friendly neighborhood hookers."

"You know her?"

"No. Don't know her. I understand she's fairly new. Hasn't been around long. Also a loner. Doesn't seem to know many of the other girls."

"She say if any of the other girls knew Chesbro?"

"Yeah. Just one that she knows of. Vickie Torrez."

"Ah, old Vickie," Frank said.

"You know Torrez?"

"Yeah. Known her for a long time. She works the streets and bars in Midtown. Tough cookie."

"Yeah, I know her, too. Anyway, I went to her apartment. The doorman says she hasn't been around for a couple days. Seems she does that."

"Does what?"

"Disappears from time to time for a few days or so. We'll find her. She can be real helpful, Frank. She knows everybody. If anybody's gonna recognize a hooker's name, Vickie will."

"What about the other one, Sandy?"

"Says she's seen Chesbro a couple or three times at her place. Strictly business. Never heard of Nemerow."

"What's she look like?"

"Sandy-colored hair like her name. She's tall, about five-nine or so. I showed her picture around all the bars in the neighborhood. Some of the bartenders recognize her. No luck in Barney's or the other two joints Joey hung out in. She says she didn't know Joey, never heard of him. She's got no solid alibi for any of the nights in question, including Chesbro."

"Let's get them both in for prints."

Harry looked uncomfortable.

"Harry, it's OK," Frank said. "Any hooker knows we can get a court order if they don't cooperate. They'll come in, believe me. We'll get prints on all of them who can't account for that night."

Harry nodded.

"Come on," Frank said. "Let's get on it."

DENISE HAD WAITED all day Monday for Frank to call, and now, late in the afternoon, feeling let down, she prepared to leave for home. The phone rang, and she picked it up on the first ring.

"Hello."

"Hi, this is Frank. Sorry to call so late, but we may have some new developments with this wine bottle case, and there's a lot going on. I did want to touch base, though. I miss you already, Dennie, and I'll call you later or tomorrow. Okay?"

"Sure," she said with mixed feelings—happy that he called, disappointed that he'd not suggested a time for them to get together. "Sure, I understand. Miss you, too."

After they hung up she closed her eyes for a moment and reflected on Saturday night and Sunday morning, wondering where their relationship might be heading.

"Hey, daydreamer, wake up."

She turned to see Gina standing in the doorway. She walked in and slumped heavily into the chair. "Been a long day. How are you doing? You still seeing that gorgeous cop?"

"Yes."

"I saw his picture in the paper the other day. He's working on that wine bottle case. How come you didn't mention it?"

"I saw no reason to."

"He ever talk about it?"

"No, not really."

Gina sat as though waiting for more conversation from Denise. When none came she said, "Well, I'm out of here. Got a heavy date." She hauled herself up and left.

38

COME ON, FRANK." Harry Leonard stopped at Frank's desk. "The doorman at Vickie's apartment called. She just got home."

Frank grabbed his coat and they took the stairs two at a time, their shoes clacking in unison like tap dancers'.

"I DON'T KNOW what you guys are buggin' me for. You got no right." Vickie Torrez sat in her living room, chain-smoking. "Harry, you know me for a long time. I never give nobody trouble. You know that."

Harry wished she wouldn't cross her legs like she did. He could see all the way up her thigh and it wasn't helping his concentration.

"I know that, Vickie," he said. "Nobody's suspecting you of anything. You tell us that you and your boyfriend were in Puerto Rico the night Chesbro was killed, I believe you. And I'm sure you can prove it. The only reason we want to talk to you is I know you know everybody.

I figure you can help us. Who else did Chesbro see besides you? Any of the girls know Mr. Nemerow?"

Vickie squashed her cigarette out and put another in her mouth. Frank beat her to the lighter on the table and flicked it under her cigarette. She peered down the cigarette and smiled at him.

He looked around the small apartment. Cheap pieces of furniture plopped down in no order. Functional and threadbare. A picture of Jesus on the living room wall. Vickie didn't seem to be a big success in her work.

Her clothing reflected her profession. Even relaxing at home, she wore the uniform. Tight miniskirt, peekaboo blouse, long earrings, a musky availability about her.

"Vickie, what kind of perfume do you wear?" Frank asked.

"Perfume? Why?"

Frank smiled. "You smell nice. That's why. I'm just curious what it is."

She softened and let a flicker of a smile escape. "I wear Opium. Glad you like it." Again a smile. She was warming up to Frank.

"I guess I like all kinds of perfume," Frank said. "If I had a favorite, though, I'd have to say Jean Naté. It's what my grandmother wore. I always remember it as a kid."

Vickie looked quizzically at him. "Your grandmother?"

"Yes. She's gone now, but I can never think of her without thinking of that wonderful scent."

"Well, nobody wears that shit anymore. Sorry about your grandmother."

"It's too bad that nobody wears it anymore, though. Hard to believe. Nobody?"

"Shit, no. It's got no sex appeal, you know?"

Frank nodded and looked at Harry.

"We've got no quarrel with you, Vickie," Frank said. "Nobody harasses you, do they?"

Vickie shook her head.

"And you don't want anybody to start now, do you?" Harry asked.

She shook her head again.

"OK, then. Let's have some names."

Vickie's demeanor changed. She was no longer cool, no longer flirting with Frank. She lit another cigarette, even though she'd just lit one and it was sitting on the ashtray. Frank noticed her hand shake when she lit it.

"I ain't talking to you no more. Get out of my apartment."

"I DON'T GET it, Frank," Harry Leonard said, as he finished off the last of his second cheeseburger. "Vickie's always been cooperative. I've never seen her like this."

"She's afraid of something or somebody." Frank watched Harry as he wiped the ketchup from his face, and remembered why he promised himself not to eat with him again. "Harry, you ever eat anything besides cheeseburgers?"

"Sure I do."

"Oh, yeah. I forgot. French fries, cole slaw, apple pie, and ice cream, right?"

"Right."

"You don't look like you're putting any weight on."

"I'm not."

"What about your lady?"

Harry gave him a wary glance. "What about her?"

"Well, you told me she wanted you to get some meat on you. All that crap you've been eating, you're still a bag of bones."

"She's not complaining. Still likes my stamina. Must be the cheeseburgers."

"Whatever it takes. Anyway, I think we leaned on Vickie as much as we could at her place. Tomorrow we'll get her to the station."

"Something's bugging her, Frank. We'll get it out of her tomorrow. I gotta go. You coming?"

"No, you go ahead," Frank said. "I'm going to have another cup of coffee and try to think through some of this stuff."

"OK," Harry said. "You can get the tab then. Thanks for the lunch."

The lunch crowd was gone and the small coffee shop was quiet. Frank sipped his coffee in the booth, grateful for the solitude.

Life was never simple. He missed Denise and realized that she was getting to him. And he was letting it happen, going with the flow— and feeling good about it.

And Jerry. He was drifting more and more into the background, running scared. Nail somebody, anybody.

The case was getting to him, too. They really didn't have much to go on. They might get something more out of Vickie tomorrow, but he was beginning to question the whole notion of a hooker being the perp. Silvio's right. Hookers don't wear Jean Naté and cashmere sweaters. And the untreated hair fibers they'd found. There's not a hooker alive who doesn't mess around with her hair color. What's bothering Vickie?

And Beatty. Didn't seem the type to pick up with a prostitute. He and his killer were looking at books. Not your activity of choice when you bring a lady of the streets to your pad.

And why would a hooker bother with Joey Brewer? The bartenders said they avoided him like the plague. Never had any money and was a deadbeat. Owed most of them. Revenge?

Nemerow. A different story. No common street girls. No Vickies. But a high-class call girl would be his style. Expensive, exotic perfumes. Sexy, turn-on clothing.

He'd worked so long with Jerry, he'd absorbed his intuition. And it was telling him the killer is overdue for the next one.

39

FRANK AWOKE FROM a troubled sleep and looked at his watch face glowing in the dark. Twelve-thirty A.M. He was wide awake and something was bothering him. He wasn't sure exactly what. There were so many things.

But something rattled around in his head. It was there as he was waking up. What the hell is it?

Vickie. Vickie Torrez. Tough woman. Been on the streets for ten years. Not the kind who gets frightened by a couple of cops talking to her. She'd been in and out of the station a dozen times over the years, always cocky, tough, a lady with an attitude. She knows she's not a suspect in the Chesbro murder. Not with an airtight alibi. Not really a suspect in any of them, and even if she was, it wouldn't faze her. And it sure wouldn't cause her to act the way she did when they asked her for names. She's afraid of something or somebody.

And then he got a brainstorm.

———

FIRST THING IN the morning Frank arranged a witness warrant for Vickie Torrez to come down to the precinct and answer more questions. He picked her up at noon. She was surly and uncommunicative. He tried a little small talk in the car but she didn't respond, kept her back to him, sitting sideways, biting her cuticles, looking out the window. They rode to the precinct in silence.

Frank and Vickie and Harry Leonard sat at the long table in the conference room. It was also the interrogation room. What they called it depended on who was in there and why.

They sipped coffee for a few minutes before Vickie broke the silence. "The fuck you want with me, draggin' me down here like this?"

Frank watched her nibbling on her nails, eyes flashing around the room, already on her third cigarette. He wasn't looking forward to this.

"Vickie, you know and I know you aren't yourself. I've been around you too long. I know you. So does Harry. We've always been fair with you, haven't we, Vickie?"

No response. Only her glare.

"You've always been cooperative and straight with us. That's why we never crowd you."

Harry sipped his coffee and eyed Frank. He liked watching him operate.

"Vickie, I know why you're afraid. I know why you're not yourself. I know what you're hiding." He stopped and stared hard at her.

The room was not warm, but perspiration rolled off Vickie's forehead into her eyes. She dabbed at them, smearing mascara. The perspiration trickling down her face turned light brown.

"Vickie, everybody knows your turf. You don't stray more than a few blocks. Forty-fourth, Forty-fifth, Forty-sixth, Seventh Avenue, Eighth Avenue. That about right, Vickie?"

She stared sullenly, looking more and more like a cornered animal. Harry offered her a clean handkerchief. She refused it.

"Vickie," Frank continued, "five weeks ago, a man was found in an alley off Forty-fourth Street. He'd been knifed to death. Last night when you were acting funny and then clammed up on us, it bothered me. It just wasn't like you. So, I got to thinking. And guess what I thought of?"

She took five or six quick, deep draws on her cigarette. Her eyes searched the room.

"Vickie, there was a man on the street that night at about the time of the murder in the alley. After our little talk last night, I called the man again. He was kind enough to come by this morning and I showed him a picture of you. You know what, Vickie? He says he saw you on the street that night. At about that time."

"Fuck you, Russo." She was on her feet, shaking violently. "I didn't do that," she screamed. "You're not gonna pin that on me." She sat down and popped up again. Harry stood up next to her, ready for anything.

Frank remained sitting. "We've been taking a lot of heat on this, Vickie, Harry and I. The man was an important businessman. The chief is busting our asses to arrest somebody on this." He stood up. "And we're getting goddamned sick of the pressure. You know how easy it would be to nail you for this, Vickie?"

He walked over to the door. "Stick around, Vickie, I'm going to get our witness back in here to take a really good look at you." He turned to Harry. "Shouldn't take much to pin this one down, Harry." And he left.

DENISE LOOKED AT her watch. She'd been doing it all day. Three o'clock. Late enough. Mike was away anyway. Time to go home, relax in a nice, long hot bath. Wash her hair, do her nails, maybe take a nap.

She turned off her computer and dropped by Gina's to tell her she was leaving in case anyone asked. Her secretary was rummaging around on Gina's desk looking for something. "She's not here, Denise. Didn't come in today. I haven't heard from her all day."

WHEN FRANK RETURNED to the conference room, Vickie was crying. Her eyes were red and puffy. Her shoulders sagged and she was no longer glaring. She recoiled when Frank entered and gave him a frightened look.

"Sorry about this, Vickie," Frank said softly.

"You get him?" Harry asked.

"Yeah," Frank said. He sat down and said nothing more to Vickie. Waiting.

Vickie began sobbing. "I didn't do it. It wasn't me." She squeezed the words out through the heaving and sniffling.

Frank went over to her and put his arm around her. "You want to tell us about it, Vickie?"

She nodded, and between sobs described the night with Crystal and Crystal's trip into the alley with the john. And she told them about the yelling and arguing and what she found when she went into the alley.

"He tried to screw Crystal out of the money. I guess she went bananas. When I got there, she was just pullin' the knife out of him. And then she stuck it in again. I tried to run but she grab me and hold the knife at my throat. She tell me I ever say anything she kill me. She say even if the cops have her, she knows people who will get me for her." She hunched her shoulders and covered her eyes with her hands.

Frank called in a policewoman. "Stay here with Vickie. Get her anything she wants. Come on, Harry."

They went into Jerry's office, which was empty. "You know, Harry," Frank said, "there are times when I really hate this fucking job."

"Frank, how did you know Vickie was connected to the murder of that guy?" Harry asked.

"I didn't. I knew something was bugging her bad. And then, I don't know. I just had a hunch. The guy was found in her area. Shit, she practically lives on those two or three streets. You can walk down to Forty-fourth Street and make book that you'll see Vickie cruising along. Why should that night have been any different? So I just threw it at her. What'd I have to lose?"

"And the guy, the witness you had in here? The guy you went to call. Just bullshit?"

Frank nodded. "I doubted Vickie would have killed the guy. She's not the type. But I was hoping she might know something."

"And you hit the jackpot. That was Tommy Sullivan's case, wasn't it?"

"Still is. He talked to Vickie early on but nothing came of it. Anyway, let's find Crystal, fast."

Harry called the number Vickie had given them. He got the machine. "Come on, let's get over there," he said.

"I can't," Frank said. He held up his hand to quiet Harry. "I've got to go downtown with Jerry. Nolan's on us again." He looked at his watch. "In fact, I've got to fly now. Find Crystal. Use as many people as you need. Get inside her apartment if she's not there. Get a search warrant. Look for pictures of her, cashmere sweaters, Jean Naté. Take the pictures over to Barney's. Show 'em to Billy.

"We're going to find her and get her in for prints. I've got a feeling we'll find some matches. I should be home by nine or so. Call me if you get anything or need me."

THE WOMAN LAY quietly across her bed. She was tired. Looking back it seemed she'd been tired since that night with Jack Beatty, when all the anger, all the memories that had lain buried for so many years tumbled out.

She knew there was rage inside her. The doctors had prepared her, helped her to understand and accept it. She knew she hated him, but she never knew how much until that night with Beatty. Now, she just wanted it all to end, the only way it could, and she could move on with her life.

She had been aware of his presence for weeks: the phone calls, the phony UPS man, the times on the street where she sensed him so strongly, she could almost reach out and touch him.

The phone rang. She picked it up halfway through the first ring. "Hello." A harshness in her voice. "Oh, hi! A drink?" She was about to say no. A drink was the last thing she felt like. But something made her say yes. "OK. See you there in twenty minutes."

Fifteen minutes later she emerged from the building. She stood on the sidewalk, looking in both directions, her head moving back and forth. The street was empty, resting quietly in that period between workers returning home and the night crowd getting ready for an evening out. A light wind blew the few straggling leaves of late fall across the street and out of sight. A street vendor beckoned her to look at his ten-dollar cashmere scarves. She shook her head and continued walking, enjoying the comparative quiet of the evening. By the time she reached the bar, she was looking forward to a relaxing drink.

The place was big and comfortable-looking. Large easy chairs and tables were lined along a row of windows with booths along another wall and more tables and chairs grouped closer to a grand piano. A pianist played softly. The long, semicircular bar stood at the end of the room up two stairs.

She spotted her friend, sitting at a table off in a corner in semi-darkness. Comfortably secluded. The way she liked it. They waved at each other and she moved quickly across the room and sat down.

They chatted over drinks, but she was edgy, tugging at her hair, changing positions, taking quick little sips of her wine. Her friend noticed.

"Rough day today?"

"Yes, sorry. Afraid I'm not very good company tonight. Hopefully, the wine will relax me."

It didn't. Two men across the room—leering, nodding at her, never taking their eyes off her, ruining her efforts to relax with a friend—made it impossible. The hostility began building.

FORTY MINUTES LATER they signaled for the waiter. He brought the check and they left. The two women stood in front, chatting for a few minutes before parting and walking in opposite directions.

She walked aimlessly along the avenue, nearly bumping into a passing couple, not certain where she was going, her mind drifting, something building in her. She approached another bar, not unlike the one she had just left, stopped, looked in the window, and entered.

THE NEW PLACE was dark and faceless. The night at Barney's flashed vaguely across her mind—a hundred years ago. She tensed the muscles in her genital area, systematically applying and releasing pressure. Her eyes closed.

After ordering a white wine, she noticed two well-dressed men enter. They stood for a moment, scanning the bar. She looked away and sipped her wine.

"May I join you?"

She turned to see one of the two men smiling at her.

Her practiced eye evaluated him—dark brown curly hair, neatly trimmed mustache, designer eyeglasses, stylish topcoat and scarf, medium build. She returned to her drink, lost again in her drifting thoughts.

"Mind if I join you, miss?"

She turned and faced the man who had just entered.

He nodded toward the empty stool next to her. "May I?"

She stared at him with blank eyes and turned back to her drink.

He removed his coat and sat down. "Chilly out there," he said, setting his coat and scarf on the empty stool next to him.

She ignored him.

"My name's Dave," he said, extending his hand. "What's yours?"

Again she turned, this time more alert, more responsive. "My name? My name is . . . my friends call me Lucky."

Dave laughed. "That's a nice nickname."

She didn't respond and they sat in silence for a couple of minutes, Dave thinking of some new approach to try to get her talking. "Hmm, you smell good. What kind of perfume are you wearing?"

He seemed to have struck a chord as she smiled for the first time and replied softly, "It's called Jean Naté."

He nodded toward her nearly empty glass. "Can I buy you another?"

She studied him again and her dead eyes showed some life. "Yes, why not?"

IT WAS TEN o'clock when Frank arrived home. No word from Harry yet. He checked his messages. One from Susan Lehman and one from his father. He hauled out the notes on his book and turned on the computer. But nothing would come. He picked up the phone and called Denise. No answer. After leaving a message he tried her cell phone. No answer.

He felt frustrated, tired, and suddenly lonely. He eyed the phone again but left it alone, took a shower, had a nightcap, and climbed into bed. Wide awake, his mind whirled. He sat up, picked up the phone, and tried Denise again. No answer. He hung up, started to put the light out, but instead dialed Carla's number. Her machine told him to leave his number and she'd call him back. He tried Susan but again no luck. He hung up and thought of Denise, glad he had called and made a date for tomorrow night, smiled, and put out the light.

THEY HAD BEEN sitting together for nearly thirty minutes. The bar was warm, and she had slipped her coat off her shoulders and let it hang over the bar stool. Dave had difficulty taking his eyes off the firm breasts protruding from her sweater. The V formed by her crotch looked tight and inviting. He coughed and took a pull on his beer. Feeling confident in the relationship he thought they had developed, he gently caressed the back of her neck.

She stared straight ahead, feeling his eyes moving up and down her. He was as disgusting as all the rest.

"Lucky. What're you thinking about? You keep drifting away. Talk to me." He put his hands on her shoulders and turned her toward him, leaning his face in close to hers. His hands went up and cupped her face. "You're a pretty lady, Lucky."

She recoiled from him.

"Hey, you look so serious. How about a smile for Dave?"

She studied him. The smile came, but it wasn't for him.

"That's better. You're even prettier when you smile." He smiled back at her.

She blinked. The room turned hazy and she felt dizzy. Slowly, the room came back into focus and he was on his feet holding her.

"Hey, Lucky. I think maybe you've had just a tad too much wine. How about if we go outside and get you some fresh air?" He held her shoulders, nodding. "Would you like that?"

She nodded.

Dave paid the bill, helped her on with her coat, and they left. Outside, the fresh air began clearing her mind, reinforcing what she had decided in the bar. "Dave, I feel a lot better now. Can we go somewhere?"

Dave's eyes lit up. "You bet we can, Lucky. Where would you like to go? Shall we go to your place?"

"I don't take men to my apartment. How about yours?"

Dave grinned and shook his head. "I live across the bridge in Jersey. Would you like to go to a hotel?"

She thought for a moment. "OK, but can we walk for a while, help me clear my head? It's such a nice night and the fresh air feels good."

"Sure, that's fine."

Two blocks later they came to a liquor store. "Dave, can we buy some wine?"

41

FRANK HAD GIVEN up trying to sleep. He was up, sitting in his kitchen drinking coffee. Not too smart; now he would never get any sleep. The goddamn case kept eating away at him. The only decent lead they had was Crystal Wilcox, but where the hell was she?

He checked his address book and picked up the phone. Gingi Nelson considered herself a friend of Crystal's. He punched in her number and was surprised when she answered. "Gingi, this is Frank Russo. Hope I'm not calling too late."

Her voice went up a couple of octaves. "Frank, my God, what a surprise. 'Course it's not too late. Hell, it's only ten-thirty. I might even go out for a while."

Frank smiled, knowing what she meant. "Gingi, I'm trying to locate Crystal Wilcox. I just need to talk with her about something. Any idea where I might find her tomorrow?" He waited through her hesitation.

"Have you tried calling her?"

"Yeah, never get an answer. I know you and she are sort of pals, and I thought you might know how I could reach her."

"I don't know, Frank. Whenever we get together she's the one who calls me. And yeah, we are somewhat friendly—as friendly, I guess, as anybody can get with her. Why are you looking for her?"

"No big deal. I just want to talk to her. When did you see her last?"

"I don't know. About a week ago. We had a couple of drinks together."

"What time?"

"Hmm, it was about eight or so."

"Where did you have your drinks?"

"Place on the West Side, Midtown. Seasons. Nice place. She likes it there."

"How'd she seem?"

Gingi laughed. "She was pissed off. She usually is about something."

"Why was she pissed off?"

"Well, I guess she was holed up in a fancy hotel suite with one of her rich dudes. Getting high on some coke, champagne, room service. You know, the whole bit. She was going to milk the guy for a couple of days or more."

"And?"

"The guy gets a call from his wife. Their kid got hit by a car and he has to take off right away and go home to Chicago. So he checks out and her little gig is over. I mean, I guess she got some money from him but she had big plans for this guy. Anyway, that's the last time I saw her."

"What hotel was it?"

"She didn't say."

"What time did you leave the bar?"

"We weren't there that long. Maybe an hour. Yeah, I'd say we left about nine."

"Where'd you go?"

"I went home. I don't know where she went. That was it. That's the last time I saw her."

"OK. Don't leave town, Gingi," Frank said. "I might want to talk with you some more. Oh, by the way, do you know if Crystal dyes her hair?" He waited through another pause.

"You sure do ask some funny questions, Frank. Anyway, yeah, she dyes her hair. I never knew a hooker who didn't. She's had three different colors since I've known her. How come you want to know all this stuff?"

"I'm nosy. You wear a diaphragm?"

"You want to find out for yourself?"

"Gingi! I'm on duty."

"You're always on duty."

"Tough life, being a cop."

AFTER BUYING THE wine, Dave and Lucky entered a small, vintage fifties hotel just off West Forty-third Street. It wasn't fancy but it was close and neither of them seemed to care.

When they entered the hotel's small lobby, she kept her head turned away from the front desk and waited at the elevator with her back to the clerk as Dave registered.

They got off the elevator on the fifth floor and she followed slowly behind him as he searched the door numbers for their room. Her heart pounded. She was going on pure adrenaline now.

They padded along the carpet in the semidarkness of the hallway. "Here we are, Lucky. Five-o-nine." He unlocked the door, snapped on the light, and they entered.

She stood at the door watching him set the two bottles of wine on a table next to a small sofa. The room reflected the age of the hotel. The rest of the furniture consisted of a queen-size bed, two bedside tables, each holding a lamp, a bureau, a television cabinet, and a small desk. The decor was immaterial to her.

"Open the wine, Dave, while I slip in here for a minute." Inside the bathroom she rationally thought through her strategy. She knew what to do. It had become that simple—even simpler with Nemerow, who handed himself to her on a silver platter. All of them pigs.

She took her time in the bathroom, letting the need build, enjoying the sensuality of the anticipation. She was in her element now, ready.

She smiled, opened the door, and entered the bedroom. The room was now in near darkness, the only light coming from one of the bedside lamps. The two wine bottles remained on the table, barely visible.

The soft sounds of Frank Sinatra singing "Strangers in the Night" drifted across the room. Dave stood in the middle of the room and nodded toward the TV-radio cabinet. "Beautiful song, Lucky." He moved toward her and took her in his arms. She recoiled, but he was strong and pulled her into him.

"Shall we dance?" he asked, and clumsily moved her across the room.

Oh, God! she thought. *I can't believe this.*

Dave continued moving her across the floor. He held her body close to his, slid his face across hers, and kissed her on the lips.

She gasped and broke away from him.

"Slow down, Dave," she said. "Let's just relax for a while—have some wine and let things develop nice and slow."

The cloying music continued, now barely audible, competing with Dave's harsh, heavy breathing as he pulled her into him again. "Hmm," he purred. "Lucky, I want you." He began maneuvering her toward the bed.

The moon broke through the clouds and beamed into the window, briefly illuminating the room before disappearing again. Dave continued directing their slow dance toward the bed.

Lucky eyed the wine bottles as she and Dave moved farther from them. They stood over the bed, Dave dancing them in place.

He leaned their bodies toward the bed, but she broke away from him and turned toward the bathroom. "Dave, honey, I'm sorry, but I have to pee again. Sometimes I get a little nervous."

He started to speak, but she moved quickly into the bathroom and shut the door, pondering what to do. She was not about to get on the bed with that pig without her weapon.

"I'll be out in a minute, Dave. Are you in bed yet?"

"Yes, I am, Lucky. Now get out here. I miss you," he purred.

She stood at the door, took a deep breath, opened it, and stepped into the bedroom.

Love was just a glance away, a warm embracing dance away.

Dave was not in bed. She started toward the table with the wine bottles when a voice came out of the semidarkness.

"Hello, Tookie."

42

FRANK POURED HIMSELF another drink. He was still wide awake, his mind too active to let him get any sleep.

He thought of Susan Lehman and the last time he saw her. She had come by his class again, and they'd had a drink and a bite to eat. Their conversation inevitably got around to the serial killings.

"How are you coming on the Wine Bottle Killer, Frank?"

"I think we're getting close but no cigar yet. We're pretty sure it's a woman, one who may have been traumatized as a child. Any thoughts on that?"

"Of course I would have some thoughts. That happens to be one of my areas of interest."

"I didn't know that. I thought your main shtick was dealing with screwed-up people like me."

She smiled and touched his hand. "You never asked, Frank. All the time I was counseling you, you were my focus. And since we saw each other only once after you stopped coming—when I tracked you down outside your classroom—why would you have known? Anyway, I thought the department had a staff profiler."

"We do, but she's been on indefinite sick leave since the first murder and hasn't been replaced yet. So . . . what are your thoughts?"

"Well, first of all, serial killers have often been characterized as antisocial-personality types manifesting aggressive, hostile behavior and have a tendency to be loners. But not all—remember Ted Bundy?

"Some serial murderers can appear to be well-adjusted persons leading rather normal lives. Their closest friends and family members have been shocked by their confessions of multiple homicides."

"Go on."

"Well, what I'm saying, Frank, is that some offenders may never reveal enough of themselves in daily life to allow the identification of their particular personality disorders. It's often only in hindsight that we're able to identify their fatal flaws.

"I know you're familiar with the case of Edmund Kemper, who hated his mother, and because of his feelings toward her he went on a killing rampage. When he eventually killed his mother and decapitated her, he believed that having finally resolved the conflict with her, his rages would subside and he would no longer feel the need to kill. Anyway, I'm probably not telling you anything you don't already know. But you asked."

"Susan, you never cease to amaze me."

"Oh, yeah? Then why do you stay away so long?"

"Good question."

"Yes, it is. Anyway, this one is on the house—no, not really. You can pay me back by taking me out to dinner to a real restaurant. This one doesn't count. I'll look forward to your call."

————

LUCKY STAGGERED, THEN stopped, trying to control the harsh breathing pounding inside her and the vertigo. She took a tentative step toward the table holding the bottles, but the figure stepped out of the shadows and stood between her and the table. She now saw him clearly.

Her knees buckled. The person facing her was not Dave, with whom she had entered the room.

The man now facing her was totally bald, no mustache, no designer eyeglasses. An ugly leer had replaced Dave's friendly smile.

Her mind drifted back to the house on Hathaway Street, the beautiful woman lying bleeding on the floor, her father's chilling words in the courtroom. She tried to think clearly but her mind remained fixated on another time, another place. And she was afraid.

He looked toward the two wine bottles. "You were going to hurt your daddy, weren't you?"

She began to cry and started backing away.

He moved closer, and she noticed something in his hand. Something in the other, too?

Her father raised a brown wig and mustache, then dropped them on the floor. "Don't need these now, do I?"

Something in the other hand. What was it? She tried to focus, but distant echoes got in the way.

He moved toward the table lamp and switched it on. "Come to me, Tookie. Daddy has missed his little girl."

She held her ground, but she grew dizzy, and again, her knees threatened to give out.

"I've been watching you, Tookie. I know you've been bad. You're not the daughter I thought you were, Tookie. No, you're a very bad person. And you disappointed me, Tookie."

He continued slowly moving toward her.

"I followed you to those bars tonight—even spent my money buying clothes to impress you." The voice soft, soothing. "Did I impress you, Tookie?"

She began to moan, a sound that quickly accelerated into a keening, little girl's wail, while she stood helplessly, watching him move toward her. And then she saw what was in his other hand.

Her father held a knife, its long ugly blade gleaming under the lamp's light. He crouched and moved it expertly back and forth, smiling, enjoying the moment. The moonlight flickered in and out of the room, and the soft sounds of Sinatra crooning "Summer Wind" mocked the ugly scene.

She instinctively backed away, but her mind continued to drift in the eerie silence of the room, broken only by the *click, click* of the ceiling fan and the hissing of the old radiator.

Her eyes glazed over. She was back again into that other time—other place.

Gale moved slowly toward her and stopped. He spoke softly, gently. "It's Daddy, Tookie. Daddy's here. Come to me, Tookie."

Tears formed in her eyes and trickled down her cheeks. She nodded and walked toward him.

"Daddy missed you, Tookie. He wants you to take off your clothes and come to him." He motioned her forward, slowly bending his palm toward himself. "You hear me, Tookie? Come to Daddy."

She nodded and shuffled toward her father until she was close enough to smell his foul breath. Another time, another place.

"That's my girl. Now, take off your clothes for Daddy," the voice commanded.

Slowly, never able to move her eyes from him, she began removing her clothes. When she was down to her bra and panties, she stopped.

"Take off your bra, sweetheart. Do it for Daddy."

She sobbed and took a step backward.

"Tookie!"

Still sobbing, she obeyed her father, unhooked her bra, and let it slide to the floor. Gale's tongue flicked across his lips.

43

JERRY BLODGETT SAT in his den, chewing on an unlit cigar, too keyed up to go to bed and try to sleep. It seemed like his entire career hung in the balance with this fucking Wine Bottle Killer. He knew he was getting paranoid, but what the hell was he supposed to feel with the kind of pressure and cheap shit being laid on him now after all the good years he'd put in?

He wasn't the type to whine, but goddamn it, it just wasn't right. He wanted to close this case so bad he could taste it. But somehow, they had to get a break. Just give me something, he thought. Anything. He put the cigar down, lumbered off to the kitchen, and opened the refrigerator. He would have a cold beer and then take a shot at trying to get some sleep.

———

PAUL GALE CARESSED his daughter's face. "Now Daddy wants you to move over to the bed and sit down."

Still staring blankly, she moved sideways to the bed.

He moved along with her. "Good girl. Now sit down."

She hesitated and searched her father's eyes. He nodded and spoke softly. "Sit down, Tookie. Daddy wants you to sit down."

She did as she was told. Her father positioned himself behind her and sat with the knife at the back of her neck.

"That's my girl. Now, I want you to lean against Daddy, and take off your panties."

She felt his hot breath against her neck and the ugly sounds from so long ago. Tears trickled down her face; she was a little girl again alone in her small bedroom, obeying her Daddy.

His hands moved up and down her body, and she heard the words again. "That's my Tookie. Daddy's here to tuck you in. You know Daddy loves you, don't you, Tookie? Yes," he purred. "Daddy loves you."

She wanted to cry out for her mother, but he would hurt her if she did. She closed her eyes and sobbed.

Her father continued moving his hands along her body, caressing, fondling. She smelled the whiskey and beer and his foul body and she was afraid, knowing he would do the dirty things to her.

Gale was enjoying himself. He now realized it was what he'd been really wanting all along. He continued caressing her, gently stroking the female softness of her pubic hair.

Slowly, gently, he spread her legs farther apart and trailed his fingers along her inner thighs. "That's the girl, sweetheart," his voice now hoarse and wheezy, "Daddy's gonna take good care of you." He was in no rush. He had waited years for this moment. His hand moved back and forth along her stomach, slowly moving downward. And then he penetrated her with his fingers.

A scream of horror and rage erupted from somewhere inside her. Her arm flailed and her hand wrapped around the lamp on the bed stand. Before her father could move, she smashed the full force of the heavy lamp backward into his face. Again, she swung the lamp flush into his mouth.

His lips parted and a tooth, surrounded by blood, dangled like a piece of spittle.

She rolled away, turned, and swung the lamp again. The tooth tore from his mouth and arced across the room, trailed by a bloody spray.

With the last blow, the lamp slipped from her hand and rolled over the side of the bed. She stared down at her father. Blood gushed from the hole formerly occupied by the tooth. Thick clots of blood and bone seeped from where his nose had been. The bulging eyes were no longer visible, covered with blood and pieces of peeling flesh.

Miraculously he still held the knife. Even more miraculously he sat up and moved his arm clumsily toward her. She lashed out at his hand and the knife fell to the floor. He struggled toward it, groping, and she pushed him off the bed. He fell on his back next to the radiator.

Quick as a cat, she straddled him, pounding his head against the radiator.

That was when she saw the knife. She drove it into his stomach. He gave a little cough, and fell sideways onto the floor.

She crawled to her feet and stared down at the thing that had been her father. He was dead. It was over. But she wasn't finished with him.

44

GERARD WILLIAMS, THE night clerk at the Haven Hotel, arrived for duty promptly at 7:00 P.M. As usual, Ned Haskins, the day man, was only semisober when Gerard arrived to relieve him. "Hey, Williams, where the hell you been, pal?" Haskins's speech was slurred, and he stumbled, making way for Gerard behind the counter.

"Ned, you reek of booze again. Don't you ever stay sober?"

"Who wants to stay sober, workin' this dump? Guy needs a coupla pops get through the day here. Goddamn maid didn't even show up to clean the rooms."

"What? Did you call a temporary service?"

"Nope."

"You mean none of the rooms have been cleaned today?"

"Nope."

Gerard picked up the check-in-checkout register. "How about checkouts?"

"Um, I don't know. Yeah, I guess we had a few checkouts."

Gerard looked again at Haskins and realized he was worse than usual. "Ned, you're drunk. You've been drinking all day. Get out of here."

Haskins grabbed his bottle and stumbled out the door.

Gerard called a temporary agency he'd used in the past and they promised to have a maid there by 6:00 A.M. If the hotel's own maid showed up, all the better. They'd have the place shaped up in no time.

He checked the register and confirmed that eleven rooms had apparently been occupied. Five of them held permanent residents. So he was only dealing with six rooms. He still had nine rooms free that he could rent until the others were made up in the morning. Things weren't so bad after all.

DENISE ARRIVED AT Frank's promptly at seven. She stood in the doorway, a tentative, uncertain smile on her face, a tiredness in her eyes that dulled their usual sparkle. "Hi!"

He hugged her and everything else in his life stood still. "It's OK. You can come in."

She leaned forward and kissed him gently on the lips.

He wanted more, pulled her into him, and kissed her hungrily. He hadn't realized how much he'd missed her.

"Well." She caught her breath. "I'll have to drop in more often."

He handed her a glass of wine and stood for a moment admiring her. She wore a pale blue turtleneck, form-fitting jeans, little or no makeup—hard to tell with her—and a pair of whimsical multicolored earrings.

"You look like a college kid."

She slumped into a chair at the kitchen table. "I don't feel like one. God, last night I slept like I was drugged. Come to think of it, I was. I wasn't feeling well and took a sleeping pill. It's had me punchy all day."

"Well, you look terrific tonight. How come you weren't feeling well last night?"

"Oh, I was OK . . . I guess. I think it was more disappointment than anything else." She paused for a moment, letting it sink in. "After you left Sunday, I thought about you a lot. I know you called me on Monday, but still, I missed you. I don't know. I guess I felt . . . a little let down, and just wanted to sleep." She wrinkled her brow and grinned. "Like I said, I missed you."

She just laid it right out. No subtlety. No games. Just blunt honesty. "Sorry, Dennie." He really was sorry. Sorry he'd let two more days go by without seeing her or even talking to her. She was the best part of his life and he was screwing it up. "No excuses. Just the same old reason. My days and nights get away from me. Last night I had an early night. Got home about ten. That's when I tried to call you."

"I know, Frank. Intellectually, I know why you don't call. But I'm a woman. I don't always think intellectually, when it comes to . . ." She groped for a word but let it drop. "How's the case coming? Any progress?"

"A little."

"Want to talk about it?"

He grinned. "No."

"OK. Want to pour me some more wine?"

"Yep. And in a little while, I'm going to make you some of the best pasta you've ever had."

"You're so modest when it comes to your cooking."

"Nothing to be modest about. How does pasta with fresh tomatoes, capers, garlic, black olives, and a touch of lemon sound?"

"Ah, putanesca."

"Right. Know how it got its name?"

She shook her head.

"The *putanas,* the Italian harlots. In between tricks, if they got hungry, they'd whip this little number up because it was quick and easy. Then back to work."

"You're a fountain of knowledge."

"Yeah," he said, and slid his arm around her waist. She leaned into him and he felt the heat coming from her. It would be a late dinner.

AT 6:05 A.M. the maid from Diamond arrived. Gerard gave her the list of rooms to be made up. There were two on the second floor, three on the third, and one on the fifth. She decided to start on the fifth and work her way down.

IT WAS 7:00 A.M. when Frank's phone exploded in his ear. The obnoxious ring was relentless.

"Frank, the phone." Denise's voice was foggy with sleep. She barely heard him answer it. Her mind floated with memories of last night, the spontaneous passion of their lovemaking, dinner, and sweet conversation, followed by more gentle, loving sex.

"Dennie. I've got to leave right away. Something's come up." He was out of bed and moving toward the shower.

She sat up on her elbows. "What is it?"

"Can't say right now." He closed the bathroom door and was out of the shower and dressed in ten minutes. He said nothing, nor did she, as she lay in bed watching him.

When he was dressed, he sat on the bed and took her in his arms. "Last night was wonderful. Perfect in every way." He kissed her. "And so are you." He started to pull away, but she held him.

"Frank, what is it? Can't you tell me?"

"Nope, no time. Gotta go."

She still held him in her arms. "Frank, last night was wonderful. I . . ." Her voice trailed off.

He hugged her for several moments, thinking of what she wanted to say, but didn't. He took her face in his hands and studied her. Something in her eyes. A sadness. Was she waiting for him to respond to what she was attempting to tell him? In a perfect world he would have taken off the clothes he had just put on, and snuggled back into bed with her and made love again. And again. Instead, he kissed her gently and released her. "Bad time to leave, Dennie, but I have to. I'll call you tonight."

She nodded blankly, managed a little smile and a half wave. After a long hot shower she dressed slowly, and left his apartment.

45

THE SCENE INSIDE room 509 of the Haven Hotel was not pretty. They never were. Even with all the windows open, the air was putrid. Blood was splattered everywhere, the room in disarray. Frank saw the uncovered body, lying on its side next to the radiator.

A wine bottle protruded from the rectum and a knife was still embedded in the victim's stomach. His face was covered with dried blood and large welts. There was not much left of the nose and there were two ugly gashes in his head.

The small room overflowed with a battery of specialists. CSI officers with their fancy evidence-collection kits crawled around the floor. Fingerprint specialists, a photographer, video taper, criminalist, and the medical examiner with a forensic pathologist at his side all did their thing, somehow managing not to get in one another's way. The department had pulled out all the stops on this one. He thought of Silvio's stories of the old days when he and a partner were pretty much it at a murder scene.

Jerry stood in a corner of the room talking with a man Frank didn't recognize. He was glad to see his friend back on the job. He spotted Frank and came over. Jerry hadn't shaved. He looked jowly and tired.

"How're you feeling, Jerry?"

"I've been better." He looked over at the victim. "Maid found him at six-fifteen this morning. The medical examiner says he's been dead for about thirty, thirty-six hours. Probably killed sometime two nights ago."

"When'd you get here?"

"Harry and I arrived a little before seven. The patrol officer was here at six-thirty."

"What have you got?"

"No prints so far. Everything's been wiped clean as a whistle. Our killer is getting more thorough. The knife's a big break, by the way."

"What do you mean?"

"It's got an unusual handle, covered with some kinda thick woven thread. Made by Talex. Never heard of them as knife manufacturers. It's definitely not your basic, run-of-the-mill knife."

Frank looked around the room. "Looks like there was a hell of a fight in here."

"Yeah," Jerry said. He nodded toward the lamp lying on the floor. "The victim was bashed pretty good with that table lamp. There are pieces of flesh and dried blood all over it."

Frank walked over to the pile of bed linens, bent over, and smelled them. "You've got a very faint odor of the same perfume in here. Come here and take a whiff."

"Yeah, I know. Faint, but it's there. Same smell as Nemerow's."

Frank went into the bathroom and returned. "There's some on the towel in the bathroom, too. Some pieces of hair also. Any ID on him?"

"Nothin'. Not even a house key."

Frank motioned to Harry. Jerry nodded and said, "Yeah, Harry's got something interesting that you're going to want to hear."

Harry came over. "Frank, I went over to Crystal's. The super of the building hasn't seen her since he saw her go out Sunday night."

"What time?"

"About eight-thirty. He let us in her apartment. She's got four cashmere sweaters in her closet."

So much for one theory, thought Frank.

"And are you ready for this? One of them is red."

"You find any Jean Naté?"

"No, but she could be out. Or maybe she carries it with her in her purse. You know, keep freshening up?"

"What else?"

"Not much. I mean, clothes, shoes, purses, toiletries, books. Nothing so far that's going to offer any help."

"You lift prints out of there yet?"

"Yeah, the prints we took out match prints we got at Beatty's and Joey Brewer's. We also got a match at Nemerow's. When we find her and print her, you can bet her prints will turn out to match the three murder scenes."

"All right! Find any pictures?"

"Nothing. We've got a good description of her from Vickie, and the police artist is working up a final sketch with Vickie. We've got a rough one for now."

Frank looked at the sketch. "Mean-looking broad. How'd she get the bad scar?"

"Nobody knows. Oh, we picked up some wigs that were in the apartment. Sully brought them over to the lab to compare with the fibers we picked up at Joey's and Chesbro's and Nemerow's. No report yet."

"How'd Vickie describe her?"

"Tall, about five-ten or -eleven. Well built. Very long black hair. She says the long hair's a wig, because she's seen her with her real hair, which is much shorter, and she's seen her as a blond and as a redhead."

"So she dyes her hair."

"Right. She's got blue eyes and wears a lot of makeup. And the scar. Vickie says she's a real looker, even with the scar. She says it makes her look even more sexy."

"OK. When's the sketch going to be finalized?"

"Probably done now. We'll take it around to Barney's and the other bars and the victims' apartment buildings."

Jerry said, "She knows we're looking for her. No point in being subtle now. We'll plaster that sketch all over this city. Frankie, we're closing in. We're going to get her."

Frank had never seen his partner so worked up. "Slow down, Jerry. You'll have a coronary."

"We've got her name in the National Crime Information Center Computer," Harry said. "Nothing yet. We've also got an APB out on her. And we've got the word out on the street. We'll find her."

"You bet your ass we will," Jerry growled. He took Frank by the arm. "We're about to put this one to bed, Frank. Come over here." He nodded toward Gerard Williams. "He's the clerk who was on duty the night the victim and a woman registered. She was tall and wore the same coat and scarf as the others. Said the guy registered with the name John Jackson—most likely a phony. He paid in advance with cash. The woman stood over by the elevator with her back to Williams. He never got a look at her face. Later in the evening he said he looked up and caught a glimpse of the woman leaving alone. Again, her back to him."

"What time?

"About ten o'clock. She's out there somewhere, Frank."

46

FRANK SPENT THE rest of the day trying to track down Crystal. He tried her apartment again, talked to maybe a dozen prostitutes, some of whom either knew Crystal personally or knew of her. Nobody had seen her for several days.

Although he'd never met Crystal he was beginning to feel like he knew her. He'd studied the sketch, committing it to memory: the long hair hanging well below her shoulders, the blue eyes highlighted with mascara, lips bright with red lipstick, the lashes too long and thick to be real, and the scar on her left cheek.

THE PHONE WAS ringing as Frank entered his apartment. "Hello."

"Hello, Frank." The unmistakable voice. Carla.

Oh, God. He wanted to hang up the phone, but at the same time he felt the same contradictory confusion that she always caused him.

"Carla, I thought you'd be in Hollywood by now, rehearsing your Academy Award speech."

She ignored the dig. "Frank, I wanted to call you. I need to talk with you. Do you have a few minutes?"

It was a while before he answered. "A few minutes? Let me give you a direct quote. 'Having told you all this, if I should call, it shouldn't be hard for you to say no and hang up.' That sound about right?"

"Frank."

She was struggling. He could tell.

"Frank, please listen to me. This morning I made reservations for Milan for next week."

"Good for you."

"But I've been depressed all day for some reason. And I couldn't figure out why. I was sky high when I accelerated my plans and decided to leave now instead of waiting till February or March."

"Carla, why are you telling me all this?"

"You haven't figured it out yet?" She gave a little mirthless laugh. "Why should you? It took me all day. Frank, it just hit me smack in the face. I don't want to leave and lose you again. I could chuck this whole thing for you. Does that tell you something?"

The phone line was dead silent. He could hear her breathing, waiting for his reply. He reviewed the words he'd been hoping one day to hear, while trying to steady his shaking hands.

"Carla, I'm going to get me a drink. I'll be right back."

"OK."

He poured some scotch, drained it in two gulps, and poured some more. He waited for it to kick in, then sat for several moments before picking up the phone.

"Carla, I once loved you very much. I thought I would never get over you, and I'm not sure that I have. But I've met someone who is moving me in the right direction—someone I care for very much." He paused, finished the drink, and stared into the phone, memories flashing through his mind. Good memories. He forced them away.

"Frank, are you there?"

"Yes, I'm here. I . . . I . . ." He took a deep breath and held his hand over the receiver for several moments before speaking. "I think you should go to Milan, Carla," he said softly. "I'm sorry."

He waited through a few beats until she responded, coldly, without emotion, "It's OK, Frank. It's been nice knowing you. Good-bye." And that was it.

He finished his drink and sat by the window, staring into the late-afternoon darkness, tears welling in his eyes. He wasn't sure how long he'd been sitting, staring at nothing, when the phone rang. He eyed it for several rings before answering.

"Hi, it's me. What are you doing?"

He smiled at the sound of Denise's voice. "Nothing. What are you doing?"

"Lying here missing you. How about if I come over?"

"I'll give you five minutes to get here."

47

WALKING TO THE precinct on Friday morning, Frank knew beyond a doubt, if there ever was one, that he had made the right decision. Last night was the best yet. He couldn't get enough of her. It was great to feel something again.

Jerry was in a surprisingly good mood when Frank reached the station. "Good news, Frankie. We got an answer back already from the bureau. Amazing what the commissioner's signature will do."

"You got an ID on the victim?"

Jerry nodded. He didn't have to. The smirk on his face said it all. "He's an ex-con named Paul Gale. Paroled from Massachusetts State Prison in Norfolk just six weeks ago. Served twenty-one years for killing his wife in North Adams, Massachusetts."

"Nice guy."

"Yeah. Anyway, that's as much as we know. The information just came in."

Lieutenant Nolan came out of his office and spotted Jerry. "Blod-gett, come into my office," he yelled.

"The hell's he want now?" Jerry muttered, and headed for the wait-ing Nolan.

Frank watched Jerry scurry over to answer Nolan's summons. No matter how many years in the department, how solid your work was, how much respect you deserved, there was always somebody who was going to make you snap to; somebody, depending on his mood, who could push his weight around and make you feel like shit. He hated the way Nolan could do that to Jerry. But then, he felt sure it was no different in big corporations. They just made it seem a little more civilized and used bigger words to carve people up.

He went to his desk and called the North Adams police. The offi-cer he talked with didn't remember much about Gale, but said he'd check the records and call him back. Fifteen minutes later the man called and told him Gale had a sister-in-law named Janet Kateley still living in North Adams.

"She the sister of Gale's wife, the woman he killed?" Frank asked.

"I believe so," the officer replied.

He hung up and spotted Jerry, head down, moving quickly toward his office. He went in and slammed the door.

Frank followed and opened the door. "Can I come in?"

Jerry sat, studying the top of his desk, his face in his hands. He nodded.

Frank told him about his phone conversations. "I'm going up to North Adams and poke around a little, see what I can find out about Paul Gale."

Jerry nodded again. Frank wasn't sure he'd even heard what he said. "I'll call you either from there or when I get back." He stopped at the door and turned. "What'd Nolan want?"

Jerry brought his head up and looked at Frank for the first time. "If we don't come up with the killer by the end of the year, he's going to put somebody else in charge of the case. Take me off it completely. End of the year. That's five weeks from now. The son of a bitch."

Frank started to say something but thought better of it for now. Jerry was hurting too much at the moment, and he knew nothing would penetrate. "We'll talk when I get back," he said, and left.

IT WAS 4:30 when Frank arrived in North Adams, an old mill town that once had a dozen thriving cotton, wool, and shoe factories, now long gone. The town sat at the foot of the scenic Berkshire Hills.

He drove down Main Street, a step back in time. The buildings were the old redbrick of decades ago. A half dozen church steeples pierced the evening sky. The town had the nostalgic look and feel of the forties. He checked into a small hotel at the end of Main Street and called Denise.

"Dennie, I can't see you tonight. I had to go on a little business trip this afternoon. I'll most likely be back sometime tomorrow or Sunday. I'll call you."

"Where are you?"

"I can't really say right now, but it's no big deal. Just some police business. I do have to run now. I'll tell you about it when I get back."

"OK."

Frank thought she sounded disappointed and maybe even a little peeved. He'd heard the tone before.

"Be back before you know it. Miss you and can't wait to see you."

He called the number the cop had given him for the sister-in-law.

"Hello."

"Ms. Kateley?"

"Yes."

He thought she sounded fragile, even a little wary. "Ms. Kateley, my name is Frank Russo. I'm a detective with the New York City

Police Department. I'm sorry to bother you, ma'am, but do you have a brother-in-law named Paul Gale?"

There was a long pause. He waited. No answer.

"Ms. Kateley?"

"Why do you want to know that?" she asked in a tremulous voice.

"Is Mr. Gale your brother-in-law, ma'am?" he asked again. And again he waited, not sure if she would hang up on him this time or what.

"Yes, he is, but why are you calling me? I've had nothing to do with that man in years."

"Well, I'm sorry to tell you, Ms. Kateley, but Paul Gale was murdered in New York on Tuesday night, and I wonder if I might talk with you."

"Oh, my God!"

He waited for it to sink in. "Ms. Kateley, I'd like to speak with you, if I may. If not tonight, then tomorrow morning. I need to ask you a few questions about Mr. Gale."

"Yes," she said softly. "You might as well come over now and get it over with. I'm not going to relax much anyway, after what you've just told me. By the way, it's *Miss* Kateley, not *Miz*. I hate that word."

HARRY LEONARD WALKED into Jerry's office carrying two Styrofoam cups of coffee. No matter how long they'd worked together, Harry still felt intimidated by Jerry. He looked upon him as his boss, which he was, and he'd never been able to connect with him the way Frank did. And when Jerry was in a bad mood, he always seemed to take it out on Harry. He was particularly wary today.

"Anything on Crystal yet?" Jerry asked. He took the coffee from Harry with a little nod.

"Nothing yet, Jerry. Nobody's seen her since Sunday."

Jerry frowned and cursed. "I told you, didn't I, that we don't have any record of her prints here or anywhere. Looks like she's kept herself clean."

"Doesn't surprise me," Harry said. "From what I hear, she's a pretty slick customer. When we pick her up and print her, you know her prints'll match the ones from her apartment and the murder scenes. I'm going over to the Iburgs', Nemerow's neighbors. See if they recognize the sketch."

"Don't count on it. According to Frank, they never got a good look at her face. Anyway, we're making some progress with the knife," Jerry said. "I got the Talex people on the phone yesterday. The knife at the murder scene was a limited anniversary edition. They only made a couple thousand of them. Big break. Only five retail stores in New York carried them. Four in Manhattan, one in Brooklyn."

"That's fabulous," Harry said. He nodded toward Jerry's cup. "You want more coffee, Jerry?"

Jerry shook his head. "A lot of stores will keep records of people who buy knives like this. Or somebody might remember a buyer of an unusual weapon. Anyway, you keep looking for Crystal. We'll get these stores checked out. Any word from Frank?"

"No, I was going to ask you."

SHE LAY IN bed, trying to focus. The last few days seemed almost too much for her. The newspaper articles. Optimistic?

It was over now. She knew it was. But had she gone too far? Been too careless? Of course they were going to find out who he was. She always knew that. But she couldn't let it stop her. She had to do what she had to do. It was always that simple.

DENISE'S PHONE RANG.

"Hello, Dennie. This is Gina."

What in the world did Gina want? "Gina. How are you feeling? I heard you've been sick."

"Yeah, I have." She sounded subdued, nowhere near the Gina she knew. "I think I'm going to live, though. Listen, Dennie, I wonder if I could talk with you today."

"What's up?" She was waiting for Frank's call and she didn't feel like a session with Gina anyway.

"I don't want to talk on the phone. Can I meet you somewhere? I really do need to talk with you. You'll be back in less than an hour. Please, Dennie, it's important."

"All right. There's a place called Jason's a couple of blocks from here." She gave her the address. "It's sort of a coffee shop. I'll meet you there."

"See you there in twenty minutes," Gina said.

LATE THAT AFTERNOON Jerry hit the jackpot. At about the same time, Harry Leonard got a tip that sent him sky high.

48

JANET KATELEY'S DIRECTIONS were easy and Frank was there in ten minutes. The porch lights were on. He rang the doorbell and a nervous-looking woman who appeared to be in her late fifties appeared behind the glass storm door.

"Mr. Russo?"

"Yes, ma'am."

"May I see your identification, please?"

He held up his badge and picture and followed the woman into the living room. The venetian blinds were closed, the only light coming from a small table lamp. The absence of any color in the room gave the impression of someone who had bled the emotion from her life. The house smelled of fried potatoes and mothballs.

He watched the nervous little woman straighten the doilies on an overstuffed chair before beckoning him to sit. In her faded housedress and with her hair tied back in a bun, she and the room looked like they were frozen in time in the forties.

"What a terrible thing," she said, sitting on the edge of the sofa. "But I guess I'm not totally surprised. He was a violent, twisted man and I suppose it's fitting that he should die in a violent manner."

"I gather you didn't much like Mr. Gale."

"No, I didn't. There wasn't much to like. You probably know by now that he killed my sister?"

"Yes," he said, and asked her to fill him in. She did, providing him with a vivid description of the events leading up to her sister's death. She spared no details.

The room was hot. She must have had the thermostat turned up to ninety. No matter how hard he tried to slice through her rambling and keep her on track, she was not to be denied her catharsis. He was tired and beginning to wonder what the hell he was getting out of all this. Until she mentioned the wine bottle.

"Tell me some more about the wine bottle business, Miss Kateley. You say he abused her with it?"

"Yes, he . . ." She stopped.

"I understand," Frank said, touching her hand.

"He'd done it before. Sarah told me about it. And then it all came out in the trial. Oh, God. It was so disgusting."

He was no longer tired. "Miss Kateley, can you tell me about his daughter?"

Janet Kateley's eyes clouded over. "She was such a sweet little thing. The poor baby, God love her, she tried so hard to be a good girl for her mother. And she was." She stopped and looked out the window into the darkness.

"Yes, go on."

"Well, it seemed like all of a sudden her father started taking an interest in her. At night when he'd come home from work, he would go into her room and lie down and play with her. Even if she was asleep, he'd still snuggle up with her. At first Sarah thought it was nice that Paul was finally showing an interest in the child. But then she started hearing dirty sounds coming from the bedroom."

"What do you mean, dirty sounds?"

"Well, Paul would be groaning and moaning. You know, like sexually? And the poor little thing would start to cry and Sarah, when she realized what was going on, had trouble believing it."

"Gale was sexually abusing his daughter?"

She nodded and her lips quivered.

"Did Sarah tell you all this?"

"Well, a couple of times I was actually there. I'm the one who first told Sarah what I thought was happening. And then one night when the baby was about five and a half, she caught him red-handed. When she confronted him, he beat her terribly. Beat the baby, too, when she started crying."

He thought of the battered mess lying next to the radiator in the dingy hotel room and felt some satisfaction. "How long did all this continue?" he asked.

"Right up until the night he killed Sarah. He would abuse that poor child almost every night. And Sarah was by then so terrified and confused, she just started ignoring what was going on, hoping it would end eventually. My kid sister was not a strong person, Mr. Russo."

"Why didn't you report it to the police yourself?"

Her eyes flared and for the first time this mousy, gray lady showed some passion. "I did, Mr. Russo. I did. The police went over and Paul told them I was a meddling busybody. Of course he denied it. And sadly, so did Sarah."

She looked away from him again and they sat in silence. For the first time, he noticed the smell of dampness in the house, and mildew, the kind you find in a cellar. He studied her for a moment. The loneliness and sadness in the woman was palpable. She had kept every detail close to the surface all these years. "Go on, Miss Kateley," he said quietly.

She turned back to him. "Can you possibly imagine, Mr. Russo, what a night that must have been for that poor little eight-year-old? Watching her mother beaten and murdered, and then sexually abused herself? Well, I can tell you, she wasn't ever the same again."

"She came to live with you?"

"Yes. Somehow, she got through the trial. I stood not two feet from Paul when he told her he would kill her some day for turning him in and testifying. She just fell on the floor of the courtroom and cried her eyes out. We had to carry her out of the room."

Frank closed his eyes and shook his head. He'd been a cop for so long he thought he'd heard everything. "It must have been hard for you, bringing her up."

"Yes, it was. She was not an easy child to get close to. I tried my best but it was so sad and a little frightening to see the resentment and hatred for her father start to build and build as she grew older."

"Jesus." Frank muttered to himself. He was getting more than he bargained for. She suddenly looked very tired. But he had to keep it going.

"Tell me more, Miss Kateley. Where is she now?"

"She's in New York City. Been there for seven years." Janet Kateley looked away again, the sadness clouding her eyes. "I never see her and rarely ever talk to her. She's in her own world and wants nothing to do with me or anyone or any memories of North Adams."

"How long since you've seen her?"

"Over seven years. She'd be almost twenty-eight now, and I'm sure she's even more beautiful than when I last saw her. So tall and shapely, so lovely."

He watched her fight back the tears, an aging, lonely lady, still suffering for what happened after all these years. She deserved more than the kick in the teeth she got for bringing up her niece. "When did you last talk with her?"

"Well, she called me about two months ago and asked if her father was out of prison yet. I told her I'd heard he was due for parole any time. She asked me to be sure to call her when I knew. I called her about a week later to tell her he'd been released. Then, a couple of weeks later, I tried calling her and found that her number had been changed to an unlisted number. I hadn't talked with her for about a year before that."

Frank sighed. He felt for her, but the constant whine in her voice was getting tiresome. He pressed on. "Do you know where she lives and works in New York?"

She looked around the room. He tried to make eye contact but she avoided looking at him. He felt he might be running out of time with this strange, nervous little woman.

"Mr. Russo, I don't even know that. I did have her address up until a few years ago, but then she moved and never told me the new one." She started to pucker and sniffle again. "She's all I have, and now I have no way to reach her. I tried so hard for that girl and . . ." She gave up fighting the tears.

"Miss Kateley." He tried not to let the impatience show in his voice, but the mildew smell was getting worse and he had a headache. He doubted she was telling him the complete truth, but he knew he had to handle this brittle lady carefully or she could blow completely. "Do you know where she works?"

She took a crumpled handkerchief from her sleeve and blew her nose. "No, I don't know where she works. I never have."

"Did she go straight to New York after college?"

"I think she worked in Boston for a while, but I don't know where or for how long. Like I said, we just completely lost touch."

"Let me have her old address, please."

She wrote it down and handed it to him. Her eyes told him she was about at the end of her rope. He had to wrap this up and get back to New York. The hell with the hotel room. "Miss Kateley, what was her phone number before she had it changed?"

She gave it to him and he noted it was a Manhattan exchange.

"Do you have any pictures of your niece?" he asked.

"No, her father took the only few I had."

"You don't have any of her at all, even when she was a child?"

She looked up sharply at him and appeared wounded that he seemed not to believe her. "No. We weren't much of a picture-taking family."

"How about her high school or college yearbook?"

"I'm sorry, but she took everything of hers with her when she left. I have nothing, not even good memories."

He wasn't surprised. He doubted there had been much joy or fun in this woman's life. "Miss Kateley, can you give me a description of what your niece looks like today?"

She frowned. "I'm afraid I'm not very good at describing people. She's tall, maybe five feet nine or so. Has dark hair, and is really quite pretty. When I last saw her she had a very nice figure."

"What color are her eyes?"

"Brown, her eyes are brown."

"Any distinguishing characteristics you can think of?"

She shook her head. "No, none that I can think of."

"OK, just one last question. What's your niece's name?"

She stared at him for a moment and the sniffles came again. "Well, she changed her name some years ago because . . . well, again you see she just wanted to erase everything from North Adams, so . . . well, it's not Gale anymore."

"Miss Kateley! What is her name?"

49

AFTER FRANK LEFT, Janet Kateley sat in her living room, trying to pull herself together. So many things had happened and now this. She wondered how Lucky was handling it and wished she could talk with her.

The phone rang, and she looked at her watch. Eight forty-five. Who could be calling at this hour?

"Aunt Janet, this is Lucky."

"Oh, Lucky. Have you heard the news about your father? Oh, God, I'm so—"

"Yes, I have. How did you hear?"

"A New York City police detective came to see me. He just left about a half hour ago."

"Yes. I thought the police might be contacting you. What did he want to know?"

"Well, he asked about your father, and I told him about all the things that happened way back and all. And he wanted to know all about you."

"I see. And did you tell him all about me?"

"Yes, I mean, I told him everything I could. But . . ." She started to whimper.

"What is it, Aunt Janet?"

"Well, I was worried about you, and I was afraid to tell them where you live. It was foolish, I know, but I just wanted to have a chance to talk with you first. I was hoping you would call me. But now I'm afraid I'm going to get in trouble. I've got to call him back and tell him the truth."

"What did you tell him?"

"I gave him your old address, the one you had about three years ago."

"That wasn't very smart, Aunt Janet."

"I know," she wailed. "I just wasn't thinking. Oh, God, I'm going to call him first thing in the morning."

"No. Please don't do anything until we talk again. I'll call you in the morning."

"All right, Lucky. Oh, sweetheart, I'm so glad you called."

"Yes, I am, too. Aunt Janet?"

"Yes?"

"What was the detective's name?"

"Oh, let's see. I have his card here somewhere. Yes, here it is. It's Russo, a nice young man named Frank Russo."

FRANK ENTERED HIS apartment and slumped into a kitchen chair. It had been a long day. The answering machine blinked relentlessly. He pulled himself up long enough to pour a drink and fell back into the chair. The apartment was raunchy. Dirty dishes from his dinner with Denise still sat in the sink. Even now, he could smell the garlic. A roach skittered across it all and disappeared down the side of the sink cabinet.

He took two long pulls on the scotch and closed his eyes. He'd had better days.

The trip back from North Adams was long and ugly. He had managed to catch the last flight out of Albany at eight-thirty, but the weather turned bad and the flight was ragged and bumpy. And his cell phone kept losing the signal so he'd been out of touch with Jerry all night. Then La Guardia was socked in and they had to circle for nearly an hour before getting clearance to land. Now, at 1:00 A.M., he was exhausted. But he was also wired.

The session with Janet Kateley rattled around in his head. Her niece, Gale's daughter, could be the key to the whole goddamn case and could very possibly be the killer.

He closed his eyes and was back in the small, stale living room in North Adams. "What is your niece's name, Miss Kateley?"

"You may find this hard to believe, Mr. Russo, but I don't know."

"You don't know?"

"I told you she changed her name, both first and last, and she would never tell me what she changed it to. Whenever we talked I simply called her Lucky, the nickname her mother and I used when she was little. I never even knew her address. What little communication we had were the few cards she sent and by phone."

He opened his eyes and they landed on the answering machine again. He reached over and turned it on. Three urgent messages from Jerry. "Call me at the house no matter what time you get home. Check your goddamn cell phone. The battery must be low. I've been calling you all day and evening."

Two messages from Denise, and two from his father. He dialed Jerry's number.

"Yeah?" Jerry's voice was a hoarse whisper.

"Jerry, I just got back. You said to call you no matter what time."

"Frank!" Jerry's voice came alive. "What time is it?"

"Ten after one."

"Frankie. It's over."

Something had happened while he was gone. "What do you mean, it's over?"

"Hold on, let me pick up the phone in my den."

Frank poured some more scotch and paced around the kitchen. He was no longer tired. He'd been away from the city for about thirteen hours. What the hell happened?

"Frank?"

"Jerry. For Christ sake, what happened?"

"OK, kid, listen to this." There was a pause and some puffing. Frank knew what Jerry was doing. He was lighting his victory cigar. And then he got going. First he told Frank about their good luck with the knife, about it being a limited edition. "We traced it to Haley's Gun Shop on West Fortieth right after you left yesterday. The owner, Ben Haley, remembers it. He only had a few of them and they sold fast. He's always kept records of who buys his knives and handguns. I've known the guy for a long time. He's very thorough. You still with me?"

Frank continued pacing around the small kitchen. "Yeah, 'course I am. Go on."

"OK, he's absolutely certain who bought this knife. The serial number matches with his records. And he remembers her. You got it, Frankie, the lady who bought the knife at Haley's Gun Shop is none other than our hooker, Crystal Wilcox."

"You pick her up yet?"

"Not yet, but we will. We should have her within twenty-four hours."

"Getting close. Anything else?"

"Yeah, it gets better. The knife was the same knife that Crystal used to kill the guy in the alley. It checks out with the pictures and slides from the autopsy. We measured the wounds and the knife. Perfect fit."

"Jerry, Vickie told us that Crystal gave the knife to Jenny Clark, the black hooker that was stabbed to death in a room near Times Square, remember?"

"No shit. Vickie said that, huh? Must be true then. Come on, Frank."

"What else have you got?"

"What do you mean, what else have I got? What the hell else do we need?"

"What about the hair?"

"What about it?" Jerry's voice took on an edge.

"The hair, Jerry. The hairs we found at some of the crime scenes were natural, untreated hair, remember? And some were wig fibers. Crystal dyes her hair. How do you account for the natural hairs we found all over Nemerow, Beatty, and Gale?" He waited for an answer. "Jerry?"

"We'll check that out when we find her?"

"Yeah, well, how about the wig fibers? None of them match the wigs that were found at Crystal's apartment."

"Oh, for Christ sake, you think they were the only wigs she had? She probably has others with her. Frank, she's the one. We got her on the guy in the alley. Vickie's an eyewitness, and she's going to testify. Crystal Wilcox is our killer."

Frank sat down and finished his drink, still trying to process all of what he'd just heard. He wanted to share Jerry's excitement but it just wouldn't come. Maybe he was simply too tired.

"Frank?"

"Yeah?"

"Nolan wants to see you and me in his office at eleven in the morning. Then at one-thirty the chief wants to see us. Be nice to get a little praise instead of all the shit they've been throwin' at us, especially me."

"Jerry, I hope you haven't jumped the gun on this. You don't—"

"Frank. It's done. It's over. And now I gotta get some sleep. You go to bed, and I'll see you in my office at ten-forty-five." And he hung up.

Frank looked through the phone at Jerry before hanging it up. "It's over?"

Is it? Did Jerry actually believe it? He doubted it. He knew Jerry too well. Nolan and the commissioner: Did they really care one way or the other? Too many loose ends.

He was too tired now to deal with it. Tomorrow.

50

THE FIRST THOUGHT that hit him when he awoke was Denise. So much going down but there she was, ahead of everything. Too late to call her last night or this morning or whatever the hell day it was when he got home.

"Hello." Even half asleep she sounded wonderful.

"Hi. It's me."

"Frank?"

Still a little fuzziness in her voice. He pictured her lying in bed, hair splayed out across her face, her breasts rolling out of her nightgown, the way she looked when he last left her. "Your wake-up call, ma'am."

"Frank, where have you been? What—"

"Whoa. Enough with the grilling. I'll tell you all about it tonight. I didn't get back till one this morning. Too late to call you."

"Just as well, I guess. I wouldn't have been much good. I had kind of a trying session with my friend Gina, advising her whether or not to accept a job offer out of state. She was a nervous wreck and it was exhausting. I went to bed early, started reading, and must have conked out before nine. I'm dying to see you."

"How about coming over for dinner? What time can you get here?"

"I have to go to New Haven. I'll call you when I get back."

He lay in bed for a few minutes focusing on her. He knew those minutes would be the best part of his day. He'd been so wrapped up in this goddamn case again. Good way to lose her, and he wouldn't blame her. Well, he wasn't going to let that happen. The phone rang and he bolted up.

"Frankie! Where the hell have you been? I been trying to call you. Congratulations." His father's voice crackled with energy.

"Oh, yeah, thanks, I guess."

"What do you mean, you guess? You guys have cracked one of the biggest cases this city has had. And you did it in less than two months. You should be celebrating. You sound like you just came from a funeral."

He didn't want to get into it right now. But he knew that whatever he said, Silvio would pick up on. So he might as well say what he was thinking. "I'm not sure that Crystal did all these guys. I think we've got a rush to judgment here. Maybe that's why I'm not celebrating. It's just not that cut and dried.

"Maybe she did these guys and maybe she didn't. I'd just hate to be part of railroading somebody because of public pressure. I can't shake the feeling that everybody—Jerry, Nolan, the chief, even the commissioner—just want to put this to bed and they don't care about irrelevancies like some holes in the evidence or like maybe somebody else could be doing these guys. No question it looks like we've got her on the guy in the alley, but I'm not totally convinced yet of the others."

There was a long silence. Frank knew his father, and he knew that when he was angry and about to blow, he forced himself into silence, collecting himself, gathering his cool.

When he finally spoke, Silvio's voice was low and measured. "Frank, I already heard last night that you're up for a commendation and a promotion. There's an old saying, been around the department since way before me, and I know you've heard it. 'If you want to get along, you go along.' You've got your killer. This is a big day for everybody from the commissioner on down. Let them enjoy. And you enjoy."

Frank started to reply, but nothing would come out. He needed to collect his own thoughts, gather his own cool before going at it any further with Silvio. "Yeah," he said simply. "I gotta go." And he hung up.

He had a lot to do before meeting with Jerry at 10:45. He obtained a subpoena for the phone company and presented it to Donald Ware, the assistant director of security there.

"Always happy to be of service, Mr. Russo," Ware said. He wore a gray cardigan sweater and used the bottom of it to clean his eyeglasses. After examining the phone number Frank had given him, Ware settled into one of the computers lining the room. "OK, so this number was changed to an unlisted number about three months ago, you say? And you want to know who this number was assigned to, right?"

Frank nodded. The adrenaline was flowing now and he wanted this officious little shit to shut up and just give him his information.

"Now you see, Mr. Russo, I can just dip into what we call our Coles Directory, which provides me with a breakdown of phone numbers by number, name, and street address. You give me a name and I'll give you the phone number and address. Give me an address and I'll give you a name and number. Give me a number and I give you the name and address of the person who has or had that number."

"Mr. Ware, I know how it works," Frank said. "I've had people do it before."

Ware shrugged and replied curtly, "OK, let's get to it. We're both busy people." He poked away at the keyboard for what seemed forever to Frank. Finally he pointed to the computer screen and said, "There it is. That number belonged to Crystal Wilcox, two twenty-six East Thirty-eighth Street."

Frank was relieved. It was beginning to look like Jerry and the others were on the right track after all.

Feeling better about things, he handed the address to Ware, the old address of her niece that Janet Kateley had given him. "OK. How about giving me the name that goes with this."

"Certainly, sir." Ware went into his routine again while Frank sat back, confident of what he would find. It was really now only an exercise.

Ware turned from his computer. "There you are. There's your information."

Frank looked at the screen. "Oh, my God," he yelled and grabbed his cell phone to call Janet Kateley. There was no answer. He made two more phone calls but again, no luck.

It was time to meet with Jerry, Jerry who had the case wrapped up, on the verge of becoming a hero.

Jerry was already sitting in his office drinking coffee when Frank arrived. The coat to his gray suit hung on the coat rack and he had on a white shirt with a necktie that Frank had never seen. His shirt was tucked neatly into his pants.

As usual when he felt edgy and out of sorts, Frank tried to cover with a flipness he didn't really feel. "Jerry, you look pretty spiffy in your new necktie, and I see you've got my favorite suit on."

Jerry got up and hugged him. Then he grabbed Frank's face in his massive hands. "We did it, kid. It's all over." He said it softly, his voice full of emotion. He went back to his desk and handed Frank a cup of coffee. "Here, I poured it for you just before you walked in."

Jerry got up again and walked around the office. "Frankie, we shut

up a lotta doubting Thomases in this city. We've gone from the out-
house to the penthouse, and I don't know about you, but I like that
penthouse."

Frank nodded. He'd hear Jerry out before saying anything. "Fill
me in some more on yesterday."

Jerry sat down again and went over the events in detail. "I knew we
were going to nail that bitch Crystal, Frankie."

Frank got up and walked over to Jerry's desk. He looked down
at the newspaper sitting on it and there were Jerry and Nolan, big
smiles, holding court.

Jerry pointed to the paper. "Nice, huh?"

Frank sat next to him. The room felt hot and stuffy all of a sudden.
"Jerry, we've got Crystal on the alley stabbing, but you don't believe
she's the Wine Bottle Killer, do you?" It came out more abruptly than
he had planned, but it was out.

Jerry's expression changed, all the joy and good fellowship replaced with a narrow-eyed stare. "What the hell are you talking
about?"

It was the tone he expected. "Jerry, I know you. You're too good a
cop to overlook all the holes in the case on Crystal."

Jerry's eyes were now slits, the color drained from his face. Frank
had seen the expression before, but never aimed at him. He pushed
on. "First of all, Jerry, as I said on the phone last night, the hair we
found at three of the crime scenes matched and they're all natural
hair. Crystal's hair is dyed. When Harry showed Crystal's picture to
Billy, the bartender at Barney's, he couldn't positively ID her."

He waited but there was no response from Jerry. "What are we going to do when we print Crystal if her prints don't match the ones at
all the crime scenes?"

Again, no reply, only the look of rage. "We don't have a positive
ID on the sketch from anybody yet and you don't even have Crystal in
custody."

Jerry finally spoke. His voice was hard and flat. "You finished?"

"No, goddamn it, I'm not," Frank flared. "You want to hear about my trip to North Adams, or don't you give a shit? Well, let me tell—"

"I don't give a fuck about your trip to North Adams," Jerry roared. He was on his feet and around the desk in Frank's face. "You go off on some wild goose chase to Massachusetts and don't even bother to call in. Harry and I are putting this thing to bed while you're screwin' around up there and you have the nerve to come back here and question me, question the chief, question the commissioner? How dare you?" His voice trembled with rage.

Frank walked to the other side of the small office, afraid one of them would throw a punch. They stood on opposite ends of the room, looking at each other, Jerry's harsh breathing the only sound.

But Frank refused to let it go. "Jerry, I'm troubled by this. I'm troubled that you're all in a rush to nail somebody. You're reacting to the pressure and you're going to close this thing out no matter what." He spoke calmly now, trying to reach his friend, his partner who had taught him so much. "Jerry, what if she's not the killer and next week or next month we find another guy with a wine bottle jammed up his ass? How are we going to look then? All I'm asking is let's just cool the rush to publicity and not jump to conclusions until we check a few more things out. We don't want to be embarrassed, do we?"

After a moment of studying Frank, Jerry looked out the glass panel into the bullpen. A small group stood looking in at them. Jerry glanced at his watch and walked over to Frank. He spoke quietly. "I hear what you're saying, Frank. I know there are some loose ends. But we have a murderess with an eyewitness. We have a substantial amount of evidence that seriously implicates Crystal Wilcox in these serial killings. I'm retiring in ten months. I'm going to go out the way I always dreamed I would. Don't spoil that, Frankie. Share it with me." He put his hands on Frank's upper arms and held them there for a moment.

Frank stood motionless, looking into his friend's eyes. He would say nothing further for now. All he wanted was to get out of the building as soon as possible.

Jerry looked at his watch. "It's eleven o'clock. Let's go see Nolan."

51

FRANK AND JERRY'S meeting with Nolan was very different from those of the past two months. Nolan was cordial and complimentary, especially to Jerry.

"Jerry, we've had our differences over the years, but I'm impressed with the way you and your men have pinned this case down. The department has taken a lot of heat over these murders, especially after Nemerow. I've never in all my nineteen years as a cop felt such pressure over a case.

"I'm sure I don't have to tell you what a relief it is to me that you've identified the killer. Now get out there and bring her in fast. I want to be able to sleep again."

"We'll get her, Joe. We've got every detective and half the patrol officers in the city looking for her. It won't be long."

"Good. I'll see you at the chief's office at one-thirty. I think he's going to have a little incentive for you boys to find her."

Jerry grinned and looked at Frank. Frank looked straight ahead.

Outside Nolan's office Frank and Jerry stood in an awkward silence. Jerry started to speak. "Frank, I—"

"Congratulations, Jerry," Frank interrupted. "You're going out in style." He turned and went over to his desk, sat down, and absorbed himself in a thick folder.

Jerry watched him for a moment, grabbed his coat, and left.

Frank sat staring into the open folder. He didn't know what was in it but it didn't matter. He looked up and around the precinct. The air was thick and heavy with the sweat of overworked cops. He got a whiff of the sweet, sickish smell of the cheap perfume and cologne worn by the hookers and pimps that paraded in and out all day. It was lunchtime but he had no appetite.

He tried to think through the last crazy twenty-four hours. His head felt like a chunk of wood. Jerry. Today was probably the happiest day in his pal's life.

Everybody was tense, pumped up. But his mind was back at the phone company, staring at the screen. He could focus on nothing else. He chipped away at the block of wood, trying to clear his mind. The information he had could blow everything sky high. He would have to proceed carefully, handle it in his own way. There was too much at stake. Too much. He buried his head on his desk.

It took him forty minutes to obtain a subpoena in order to get the information from the post office regarding the forwarding address for the old address Janet had given him. It was now 1:15. No time to get the new address now.

The session with the chief was much like the meeting with Nolan. The chief's little incentive was a promotion to detective lieutenant for Jerry and detective sergeant for Frank when they brought in Crystal and everything fit together, which he was confident it would.

By the time they left, Frank was sick to his stomach, feeling like he would vomit any minute. His apartment was not far. He was in no mood or shape to go to the post office. He would go home, take some Pepto-Bismol, and try to calm down a little first.

It was three-thirty by the time he arrived home. He tried the phone again, and again had no luck. Instead of the Pepto, he poured himself a heavy dose of scotch, straight up, slumped into his chair, and downed most of it. He knew why his stomach was a mess, and it wasn't medicine that would make it go away.

There had to be a simple answer that would clear things up for him. Everything pointed to Crystal. Maybe what he had was little more than a blip.

He sat gazing at the kitchen wall, his apartment now in semidarkness. The gloom of a sunless November afternoon had settled in. The empty scotch glass dangled from his hand. He got up to wash his face before heading for the post office when the phone rang.

"Hello."

"Hi, it's me. Can I come over?"

"Can you come over now?"

"Yes, I'll be there in half an hour.

52

FRANK HUNG UP the phone and began pacing the apartment. A craving for a cigarette gnawed at him. He resisted the urge to run out and buy a pack.

Not much time. He wasn't sure how he would handle this, how it would play out.

He chewed his thumbnail and wandered into the living room and back to the kitchen. It could be risky, but he had to do it this way. There was no way he was going to bring Jerry or anyone else into this yet. Not until he had more answers. And he hoped they were the right answers. They would be. His gut told him that. He sat at the kitchen table and popped up again, poured some of the morning coffee, sipped it, and spit it into the sink.

She was very possibly Gale's daughter. So? What if she was the daughter of an abuser who liked to use a wine bottle. So he got the wine bottle treatment like the other four. Coincidence? No. Crystal was the daughter and Crystal did these guys. And Janet Kateley would identify her.

From everything they'd learned about Crystal, she was sadistic, a man-hater. Abusing a man with a blunt instrument after he was dead would be consistent with her profile.

Still, he had to consider all possibilities and he couldn't shake the worst. A thought that wouldn't go away sent him to his bookshelves, where he pulled out *The Murderer* by the psychiatrist Emanual Tanay. Something Tanay had written was sticking in his mind; he had to read it again. He went immediately to the passage: ". . . the murderer appears to carry out the act in an altered state of consciousness. In such an ego-dystonic homicide a person kills against his conscious wishes and thus the murder is carried out during this altered period of consciousness. When this occurs, part of the psychic structure is split off from the rest of the personality."

He held the book, pondering the passage for a few moments before picking up another by W. I. Thomas. He quickly found what he was looking for. "In homicides whereby the individual has suffered a cycle of trauma in childhood and is faced with a psychologically irresolvable conflict, one dissociative reaction often is a quest to gain revenge, an act that can be repeated over and over until the need for vengeance is satisfied. When and if this occurs, the individual could be freed from further dissociative actions."

"In other words, the killings would stop," he said aloud.

Vengeance. It had been his theory after the second murder. *Payback* was the word Silvio used. He read on. "When the vengeance is satisfied the individual could be freed from further dissociative actions." He was tracking now into unsettling territory, but he could no more stop than he could erase the name on the screen in Donald Ware's office.

The person could go back to being a normal human being again. No more killing against conscious wishes. No more need to. No more—

The door buzzer jolted him to his feet. He reached for the intercom button but his hand stopped short. The buzz zapped through the apartment again, this time longer, insistent.

He pushed the button.

"It's me."

He waited for her, wondering what he would say, what direction the evening would take. The doorbell rang and he braced himself.

She stood in the doorway, a little uncertain smile on her face. He thought she looked as beautiful as ever.

"Hi," she said and stepped inside.

He looked at the large tote bag she carried. "Going somewhere?"

"No, I just came from working out."

He studied her face for a moment, nodded, and lowered his eyes. When he looked up again, her smile had faded.

"You seem different, Frank. What is it?"

"I went to North Adams and talked with Janet Kateley last night. Does that name mean anything to you?"

Her eyes glazed over.

He waited but there was no response. "Did you know that an old address she had for her niece, Paul Gale's daughter, had a telephone listed under your name?"

Her eyes seemed to clear just before she lowered them. "Yes," she whispered.

"Do you want to tell me about it?" He still wanted to believe she could explain everything.

"Yes," she said. "I do." She moved into the living room and he followed. "I hope you're going to give me the benefit of explaining all this to you before making a big deal out of it."

"I've said nothing to anyone, not until you and I have talked. I think you would know that."

He watched her, looking for a sign, something, anything that would help him get through this.

She turned to him. "Frank, I'm so nervous about all of this. It's all very confusing and I want you to hear me out." She started fidgeting and gave him a little smile. "I've got to go. Can I use your bathroom?"

He nodded and she headed through the bedroom toward the bathroom. He heard both doors close and the phone ring at the same time.

"Frank, this is Jerry."

"Yeah. You find Crystal?"

"Not yet. Frank, when you went up to North Adams, who'd you talk to?"

"I talked to Gale's sister-in-law, Janet Kateley."

There was a pause at the other end. "We just got a call from the North Adams police. Janet Kateley's been murdered."

"Oh, sweet Jesus! When?"

"They say she was killed sometime very early this morning, about three, four A.M.—"

Before he could respond, Frank heard the bedroom door open. "Jerry," he whispered. "I'll call you back in a few minutes."

He hung up the phone and turned. Crystal Wilcox stood facing him.

53

HE CLOSED HIS eyes, rubbed them, and opened them again, expecting the apparition he had just seen to be gone. She was still there, staring at him, smiling. The police artist had failed to capture the coldness in her blue eyes. He doubted anything could.

She wore the kind of miniskirt he'd seen in the sketch and stood over six feet tall in her spike heels. Her lips were thick with heavy lipstick, giving her mouth a cruel twist. The scar on her cheek, heavy makeup, and hair well below her shoulders gave her a menacing presence.

"I understand you've been looking for me," she said in a voice nearly as deep as his.

Where did she come from? He tried to think clearly, shake off the numbing shock that kept his brain from working.

Before he could speak or move, she produced a gun. She appeared to be holding something with her other hand, but he couldn't make out what it was.

"I'm sorry, Frank."

Her voice had changed. "Oh, Jesus Christ. Sweet Jesus. No."

She nodded.

He closed his eyes and shook his head. "No, no, no," he whispered. He had wanted everything to be explained, all the awful questions to be answered. And now they were, in horrifying clarity. The nagging familiarity of the police artist's sketches, the sterileness of Crystal's apartment. But there were still so many questions.

"Why? Just tell me why? I think you owe me that."

"Why? Why Crystal? Is that what you're asking me, Frank?"

"We can start with that."

"I liked turning myself into a woman men needed, were willing to pay money for. I enjoyed being in control. I was always the dominant one."

"What about going into alleys with drunks and—"

"Oh, yes. I'm sure you have trouble with that. If it makes you feel any better, I didn't like it very much. But I was always a lowlife. My father saw to that. It seemed fitting that I should play the role of the worst kind of lowlife for a woman, a streetwalking prostitute. I was the dirty little girl doing dirty little things. But you could never understand."

He could understand. Even with her there, holding a gun on him, he could understand and his heart ached with sadness for her. But he knew the danger he was in. He needed to keep her talking.

"What about us?"

Her face softened for a moment. "I thought I loved you when I was with you. I tried. When I was able to keep Crystal away for a while, I did love you. But she kept coming back."

Even now, looking at Crystal, it was difficult to see the real person underneath. In a way it was better that way. He preferred to think of her as Crystal. Keep her talking. "The blue eyes. Contacts?"

She nodded.

"And the scar—makeup?"

She nodded again. "Yes, I'm very good with makeup."

"How long has Crystal . . . been with you?"

She hesitated and looked away. "A very long time."

"How did the killings begin?"

Beads of perspiration formed on her forehead, trickled along her eyes, picked up mascara and continued down her cheeks, creating black stripes in her makeup.

"Jack Beatty was an act of rage. It had been building in me for a long time. He triggered it. I didn't plan to kill him. It was sort of an accident, but I liked the feeling.

"It's hard to explain the man in the alley because Crystal killed him. I . . ." Her upper lip glistened with the perspiration that had made its way down her face, and her eyes narrowed. The deep voice of Crystal returned. "When we got in the alley and he turned nasty, I saw her father, disgusting, foul, drunk, and I enjoyed sticking the knife in him."

"What about the knife, Crystal? You never gave it to Jenny Clark like you told Vickie, did you?"

The smile returned. "Yes, I did."

"Then how—?"

"Don't you understand, you fool? That animal killed Jenny and took the knife."

"And you killed him with it in the hotel room."

Her expression softened and the old familiar voice returned.

"Crystal didn't kill my father. I did. I killed Jack Beatty. And I killed the little scum Joey. And I killed Nemerow." She jutted her head toward him, her voice emphasizing each word.

She's losing it, he thought, watching her face contort each time she hissed the names. "And who killed the others?"

"I did, except for the man in the alley. Crystal killed that man."

God! His stomach turned sour and a wave of nausea swept over

him. Dark shadows cut across the room, casting her in eerie silhou-
ette. How long had they been standing there? How much longer
could she remain rational? He knew she could blow at any minute.
"What about the natural hair and the wigs? Crystal's hair is dyed.
Yours is natural. How did you work that?"

"Crystal's hair wasn't dyed. She wore different color, natural-hair
wigs sometimes, and sometimes fiber wigs. She told those stupid
women that it was her real hair dyed. They never knew any better."

"And the hair found in Nemerow's apartment—the natural, dark
brown hair?"

"I wore a natural-hair wig that night, as I have been doing lately."

"And the old phone number and address?"

"When I gave my aunt the phone number, I gave her the number
to Crystal's apartment. I wasn't there very much so it was better that
way. Later, I gave her my own address because I knew she would give
it to my father. I wanted him to find me. He had pictures of me, not
Crystal."

"Why did you kill your aunt?"

"I had to do that!" she screamed. "She was going to call you and
give you more information. And she would have identified me. And
now she can't. No one can, except you."

She started to sob. "I don't want to kill you, Frank."

He spoke softly, gently. "Sweetheart, I can help you. You're very
sick. You need help and we'll get it for you." He moved in her direction and put his hand out to her. "I know you don't want to kill me,
sweetheart."

The hammer of the gun clicked. "No." The harshness of Crystal's
voice returned. "She doesn't need you. She's finished with you. She
doesn't need you or your help. She has me and that's all she needs. I
will go away for a while but she knows I will always be with her.

"She can't kill you, but I can." She stepped toward him and raised
the gun. The phone rang, distracting her long enough for him to grab

the gun from her hand. As he did, she raised the other hand and brought the wine bottle she'd been holding down on his head.

He fell to the floor and the room turned to darkness for a moment. When he opened his eyes, he saw her about to bring the bottle down on him again. He raised the gun and fired.

The phone continued to ring. He pulled it to the floor and answered it.

"Frank. I thought you were going to call me back. What—?"

"Jerry, you'd better get over here right away."

"Why? What's—?"

"Jerry, just get over here. Please."

He hung up the phone and cradled the dead woman in his arms.

54

HE OPENED HIS eyes. The room was nearly dark. He had no idea how long he'd been sitting on the floor, holding her. Had he blacked out? He thought he'd heard his buzzer, but he couldn't be sure.

He put his hand to his face and pulled it away, covered with blood—her blood from where he had held her against him. His head throbbed, and he realized some of the blood was his own.

He closed his eyes again and felt the wetness of the tears still there. The nightmare began coming back in bits and pieces.

A commotion at the door. Someone knocking, pounding. Voices. When he opened his eyes the building superintendent stood in the doorway.

Someone behind the super. He couldn't make out who it was until Jerry pushed his way into the apartment. And stopped.

Frank looked up at his friend and partner. Jerry stood motionless, his mouth open, lips moving, making no sound. He stared at Frank sitting cross-legged on the floor, rocking a woman in his arms, both of them covered with blood.

And then the words tumbled out. "Frank, what happened? What's going on here? Who—?" He went to Frank, looked down at the woman, and blinked several times. "Crystal? Crystal Wilcox?"

Frank slid away from the body and started to get up. He staggered and Jerry helped him to his feet.

"You all right, Frank?"

Frank leaned against the wall. "Yeah, I'm all right."

"Frank, talk to me. What happened? What the hell is Crystal Wilcox doing here? Is she dead?"

Frank made his way to the window and raised the blinds. He looked out at the lights of the city below.

"Yes, she's dead," he said softly. "Only it isn't Crystal Wilcox. It's Carla."

55

THREE WEEKS LATER.

Frank leaned back on the seat and closed his eyes, still reliving the thoughts that refused to go away—the hideous day that would stay with him forever. He doubted he would ever be free of the image of killing the woman he once loved. Maybe getting away from New York for a while would help. Maybe.

He finished his drink, pushed the seat back as far as it would go, and looked down at Denise, sleeping on his shoulder. They were somewhere over the Atlantic Ocean, halfway between New York and Barbados.

It was two weeks to the day since he'd buried Carla, poor, tormented Carla. The toast of New York. And there were three people at the cemetery, Frank, Jerry, and Betty. Even her agent stayed away.

Only two weeks, but it seemed so long ago that they stood in the cold December drizzle. After a while Jerry and Betty got into the car, while Frank remained kneeling next to the casket, the rain dripping down his forehead. His lips moved silently for several moments before he blessed himself, kissed the casket, got up and left.

Although he had truly loved her, he never saw the demons eating away at her. If only he'd been with her longer, he might have been able to help her before she snapped. If only. He eased himself into the car's backseat and they drove away.

It was over now. High in the air, away from everything, he tried to peel away the nightmare and think of tropical sunrises and the beautiful woman next to him. He leaned over and kissed her. A gentle moan interrupted her soft steady breathing and a hint of a smile crossed her face. He kissed her again and closed his eyes.